LEAN IN TO LOVE

Visit us at www.boldstrokesbooks.com

By the Author

The Set Piece

Heartwood

Tread Lightly

Romancing the Kicker

Lean in to Love

LEAN IN TO LOVE

by

Catherine Lane

2024

LEAN IN TO LOVE

ISBN 13: 978-1-63679-582-9

THIS TRADE PAPERBACK ORIGINAL IS PUBLISHED BY
BOLD STROKES BOOKS, INC.
P.O. BOX 249
VALLEY FALLS, NY 12185

FIRST EDITION: MARCH 2024

CREDITS
EDITOR: BARBARA ANN WRIGHT
PRODUCTION DESIGN: SUSAN RAMUNDO
COVER DESIGN BY INK SPIRAL DESIGN

Acknowledgments

I can't tell you how happy and proud I am to see *Lean in to Love* as a published novel. It survived a number of insane challenges: a pandemic, our son's senior year on zoom, a publisher change. Any one of these could've killed the book, but the story wouldn't let me go, and so thankfully, here it is.

I am grateful to Bold Strokes Books for making the process easy and fun, and most importantly, for introducing me to Barbara Ann Wright, my editor, who made the story and the writing so much better. Many thanks to Susan X. Meagher and Celeste Castro who talked me through early versions of the story and Elizabeth Hayden, Ann Etter, and Anne Pace who gave valuable advice and critiques on multiple drafts. Ryan O'Nan, I don't know where I would be without our writer's walks and talks. I do know you gave me inspiration for one of my favorite scenes. And finally, thank you to my wife and son who give meaning to my days. I love you both.

Dedication

To PBD

CHAPTER ONE

Rory sat at the counter of the Honey Pot Bar when the heavy wooden door behind her jerked open. She didn't look up. Her gaze was glued to her mom's text on her phone:

Sweetie. Call me tomorrow. I'm in a bit of a pickle.

Rory tapped her fingernails on the counter. Her mom was calling her problems pickles now? That was new. Only when the woman beside her made an odd choking noise did she swivel to look behind her.

The phone dropped from her hand.

London Green, larger than life and breathtakingly gorgeous, stood framed by the closed door.

"Wow, Maya." Rory turned to her roommate who was serving behind the bar. "Is that a great getup or what? She looks just like her." Because there was no way the real London Green—one of the most recognizable and bankable actors in Hollywood—was standing in a lesbian dive bar in North Hollywood Arts District. More likely, a customer from Showgirls, the drag bar next door, had made a wrong turn.

"Look again." Maya stared over her shoulder, seemingly unable to rip her gaze from the woman at the door. "She's the real thing."

Rory swiveled, narrowed her eyes, and studied the person in front of her. Maya had a point. There was something not quite right about this London Green impersonator, or rather, something too right. Her huge pale eyes were the perfect mixture of green and blue and summer sky, as some reporter had written. And though Rory had little experience with makeup, she was close enough to see that this woman was wearing almost none. Her high cheekbones, strong jawline, and full, kissable lips were God-given. Seriously, if anyone could manufacture such universal sex appeal, everybody on earth would be rushing to CVS to get a beauty kit.

"Hello, NoHo." London, or not-London, laughed and tossed her signature ruffled hair. Golden bangs flopped across her forehead in the most adorable way. "What does a woman have to do to get a drink around here?"

Now that everyone's eyes were on her, she moved to the counter as if accepting an Oscar. Gasps rattled around the room. Her walk was a little masculine and a sexy contrast to her classic beauty. She bubbled with confidence and authenticity. She had to be the real London.

Rory groaned. She was not a fan of Hollywood. The entitlement of the industry upset her. It divided Los Angeles into the haves and have-nots. If it got out that London Green was a customer, all the empty seats around her would be packed, and she could kiss the peace and quiet of the Honey Pot good-bye.

Up to now, celebrities and the other upscale lesbians had stayed away. They flocked to Hollywood and the new clubs popping up there. Deep in the Valley, the Honey Pot was the perfect place for an average, run-of-the-mill lesbian to hang out, have a beer, and figure out how to get her cooking career out of the back kitchen.

Maya, on the other hand, obviously saw her chance. She leaped down the counter until she was right in front of the superstar. "You want a drink? That's easy." She paused for effect as a dazzling smile jumped to her lips. "The woman just has to tell me what she wants."

Rory's eyes widened. Maya was shameless. While they'd only been roommates for a few months, Rory was not surprised. Maya talked about the A-lister all the time. It had been London Green this, and London Green that. Now that she thought about it, Rory threw Maya props. Her idol had walked through the door, and she was not going to let the opportunity of a lifetime pass her by.

London gave Maya a slow once-over. With a smoldering stare, she traced the sexy curves of Maya's hips and lingered on her breasts stuffed into a tight Honey Pot T-shirt. Finally, London settled on Maya's dark, glittering eyes and returned her grin. The air was electric. As clichéd as it was, Rory looked for sparks flying between them.

"What do I want?" London's tone was deep and husky. "Let's start with a vodka tonic and see where that takes us."

Sharp intakes of breath buzzed around the bar. Everyone gasped as if watching a movie premiere. Rory could almost hear a deep male voice setting up the storyline for the trailer. "One cold winter night, the Princess of Hollywood walks into a bar and finds true love with a common bartender." Or maybe that was the beginning of just another bar joke.

Whatever the case, these people were fools. There was no such thing as insta-love. No one could recognize their soulmate by stepping into the same room with them.

"London," a voice at the door called. "Are you in here?"

London released Maya's gaze and waved casually. "Over here."

A pretty, garden-variety blonde scurried to London's side. She peered into the darkness of the bar and wrinkled her nose as if she smelled something rotten. "I thought we were going to Sue's."

"Sue will take her sweet time getting back to the Westside. Besides"—she gave Maya another once-over—"I've placed an order for something I really want."

The blonde jerked back as if she had been slapped. She glared at Maya as if she owned London, and her mouth screwed into a tiny knot. Even in the dim light of the bar, Rory could see the truth. London only had eyes for Maya, whose dark beauty was the perfect contrast to her own shimmering light. They fit together like yin and yang. If this woman was hoping for something with London, she was completely screwed.

"Sue's expecting us." A slight panic crept into the blonde's voice.

Rory had to give it to her. She wasn't giving up.

"You go, then." London reached out a hand to Maya. "I'm staying here."

Maya pushed the drink across the bar, and London plucked the lime from the rim. She rubbed it slowly across her lips and dropped it back into the glass. The action would have been ridiculous on anyone else, but Rory had to admit that London had totally pulled it off.

"Sorry, It's the best vodka we have here." Maya leaned over the bar slightly. "We don't have a big selection."

London took a sip. "It's exactly what I wanted. I didn't know it until I came in."

The blonde went rigid. She stared, wide-eyed, at the drama playing out in front of her, in front of them all.

Rory bit her lip, pitying this stranger. Living out the end of her relationship so publicly couldn't be easy. "I'm sorry." She reached out and touched the woman's elbow.

The blonde pulled her arm back as if she had been burned. "Fuck off," she said. To Rory, maybe. To London, probably. To life in general, definitely. She rushed off, and the front door slammed behind her with a heavy thunk.

"Don't go anywhere," London told Maya and slipped out of the room.

The bar erupted in chatter. The dozen or so people buzzed with the excitement of a large crowd. A couple in the front argued about which selfie with London in the background to post on Instagram. Another woman shouted into her phone, "You will never believe who was just standing ten feet from me."

Rory leaned over the counter and poked Maya in the shoulder. "Oh my God. What're you doing?"

Maya grimaced and giggled simultaneously. "I don't know." And then, she shrugged. "It's London Green," she said as if that was the only explanation needed.

"You can't flirt with her. She's with her girlfriend. There are rules. And if you don't believe in them, you should at least believe in human decency."

"Nuh-uh." Maya grinned. "They broke up months ago. It was all over *Hollywood, Now*."

"Someone needs to tell her, then."

Maya pointed to the shadows outside the bar's frosted windows. "I think that's what's happening."

Sure enough, they were arguing. Or more accurately, the woman was shouting and swinging her arms wildly over her shoulders. She moved in jerks that reminded Rory of shadow puppet theater. London stood quiet and still until she raised her hand, face height, palm facing out in the universal gesture of *stop this shit right now*. The woman froze as London spoke. Deflating little by little, her head, her shoulders, and finally, her whole body sank in on itself. Eventually, she slunk away into the night.

"She'll be all right," London announced when she returned inside. "I sent her to Sue's. The car service is taking her there. She won't be alone. I guess she thought being broken up was on a sliding scale, and we weren't at the final stage yet." London laughed, and somehow, it was sympathetic. Her head whipped around the room at lightning speed. She gave each patron a tiny private moment, and for half a heartbeat, invited each of them into her world.

Rory marveled at the performance. It didn't matter whose fault the breakup was, everyone in the Honey Pot was completely on team London now. Impressive…and maybe a little scary. Were actors always acting?

London crossed to the bar. She fixed Maya with another smoldering stare and traced a finger around the rim of the vodka tonic. "Where were we?"

"Right about here." Maya drew her hand off the glass and slid London's finger into her mouth.

A soft groan drifted over to Rory. Who it came from, she didn't know. London? Maya? Carol at the end of the bar counter whose mouth had dropped into a perfect O?

London licked her own lips. "When do you get off?" The question, barely a whisper, was loud with desire.

Maya kissed the tip of London's finger. "Right now." She dropped her hand to her waist and tugged at her apron strings.

"What?" Rory couldn't bite back the reaction. "You're in the middle of a shift." Jobs were hard to come by, especially for out-of-work actors. "Are you crazy? You can't throw this job away."

"You're not my boss, Rory," Maya said.

"But I am." Terri, the perpetually frazzled manager, scooted around the bar to grab Maya's arm. "You can't do this. We're already down one server."

Maya easily sidestepped her and let her apron tumble to the floor. London reached out a hand, and as Maya intertwined their fingers, she transformed. Certainty shone from her as if she was lit by a spotlight from within.

Rory blew out a deep breath. This wasn't going to end well. How could it? But Maya was a big girl, and truth be told, none of Rory's recent relationships had lasted more than a few months. She wasn't in a position to give dating advice to anyone. And yet, Terri was right. Life was built on both responsibilities and consequences.

The wooden door shut behind the couple with a loud thunk.

Terri whipped her head toward Rory. "She can't walk out on her shift. Does she think she can drop in and out whenever she wants? What the fuck?"

Rory shrugged. "Who knows what she's thinking." Although everyone in the bar knew exactly what Maya's train of thought had been.

"What am I supposed to do now?" Terri stamped her foot like a two-year-old.

"I'll take the rest of her shift." Rory started around the bar.

"You haven't worked here for years."

"It's like riding a bike. I never forget a recipe, cocktail, or pastry." Before Terri could argue, she added, "I hate to see you in a bind. It's the least I can do."

Terri ran a hand through her frizzy hair, trying to tamp it and her anxiety down.

"I'll do it for free," Rory said.

"Fine." Terri turned her back as if she was doing Rory the favor.

Behind the counter, Rory picked up the apron with a thumb and forefinger and shook it out carefully before tying it around her waist. The floor was sticky with God knew what, and these were her good jeans. As she tightened the double knot below her belly button, she tied her past around her. Moving backward into bartending was not her goal. Like Maya, she also wanted to throw caution to the wind and embrace something shiny and new in her life. Unlike Maya, however, her new direction hadn't just waltzed in the door.

She plastered a smile on her face and called out, "Okay, Honey Pot, who needs a drink?"

❖

"She did *what?*" Ellis Turner, CEO of the Ellis Turner Agency, shouted into her phone. A familiar stiffness snaked from her jaw to her neck and settled below her shoulder blades. "Sorry, Yolie, I'm not mad at you."

"I know," her assistant said quickly. "We both heard her promise she was going to Sue's after the play."

"London's promises are often lies." Ellis knew she was being hard on her most important client. In a kinder mood, she would characterize her as spontaneous and open to whatever life had to offer, but it was late, and she had been here before. Too often. "For Christ's sake, what was Shannon doing there? They broke up three months and four days ago. I should know, I called *Hollywood, Now* myself."

"She showed up at the theater unannounced. And you know London, she's way too oblivious. She knew they were done, so it didn't matter if Shannon hoped they might get back together.

And from what I saw online, Shannon wasn't happy when they didn't."

"Online?"

"I think someone was on the street with a phone when they were arguing. London didn't say much. Shannon, though, had a few choice words."

Ellis shut her eyes and tried to not let irritation bleed into her voice. "What words, exactly?"

"Like slut, the c-word, and meat curtain."

"Meat curtain?"

"It means fat, ugly woman parts."

"I know what it means. Does Shannon? Because she signed an NDA."

Thanks to a teeter-totter accident in preschool, a jagged scar started at London's vagina and ran to her pubic bone. A blemish on an otherwise perfect body, but any flaw, especially a hidden one, was gossip gold to the tabloids, and London was especially sensitive to the scar.

Ellis pulled a to-do list on her desk closer. Next to number fifteen, she jotted, *Damage Control: L's vagina.* Sometimes, not often, she hated her job.

"She was angry, I guess." Yolie sounded tired, poor thing.

"Obviously." Ellis rubbed one temple with her free hand and hoped that a migraine wasn't on its way. Even now, she had no idea what had gone wrong. She had met with Shannon personally. They'd sat in this very office and had drunk oat milk lattes while she'd explained that London wasn't ready to settle down. It wasn't anyone's fault. She thought the meeting had gone well. Shannon had nodded, said she understood, and had even thanked Ellis for her time. What had she missed?

Forget the past. It was the present that was going to hurt them. "And London had a few drinks at this bar?" Ellis asked. "It's really called the Honey Pot?"

"Yeah."

"Jesus. Everyone's going to have a field day with that name. Please tell me that she left the Honey Pot and went straight home."

"She did, but…"

Ellis swallowed hard. "But what?"

"But not alone."

"Damn."

"And they took a Lyft."

"What happened to the driver we hired?"

"I don't know?"

London knew better. A Lyft? Now there was a witness. Dread churned in Ellis's stomach. She could only imagine what the driver had seen. London was not known for delaying gratification on any front. In the last few months, she was starting to get a reputation for a *colorful dating history*. The kind that did a man good and pulled a woman down. Fast.

Ellis hated the double standard as much as anyone, but Hollywood was a well-oiled machine that despite liberal rhetoric, wasn't going to jump the tracks for an out, queer, gender-bending actress who called her own shots, no matter how gorgeous she was.

"Who is she?" Ellis centered on the only question that mattered now.

"Sorry. I don't know that, either. There are pictures, though. I'm sending them now. Do you want me to come in?"

"God, no. It's Saturday night." Ellis glanced at the clock on her desk. Eleven-thirty. How on earth had it gotten so late? She hadn't even had dinner. "As usual, you've already gone above and beyond. I'll take it from here."

"You sure?"

"Absolutely." Ellis had won the employee lottery in a big way, and she knew it. "And don't come in tomorrow, either. The door will be locked, so don't try to slip in. Take a full weekend for once."

"Okay. But you need some downtime too."

"I'll get some. I promise." She hung up and added under her breath, "Once I figure out how much trouble we're in."

London's latest stunt couldn't have come at a worse time. January was the beginning of TV pilot season in Hollywood. This year, with new active streaming services in the mix, over thirty pilots needed actors right now. Three new breakdowns and scripts had come in yesterday. She had spent her Saturday researching the projects, jotting down notes about the casting directors, the showrunners, and the production companies, and slogging her way through the scripts. She needed to maintain her reputation for submitting the perfect actor for each audition. Already, a list matching actors with audition times sat on her desk. London wasn't her only client, just her biggest headache.

And yet.

She owed London everything. She had signed with the Ellis Turner Agency when lowly extras on film sets wouldn't give her the time of day. She had told Ellis that she liked her disciplined vibe and that she needed a queer woman who would inherently understand the hardships of navigating the Hollywood landscape as an out lesbian. London had made Ellis's career. And in return, Ellis had given her all her gratitude. And all her attention.

Total win-win, even if at times, managing London was like standing in a whirlpool with nothing to hold on to.

She grabbed her laptop and pulled up Yolie's email. Several paparazzi photos of London and a younger woman exiting the Honey Pot and climbing into a Lyft popped onto her screen. She studied the stranger with a professional eye. Shiny dark hair fell in easy waves. Ellis couldn't see her face, but her body was quite good. Curvy, athletic, and very sexy if you liked that look. And Ellis knew that London did. Thin, blond Shannon had been an inexplicable blip on the radar. This woman was a little tough around the edges and definitely badass. Yep, totally London's type.

Ellis zeroed in on the Honey Pot T-shirt. The logo—a sexy cartoon bee plunging into golden nectar—sat right on her breasts. *She works for the bar.* The realization hit Ellis with certainty.

She picked up her phone. "Hey, Siri," she said, "The telephone number for the Honey Pot Bar in North Hollywood."

"The only option I found," Siri said, "is the Honey Pot on Miranda Street. Is that the one you're looking for?"

"Yes." It was the last place she wanted to call on a Saturday night, but here she was.

A double beep and the Honey Pot's information appeared on Google Maps. Ellis hit the call button. "The Honey Pot," a female voice answered after several rings. "Where the drinks and the women are sweet. Terri speaking. Can I help you?"

"I hope so." Ellis put on a vague Valley girl accent: young and supremely self-centered. "This is crazy, and I know that you probably have rules against this kind of thing. You should know I never do this. I was in there earlier tonight and there was a…" London's flavor of the week was too tough to be a server. She took a chance. "…bartender. She had long dark hair and was really hot. I was hoping that maybe—"

"Maya's not here," the woman said curtly.

That was almost too easy. She got a first name. Halfway there.

"No?" Ellis tried to infuse her voice with longing. "I…we… well, you see, we had a moment—"

"Dear, she has moments with everyone here. She was angling for a better tip."

"That's kind of what I wanted to do. Tip her. I mean, not with money." Ellis tried for an embarrassed laugh. "You see, we talked about these cupcakes I make. She says she loves red velvet, and wouldn't you know it, I specialize in red velvet cupcakes. If you could tell me her last name, I could put them in a box with her name on it to make sure she gets them. I'll drop them off."

"Layton, but don't bother. I fired her ass tonight. She just doesn't know it yet."

Ah, that explained the easy information. This woman was the owner or manager, and she was pissed that Maya had put an exquisite face and her libido before the job.

"Why?" Ellis hoped she was mad enough to unload.

"I need someone who's reliable."

Bingo. She was absolutely mad enough.

"She took off for three auditions this week alone, and now she can't even finish her shift? I run a real business here, not someplace to hang out when your life's not working out. Look, I'm sorry. There's a better woman out there for your cupcake."

Jesus, was everything a double entendre in the Valley? "I'm going to drop them off anyway. In case she comes back."

"She won't. I'll never let her in the door again." Terri hung up.

Ellis tapped two fingers on the desk as she rolled what she had learned around in her head. Maya Layton was a big flirt, she was a wannabe actor—of course, who wasn't in Los Angeles—and she had chosen London over her job.

"Fuck me," Ellis said out loud as the weight of London's future fell heavily on her already tense shoulders.

She glanced at her laptop. The battery read sixteen percent. She could turn it off, head to bed, and grab downtime as she had told Yolie she would.

Or.

The charger sat neatly on her desk, taunting her.

As if they had a mind of their own, her fingers stretched for it.

London wasn't the only one who'd be pulling the covers off Maya Layton tonight.

CHAPTER TWO

Rory's phone woke her out of a deep sleep with a persistent, old-school ring. Barely awake, she glanced at the clock. Five-thirty? Who on earth would call this early?

Convinced that something must be wrong, she threw back the covers and grabbed the phone. It stopped ringing as soon as she picked it up. She stared at it, waiting for a voice mail. Nothing. Should she call her mom to see if everything was okay? It was early, however, maybe *pickle* was code for *deep shit*. Before she could decide, the phone rang again.

"Hello?"

"Rory. Are you up?" A quiet voice asked despite the obvious. Not her mom. "Who is this?"

"Maya."

"Why are you whispering? I can barely hear you."

"I don't want to wake London. She's still sleeping. Listen, can you come and get me?"

"What?" Surely, she had heard wrong. She liked Maya well enough. She paid her rent on time and more often than not, replaced the food she took without asking. However, this early in the morning, it was kind of a big ask.

"I'm sorry," Maya said. "I don't have my car. We took a Lyft last night."

"Can't you get another one and come home?"

"No. I don't have my phone."

She knew she was still sleepy, but nothing was making sense here. "How are you calling?"

"She has a landline. Isn't that adorable? Who has a landline these days?"

"Yeah, right, adorable. And your phone is where?"

Maya sighed heavily. "Locked up in a kitchen drawer. London's agent has lots of rules. Number one is that guests can't have cell phones in the bedroom. Crazy, huh?"

Rory had heard crazier.

Like this request.

"It's five-thirty in the morning. On a Sunday," Rory added. "Maybe you can wait until London wakes up? She can get you your phone or use hers to get a Lyft—"

"Yeah, I could do that," Maya said quickly. "But I don't want to overstay my welcome. Shannon, that woman in the bar last night…London told me that she was clingy right from the start. I don't want to make any of her mistakes."

Rory said nothing. She was going to suggest calling a taxi with the phone already in her hand. Maya had pretty much quit her job last night, though, and taxis were expensive, much more so than calling your roommate for a free ride.

"Okay," Maya said when the silence dragged out, "here's the real reason. If I leave my phone here *by mistake*, I need to come back to get it, or at the very least, she needs to get in touch with me."

"That actually makes sense."

"I hope so. Rory, I really like her. Last night at the Honey Pot, I admit, I was seeing how far I could get. But when we got to her house, something special happened between us."

"Maya, I don't want to hear about your sex life."

"It isn't that. I mean, it isn't *just* that. I think this could be more than a one-night thing." Maya paused, and when she spoke again, her voice was infused with awe. "I can't believe it. She's totally into me. And so considerate." Maya said the last word with such emotion that Rory knew now they *were* talking about her sex life. "Please, come get me. This could be everything I've ever wanted, and I don't want to blow it. I'm in love."

"After seven hours?"

"It's crazy, right? But it happens in the movies all the time. Oh my God, they wouldn't have to change a thing. It would be a blockbuster."

"You got to be kidding me," Rory said. She had to admit, she was more amused than exasperated. She too, was curious how far Maya's gamble was going to get her. Besides, she had never been able to go back to sleep once she was up.

Maya sweetened the pot. "I'll clean the kitchen and take out the trash for a month."

Rory blew out a deep breath. She hated taking out the trash. "Fine. Where are you?"

"Not far. Hollywood Hills. Sunset Plaza Drive. Google it. Take Laurel Canyon and make a right on Kirkwood. You need to go up Sunset Plaza to the top." She raced through the directions as if they were a disclaimer on a medicine commercial. "Once you get there, you can't see the house, but there's no way you can miss it. There's a black gate with cool patterns, like from Mexico or South America. I'll give you twenty minutes and meet you outside."

"You better be there," Rory said.

Maya had already hung up.

Rory yanked on whatever was closest. A pair of unwashed jeans, an ancient sweatshirt, and flip-flops. She didn't even run a comb through her short hair. No one would see her. She wasn't planning to get out of the car. London's house was close to their apartment in North Hollywood by LA standards. But Maya had only lived in town for six months and still didn't have a clue. It was going to take Rory longer than twenty minutes, and she had to get going if this goofy plan of Maya's had any chance of working.

The drive did take longer. Too many unfamiliar roads and bald tires that needed to be replaced. It was way after six when Rory found the black gate at the top of Sunset Plaza Drive. Maya had been right on one account. She couldn't miss it. Geometric Art Deco patterns interlocked to form a true work of art. Rory marveled at its bold beauty and then grumbled at the empty driveway.

No Maya.

She pulled a U-turn and parked across the street, facing downhill for a quick getaway. She killed the engine and tapped her fingers on the steering wheel. How long was she supposed to wait? For all she knew, London could have woken up and was being *considerate* again.

Annoyed as she was, she couldn't blame Maya for staying. There wasn't a lesbian on earth who hadn't a fantasy or two about London…except for, maybe, Rory. Not that anyone would believe her. London was a little too perfect for her. She liked her women real, with natural imperfections. Although her most recent ex's quirk of walking away with her favorite frying pan was one imperfection she could live without. She grimaced. The last thing she wanted to do was mull over the sad state of her love life.

Which was exactly what she would do if she was forced to sit here any longer.

She needed a plan and a large cup of coffee.

As if on cue, an electric, black-and-white BMW, looking like a monstrous Storm Trooper's helmet, glided silently around the corner. It pulled up to the gate and stopped. A hand reached out the driver's window, touched the gate's keypad, and hesitated. The driver's head tipped up and seemed to notice her in the rearview mirror.

The car's brake lights flashed red, and the driver jumped out so hastily, she tripped on the door frame. She righted herself quickly and strode over with deliberate steps, her arms swinging mechanically, as if she had been wound up with a key from behind. She was beautifully dressed, especially for a Sunday, wool slacks and a simple and elegant green sweater. Rory knew the kind: so expensive it could have put gas in her tank for a month. A thick, gold Y-chain swung between her breasts and tied the outfit together, and as Rory noticed, called attention to her curves. Her copper hair was pulled back into a high bun so tight, it pulled at a face that would be attractive if her eyes weren't screwed into a hard glare.

She whipped a closed hand in a circle and motioned for Rory to roll down her window. Rory did and gave her a smile. "Can I help you?" The woman's tone offered anything but help.

"No, I'm good. Just waiting for a friend." Rory said lightly as if hanging outside a megastar's house at the crack of dawn wasn't weird or creepy at all.

"You can't wait here." She pointed a manicured finger to the NO STOPPING ANYTIME street sign hovering over Rory's car. The tow truck was pulling a car that looked remarkably like her ancient Kia. "I don't want any trouble." The woman slid the latest iPhone out of her purse. "But I will call the police if you don't move on."

"I don't want any trouble either. God knows, that's the last thing I was looking for this morning. But sometimes, trouble comes whether you want it or not." She widened her smile and met the woman's glare head-on. "Crazy the way life works sometimes, right?"

Now she'd see how tightly wound she was. Often, people needed a kind word, a touch on the arm…or a smile…to loosen up.

The woman's irises, the color of green sea glass, sparked with annoyance. "Life has a way of testing people. That's for sure. Could you just move the car, please?"

The smile hadn't worked. Plan B then. "You'll have to do me a favor first."

The woman's eyes widened. "Excuse me?"

Rory met her stare. Maya was going to owe her big time. "Clearly, you're going in there. Presumably, you will see London Green. Can you tell her to tell Maya that Rory's out here? And I'm only waiting ten more minutes, and then, her ride's leaving. I need a cup of coffee."

At the mention of Maya's name, the woman's stiff posture softened slightly. "You mean Maya Layton?" She squinted into the car to study Rory.

Conscious that she was wearing clothes that this woman probably wouldn't be caught dead in, she held her head high and spoke firmly. "Yes, I'm a friend of Maya's. She doesn't have her car, and she needs a ride home."

The woman blew out a long breath and looked up and down the empty street. "Oh, for Christ's sake. Pull your car in behind mine. We're both here for the same reason."

"Great." She turned the key hanging in the ignition. A loud squeal and then the engine spun to life. She pulled in behind the silent BMW.

The Art Deco masterpiece swung open slowly, theatrically, even, as if curtains were parting on a Hollywood production. And it might have been. The estate could have won an Oscar for set design. The driveway wound through well-coiffed native shrubs and bushes in a xeriscape terrain. Rory had grown up in Topanga Canyon, the bohemian artist refuge outside of LA, and knew a thing or two about drought-tolerant plants. But her mom's carefully tended garden looked like an explosion of weeds next to this place.

The house popped up at the edge of the canyon. The entrance was small, demure, even, although a waterfall feature and an atrium filled with colorful plants flanked either side of the double door.

"Wait here." The woman held up a hand in warning as she slid out of her own car. "I'll get Maya."

Relief washed through Rory as she settled back in her seat. She didn't care what this woman thought of her, but the last thing she wanted to do was prolong the morning by getting out of the car. In two short conversations, the entitlement of this woman who thought she could direct Rory's every move had rubbed her the wrong way. What made her think she was better than Rory? Because she was on a first-name basis with London Green? What a joke.

As the woman pulled out the key for the front door from a leather work bag on her shoulder, it swung open, both sides at once, framing London Green as if her appearance was a sudden reveal in a movie.

Did London practice her entrances, like here and last night at the bar, or did movie stars inherently know how to pull them off? In a less dramatic version, Maya popped up behind her and waved at Rory, a happy smile on her face.

"Ellis! What are you doing here?" London asked brightly and then looked straight into Rory's car. "And you must be Rory. Come in. Both of you. Come in." London gave her a dazzling, toothpaste commercial smile.

In the car, Rory glanced at her jeans. There was a rip in one knee, and her rubber flip-flops looked like they were part of the original shipment from Japan in the 1950s.

"No," Ellis said. "No one's coming in. Maya and Rory are leaving, and you and I have business to discuss."

London laughed and waved away Ellis's objection. "This is Sunday. Until tomorrow at nine, you're my friend, not my agent."

Ah, the crazy one who locks phones away. That explains a lot.

"Sunday," London continued, "is also Carmen's day off. We're fending for ourselves. We've made coffee."

Coffee was the magic word. Rory's hand moved almost on its own and opened the car door. Ellis gave her the once-over even before she had fully exited, lingering on each offensive piece of clothing before settling on Rory's unruly hair.

She fought the heat rising in her chest. "I hadn't planned on coming in."

"Hmm," Ellis said, although what it meant exactly, Rory couldn't decipher.

Everyone followed London inside. The unassuming entrance to the house was, of course, deceptive. Crystal-white porcelain tiles flooded the entryway and ran into a large, ultramodern living room. The back walls were glass, and the view spanned the whole city. The tall buildings of downtown sat center frame. Rory stopped to admire the vista. Even with the haze of the early morning fog, the panorama was something very special.

"Can you believe it?" Maya asked as she doubled back to Rory. "Come on. You're especially going to love the kitchen."

Rory's cheap shoes slapped against the tile as she moved. She made a conscious effort not to shuffle. She wouldn't be embarrassed. Then, she turned the corner, and all thoughts of what she was wearing dropped from her mind.

The sleek chef's kitchen was stunning. High gloss cabinets ran down to white marble countertops. A grand island was made of the same glossy material and supported a huge bouquet of pink flowers. Thanks to that pop of color and several others, the room had real warmth despite its white-on-white design. Rory cast a practiced eye around the room. The appliances were top-of-the-line, as was the wine fridge and the hood over the cooktop.

Man, would she love to cook in this kitchen. Either London and her staff were neat freaks of the highest degree or no one baked, simmered, or grilled here. It was way too clean. Such a shame.

A bubbling noise did come from one corner, and the aroma of fresh coffee wafted over.

"Latte or straight up?" London crossed to a high-end espresso machine.

Rory's mouth watered. She could almost taste the nutty, bitter flavor. She glanced at Maya for directions. Were they staying or going?

Maya shrugged and picked up a full mug already on the counter.

"Any type of caffeine would be wonderful," Rory said.

"Perfect. I make an excellent latte. Sit." London motioned to the stools on the other side of the island.

Ellis, who'd said nothing since the driveway, huffed.

What's her problem? Rory pulled out the stool and plopped on it as if she was here to stay. "Thank you. I'm completely useless without coffee."

"Rory knows coffee and other flavors. She's a chef," Maya said proudly, as if Rory was her own child who'd done something extraordinary.

"You work in a restaurant?" Ellis turned to her with another cool gaze.

"No. I'm a culinary assistant for a cooking show on the Food and Flavor Network. Nothing exciting. I work in the back kitchen." What was going on here? Maya rarely shifted the conversation off herself.

"The back kitchen?" London asked.

"It's where the food on the show is actually made. Those kitchens on set, they barely work."

"She's on *Guess Who's Coming to Dinner* right now." Maya jumped back into the conversation. "The show, not the movie. You know the one where Norah Gallagher makes a meal and then invites famous people over for dinner and a side of gossip?"

"Norah Gallagher the comedian?" London asked.

Maya nodded, and a smile she was clearly trying to bite back tugged at her lips.

"Oh, we did that network show together years ago." London looked over Maya's shoulder to Ellis. "God, what was it, five, six?"

"Six." Ellis finally slid onto a stool, leaving an empty seat between her and Rory. Her back was as straight as if someone had slid a two-by-four into her sweater.

"You could go on the show." Maya handed London an empty mug for the latte.

London poured the espresso into the cup and reached for the steamed milk.

After a moment of silence, Maya added, "They would eat you up. You'd be their most famous guest ever."

Rory nodded. It made sense now. Maya had been manipulating the conversation from the start. The detour was part of the ruse. If she could get London to guest star on *Guess Who's Coming to Dinner*, Maya could be on set. Leaving nothing to fate, she was planning another chance encounter.

On the other side of her, Ellis blew out a quick breath. She had obviously figured out the endgame too. "London's very busy right now. She's preparing for her role in *Dazzled*. You know, the new live-action fairy tale from Prodigy Studios? She's Princess Carina." Pride simmered in her voice.

With good cause. Rory knew every A-lister had campaigned for that role. Prodigy was throwing big bucks and creative guns at the production. If she believed the articles in *Hollywood, Now*, actors had come out of the woodwork to audition, and by all accounts, the film was destined to shatter box office records worldwide.

And London had snagged the role. Now, sitting next to the bristling energy that was Ellis, Rory was pretty sure that Ellis, as annoying as she was, had had a big hand in that accomplishment.

"Shooting doesn't start for months." London smiled at Maya. "And all I'm doing right now is getting into shape. Sure, I need to tighten up some." She brought a hand to her perfectly toned stomach. "But I could take a day off to see Norah again. She was very good to me when I was first starting out." She poured milk into the mug with the skill of a barista and then turned to Ellis. "Can you make that happen?"

"I'm not sure this is where you want to spend your valuable time at the moment."

London slid the full mug on to the counter and pulled Maya, who matched her height exactly, almost as if she was cast that way, into a tight embrace. "That's where you're wrong, Ellis. I know exactly where I want to spend my time." They both leaned in at the exact same moment.

The kiss exploded as their lips met. Maya immediately reached up with a hand to pull London even closer. And they were lost to everything and everyone but themselves.

Only a few feet away, Rory sat mesmerized as she watched the kiss grow deeper and deeper. Why was she still watching? Shouldn't she turn away to give them some privacy? And then, it hit her.

This was a movie kiss. Not that it wasn't real. London clearly had genuine feelings for Maya as she tenderly slid a hand down her back. This embrace was somehow bigger and grander than a kiss in the real world. Rory half expected romantic music to swell in the kitchen.

"London." Ellis's voice cracked and broke the spell. "Can we please take care of some business? Before this goes much further?"

Rory swiveled toward her. A deep blush had warmed Ellis's cheeks, as red as a stop sign. Which was what Ellis clearly wanted them to do.

Rory sat back in her seat. Wow, the control freak had feelings. Who would have thought? The embarrassment softened her look. Freckles popped up everywhere on her face, and Rory realized that she had covered most of them up with makeup.

It's a better look for her. More natural, almost human.

Ellis swung to the other side of the barstool and yanked her leather work bag onto the island. She pulled out a single sheet of paper. The words Nondisclosure and Confidentially Agreement ran across the top in big, bold letters.

Rory took in a quick breath. Shit. The morning was getting super serious, super fast. Goddammit. This was exactly what she hated about Hollywood. The people in power, like this Ellis Turner, thought they could walk all over the regular people like her and Maya. She saw the entitlement on her cooking show, as insignificant as it was, and sure as shit, she was seeing the privilege now. Maya only wanted love. Didn't Ellis want her client, who'd called her a friend, to be happy as well?

"London," Ellis said again. This time louder and without the tremble in her voice.

They broke apart—the kiss had run its course, anyway—and both turned toward Ellis. London settled a possessive arm over Maya's shoulder and raised an eyebrow. "What business could the four of us possibly have together?" she asked.

CHAPTER THREE

This." The NDA scraped on the smooth surface of the island as Ellis slid it over. "And it only concerns the three of us."

Once, before she knew how easily London fell in love, Ellis hadn't demanded an NDA from the flavor of the month. That rookie mistake had totally bitten her in the ass. Revealing pictures, although not London's vaginal scar, had popped up on social media the second she had moved on. Both her and London's careers had nearly tanked before they'd begun. Ellis would never, ever underestimate a scorned woman a second time.

London pulled the paper toward her with one finger. "Oh God, not this again."

"What is it?" Maya craned her neck to look, and her face fell. "Oh."

"It's a boilerplate nondisclosure agreement. A confidentiality agreement's standard in situations like these." Ellis tried to infuse lightness into her voice. Despite the way she was coming off, she always hated this part. The NDAs had nothing to do with London, or even Maya, and everything to do with love at first sight. It flat out didn't exist. At best this was good, old-fashioned lust, and it would burn out hard and fast. As it always did for London.

"I'm sure you'd never purposely do anything to hurt London." She wished she could call a time-out and explain to Maya that it wasn't personal. Although…she had learned a few things about

Maya from her late-night research that might be red flags. In the last six months, she had booked only one commercial, and that had been group work, not as a principal. London was her big break. And more importantly, there was something about this woman that rubbed Ellis the wrong way. What, she didn't know. She couldn't quite put her finger on it. Yet.

Maya's eyes widened with this sudden development, her lips curled slightly at being center stage.

London slid the paper across the marble counter. "You better sign it, or she'll never leave us alone."

Thankful that London was playing her part, Ellis drew a pen with an ETA logo from her briefcase and handed it over to Maya.

"Um…okay. Yeah, I'll sign."

Ellis bowed her head in relief. Maybe this day wasn't going to be a complete shit show.

"No. Wait." The words were quiet, but they echoed in the kitchen with conviction.

Tension cut back into Ellis's shoulders like bands of barbwire.

"I'm sorry, I need to say something here." Rory slid off the barstool, pointed at the NDA, and grew into the space around her. "These kinds of things are exactly what's wrong in today's Hollywood. They're used to hush up bad behavior at every level."

"Excuse me?" Ellis couldn't believe her ears.

"It works because we live in a culture where extreme bullying and victimization from people in power are both totally okay—"

"I'm not a bully," Ellis shot back.

"Isn't that what all bullies say?" Putting her back to Ellis, she turned to Maya. "Seriously, you don't have to sign anything like this." She pulled the paper out from under Maya's hand to prove her point.

Ellis raised her palm and flashed it toward Rory. "Wait a sec—"

"Exactly. That's what we should all do." Rory bounced up on her toes and stood taller than everyone in the room. "You can't control relationships, or at least, you shouldn't."

"Please, let me address my client." Ellis curled her fingernails into her palm.

Rory addressed Maya. "If you start with what could go wrong, it's like you're inviting disaster into bed with you—"

"Rory," Maya's face tightened, "I really want this."

"You sign this, and you're in a relationship with her too." She motioned to Ellis. "Jesus, it's almost a thruple. She's going to be pulling the strings anyway. Don't give her even more ammunition."

Rory took a breath, and Ellis grabbed her chance. "Do you always jump in where you don't belong? You can't just say whatever you want."

Hands upturned, Rory shrugged. "See. It's already started."

Ellis mentally kicked herself. The words had come out before she had thought about them. A cold hard bitch was how she was coming off now, and it wasn't doing her cause any good. What she wanted to say was that this wasn't her first love rodeo. That she had seen this exact scenario with London play out more than once. When the relationship was over, and it would end, hurting London would be way too easy for Maya. As easy as throwing a pebble into the ocean. Above everything else, she wanted to protect London and not only because it was her job. At thirty-seven, she was only eleven years older than London, but she felt very motherly and protective of her. Both feelings pushed and pulled at every decision she made about London's career.

"You're right," Rory jumped back into the discussion. "No one invited me in, and I don't belong here for a thousand reasons. It doesn't change anything, though."

No one spoke, and a leaden silence hung heavily around them.

Finally, London snatched the NDA off the island. "She's right, Ellis." She ripped it into two pieces and let them drop to the counter. "Maybe this has been the problem with all my relationships. Let's take the training wheels off this one and see how far we can go."

Maya's whole face lit up, and Rory nodded her approval.

Oh my fucking God. Ellis closed her eyes and breathed from her belly, trying to center herself again as her meditation coach had taught her. She couldn't afford a migraine now. How had this gone sideways? And so quickly? Why hadn't she left Rory out by the curb and talked to Maya alone?

"Okay," she said finally. At least her voice was even. She would circle back to the NDA later. "How about you both stay put for the next couple days? We can send somebody over to your house, Maya, for your stuff. That will give me a chance to create the kind of exposure that we want for this new relationship. What do you think about that?" She glanced between them, waiting for an answer.

"Sure, we can do that." London grabbed Maya's hand. "Right?"

"Yeah," Maya answered, surprising Ellis with how much happiness one little word could contain.

Maybe she was wrong. God, she hoped she was, for everyone's sake, especially the couple in front of her.

"Staying in is definitely a good idea. Thanks, Ellis." London raised Maya's hands to her lips and then led her quickly out of the room. They disappeared around a corner, and with London's energy gone, the kitchen felt very empty.

Ellis scooted around Rory and flipped the switch on the coffee maker. It powered off with a low hiss. "I guess that's our cue," she said, grabbing the full cup of coffee still on the counter and dumping it into the white farm sink. It circled down the drain as if it had never existed.

She glanced up to recognize that Rory had been watching her every move. Oh yeah, that was her coffee. Apparently, no one's plans were working out this morning.

She could get back to the office and change that. She waved a hand toward the front of the house. "Can you find your way out of the canyon?"

"Look. I—"

"No need to apologize." Ellis didn't know if Rory was about to. It didn't matter. The moment was over. Outwardly, at least,

Ellis needed to show that she had taken the loss and had already moved on. "We both want what's best for our friends. I get that."

She led the way out. "Are you, by the way?" Ellis asked.

"Am I what?"

"Friends with Maya."

"No. We're more roommates than friends."

That was the first good news Ellis had heard all morning. London liked her lovers close until she didn't. Maya would officially move in by the end of the week, and with a little luck, this would be the last Ellis would see of Rory, the woman who could kill her best-laid plans.

When they got to the front door, Ellis stuck her hand out. "It was nice to meet you," she lied.

Rory hesitated and then raised her own. "You too."

They shook on it. Lies all around, apparently.

Rory slipped out and walked across the driveway, her flip-flops slapping ridiculously against the pressed concrete.

Ellis watched her go. She had to admit, the view wasn't bad. If she took away the jeans and ratty sweatshirt, not that she was undressing Rory in her head or anything, she was very attractive. Long and lean, in that androgynous, unisex kind of way Ellis had always secretly admired but had never dated. She had noticed other things too. Rory's brown hair was lush and thick and would take a trendy cut nicely if Ellis was styling her for auditions. Her eyes had also been an inviting shade of brown. And not one freckle. Her skin, damn her, was unblemished. And now, heading to her car, she moved with quiet determination. It made a very pretty picture.

For the second time that morning, heat rushed to Ellis's cheeks. What was she doing? Had she been sizing up actors for so long, she assessed everyone now? With any luck, she would never see this woman again, and she could easily protect London as she moved through this latest diversion and on to her real future: crushing her role on *Dazzled*.

London was on the track to superstardom.

And Ellis Turner was driving the train.

❖

An hour later, Rory popped the plastic lid off her coffee cup and peered inside. Only foam. She had stopped at the first coffee house at the bottom of the hill and ordered the biggest size on the menu. It had been so absurdly expensive, she almost snatched the cash back when the barista had plucked it from her hand, but she needed her fix. Scalding the inside of her mouth, she had gulped the first few sips like an addict and had nursed the rest on the way home. Now she wanted another, much cheaper pourover from her own kitchen.

First, filial duty called. "Hi, Mom," Rory said when she picked up on the first ring.

"Hi, sweetie. You got my message?"

"I did. I didn't want to call too early." She imagined her mom sitting at her kitchen table picking at a homemade cherry scone, waiting for the phone to ring. "So," Rory said as lightly as she could manage, "what's this pickle you've gotten yourself into?"

"The Grind is opening another store in Malibu and ordered a bunch of premium coffee mugs."

Her mom's home pottery business could churn them out in a week. "That's great. What's the problem?"

"Don't judge me."

"Do I ever?"

"This time, you might."

A chill ran down Rory's spine. Usually, her mom didn't announce her problems; she just slipped them in when they chatted: *I had a cheese sandwich, the kitchen faucet is leaking, and such good news, your sister got twenty cups of milk from the goats today.*

"I doubt I'll judge you, and even if I do, I'll always help you if I can. Tell me what's wrong."

"The kiln's broken."

That wasn't too bad. "Can it be fixed?"

"No, it's stalled out."

Okay, a little worse. "So you need a new one?"

"I do, and I found a great deal. They want the money up front, and I'm a little short on cash."

"What about your savings? You can dip into that and pay yourself back when you deliver the coffee mugs."

"That's where I'm a little short."

"How short?" Rory didn't have access to her mom's accounts. But she should have had enough to buy a new electric kiln for her pottery business.

"Very short."

Her heart skipped a beat. "What happened to it?"

"Your sister needed it."

"For what?" This conversation was like pulling teeth. A lifetime of experience, however, had taught her that her mom sprinted for any exit like a feral cat when cornered.

Her mom sighed deeply on the other end of the line. "The base model of that tiny house didn't have a big enough kitchen to make her cheese. And my kitchen isn't cutting it. She's been saving for so long. I couldn't say no."

Damn it. Meadow hadn't told Rory that part. Her sister had said that she wanted a place of her own. Close to the goats she was also boarding for free on their mom's land.

"That was wonderful of you," Rory said through gritted teeth.

Her mom was one of the nicest people on the planet, and her decisions were usually grounded in emotion, not reason. "Thank you. She needed a little pick-me-up," her mom said. "You know the goat cheese business isn't growing as fast as she hoped."

Rory's anger finally boiled over. She wanted to lash out about Meadow right then and there. Her sister often put her own needs before everyone else, and the most pressing question hadn't yet been asked. "Mom, was that money earmarked for anything else?"

"Maybe."

Which meant yes. "What?"

"Some of it might have been going to property taxes." Her mom cut into the silence. "Take a breath before you respond. You know how you sometimes blurt out what you're thinking."

Oh shit. Her mom hadn't paid her taxes? And the one way she could, selling her pottery, was currently not accessible to her. Rory didn't have ready money to bail her out, either. Her mom was drowning in a whole barrel of pickles, and she might be pulling Rory into the brine with her.

Several assertive raps on the front door broke into her thoughts. Her elderly neighbor across the hall probably needed something. "Mom, that's probably Mrs. Bradley. Can I call you back?"

"Why don't you come out for lunch instead? It will give you time to think and us time to talk."

"I'd like that." She hung up, peered through the peephole, and did a quick double take. Unbelievably, Ellis Turner stood straight-backed in the hallway. Her green eyes and bright copper hair shone against the dingy wall behind her. She held both a sheet of paper and a large take-out coffee in one hand.

Wow. Rory studied the dozen different copper shades in her hair in a way she hadn't earlier. *The color must be natural.* She dropped her gaze and mentally kicked herself for noticing. This woman was not a friend. In fact, she wasn't even sure she was a nice person.

She wasn't going away, though. Rory opened the door and threw Ellis's first words this morning right back at her. "Can I help you?"

"I hope so." Ellis clearly hadn't noticed the snub and handed her the folded piece of paper.

Rory opened it to find a long list of clothes and personal items written in Maya's childish, looping hand.

"Those are the things your roommate can't live without. Well, not until tomorrow, as I had hoped," Ellis said matter-of-factly. If she was annoyed, and how could she not be, she sure wasn't showing it. Her face was blank, but she pranced on her toes like a racehorse at the gate. Clearly, she wanted to get in and out as fast as possible.

"I thought you'd have people to do this for you." After their last encounter, Rory couldn't help poking her a bit.

"I do, and she works hard and deserves a full weekend for once."

"Oh." Rory was surprised. Very few of these Hollywood types thought of their assistants as real people. Rory had read in *Hollywood, Now* that London went through them like Kleenex. She took a step back and with a wave, invited Ellis inside.

As she entered, Ellis glanced around, and Rory saw the apartment through her eyes. A cookie-cutter two-bedroom, deep in an undesirable neighborhood. Sure, it was relatively new but made so cheaply, it already looked twenty years old with its scuffed floorboards and chipped kitchen cabinets. Rory shrugged. Whatever. Not everyone could live in a gorgeous mansion in the hills.

"Oh, this is for you." Ellis held out the coffee. "A latte, since I threw yours away at London's."

"Thank you," Rory said, surprised again. She wrapped her hands around the still warm cup and drank in the heady aroma. The coffee was…unexpected. Thoughtful, even.

Ellis motioned to the list. "Do you think you can help me gather her things?"

Or maybe the coffee was a calculated bribe. With the battle lines firmly drawn earlier that morning, Ellis might grab any advantage.

"Sure," Rory said. It didn't matter; she was a sucker for a good cup of coffee, and Maya, not Ellis, had set this meeting in motion. "How'd you know I'd be here?"

"I didn't. I'm meeting with a new catering company in this neighborhood, and I thought I might have a better chance of catching you if I didn't call to warn you first."

Despite herself, Rory chuckled. "Probably true. Look, I hope you know, this morning wasn't personal."

"On either side. But that hardly matters now. I'm here to do my job."

A job that was now working for Maya as well. Rory almost felt sorry for her. Barely a new adult, Maya would be a hard mistress while she was with London. "I'll get the stuff. Can you wait here?"

"Of course, and I've a recording of Maya giving both me and you permission to gather her things if you'd like to hear it."

She took a gulp of the coffee and slid the cup reluctantly onto the breakfast bar. "That's okay. I trust you. I'll be right back."

Day-to-day, Rory never went into Maya's room. They'd agreed when Maya had moved in that personal space was private, and Rory's fingers froze as she grabbed the handle as if she was a common criminal. The room was the smaller of the two bedrooms, with only one window looking across an alley to another apartment complex. Clearly, Maya thought of it as a momentary pit stop. The walls were blank, no posters or pictures. An unmade bed and a vanity table with an oversize mirror were the only furniture. Clothes littered the floor: clean ones in folded piles on towels and dirty ones in plastic woven hampers. On the other side, the biggest iPad Rory had ever seen was clamped into an articulated floor stand and ready for viewing. A fluttery feeling rolled through her belly. She felt like a Peeping Tom who was gazing into her roommate's inner life. The saddest part? Not much was here.

She made quick work of the list. Makeup she easily found in the drawers of the vanity. Rather than going through it all, she slid them out and dumped the concealers and lipsticks and perfumes into a cloth bag she found nearby. Various items of clothing, a toothbrush and cleanser and a thousand moisturizers from the bathroom, the iPad, two framed pictures, not of her family…the list went on and on. Rory loaded the items into a large empty hamper.

Full to overflowing, the hamper didn't look like a few things to tide Maya over. More like a hasty retreat. The realization fell around Rory like heavy stones. No matter what happened with London, Maya wasn't coming back.

Fuck, she was going to have to find a new roommate.

When Rory struggled into the living room under the weight of the hamper, Ellis's face drained of color. "That's a lot of stuff."

"I know. You might need a bigger car." She deposited it on the coffee table, and it hit with a surprisingly loud thud.

"Thanks for putting it together. I better get going."

"No problem." Rory headed to open the door for her.

Ellis grabbed both handles of the hamper and heaved, twisting for the door at the same time. She teetered under the weight, caught her left heel in the carpet, and lurched to one side. The hamper fell, and Ellis, all arms and legs, tumbled in the other direction.

Rory didn't even think about her reaction. Bounding over, she pulled Ellis toward her. She grabbed her waist to stop the fall, and then instinctually slid a hand under her breast to steady her. Flinching at the touch, Ellis spun in the other direction and took Rory with her. They flailed clumsily together, twisting in a dangerous dance.

Finally, Rory reached out with her foot and anchored her leg against the sofa. Standing firm again, she whispered against Ellis's ear, "It's okay. I got you."

Rory had no idea how she and Ellis ended up in a full-body embrace. Ellis might have fallen toward the sound of her voice, or maybe she had tugged Ellis to her when she'd righted herself. Whatever the reality, Ellis was now nestled into the hollow of her neck. A perfect fit.

For a tiny, single moment, neither moved. Ellis's cologne, a mixture of jasmine, cedar, and vanilla, washed over Rory and tickled her nose. The scent was sensual and strong but still hinted at vulnerability. Her pulse quickened. She fought her instinct to pull Ellis closer and lose herself in that scent. Instead, she surrendered to the wiser choice and stepped away from their embrace.

Blushing to the roots of her hair, Ellis also tiptoed back gingerly and stared at the offending carpet. When she finally looked up, freckles, like stars at dusk, had popped up across her face, and several tendrils had escaped her tight bun.

Just like in the kitchen. Rory liked her better when she wasn't on the offensive.

Ellis squeezed her eyes shut, no doubt to fight back her embarrassment. From what? Everyone tripped. Everyone had ridiculous moments. They should laugh it off and be done with it. Ellis's emotions, though, were clearly as tight as a new leather shoe.

"You okay?" Rory asked.

"Yeah." Ellis tugged at the neck of her sweater. "Good catch."

Rory chuckled. "For a moment, I thought we were going to end up on the ESPN blooper reel."

Ellis didn't answer. Instead, she straightened her sweater and centered the gold chain between her breasts.

Breasts that a few seconds ago had been pressed up against Rory. Still feeling their touch, she searched for something to say. Nothing came to mind. Ellis clearly felt exposed, and the last thing Rory wanted was to add to her distress. She didn't agree with what she stood for or her methods, but that was no reason to be rude.

In fact, the simmering irritation from London's kitchen was gone, replaced by...what? Rory couldn't put her finger on it. Fine lines radiated out from Ellis's eyes, and underneath, dark circles hid under the concealer. She looked...tired.

The kindest thing would be to get her outside as soon as possible. Rory dropped to the ground and stuffed Maya's possessions back into the hamper. Ellis joined her, and they worked in awkward silence as she rooted under the sofa for a runaway lipstick.

The last item, a framed picture of a solo Maya grinning at her college graduation, hit the top of the pile.

"Here," Rory grabbed one side of the hamper. "Let me help you down with this."

"Might be safer." Ellis gripped the other side.

Together, they headed out the door. Neither spoke on the ride down in the elevator or on the walk to the BMW parked curbside. The hamper didn't fit into the tiny trunk. They had to shove it sideways into the back seat. Some of the makeup fell to the floor with metallic clinks. Ellis jumped in to collect them, and Rory wondered if she would repack the entire hamper before she gave it to Maya.

"All right, that looks good." Ellis moved around to the driver's side and met her gaze.

"You're good to go." Rory ran a hand through her messy, unwashed hair and wished she had taken a little more time with her appearance before she'd raced off at the crack of dawn.

"Thanks for your help." Ellis gave her a little wave and jumped into the car. She pulled quickly into the heavy traffic of Lankershim Boulevard.

Rory stood on the sidewalk and watched the BMW expertly cross two lanes and zoom away. She had her errand, and she wouldn't want to spend one more minute in the Valley than she had to. Although…who knew? So much of the morning had been unexpected.

The delicious coffee. Ellis had gone out of her way to stop somewhere nice rather than a chain. Her alluring scent. And the most surprising thing, she had just thrown herself into Rory's arms.

Not entirely the truth, but something fun to lead with when she and her mom sat down for lunch before they got down to the hard conversation about money.

CHAPTER FOUR

"Yolie? Did Mark get back to us?" Ellis called out the next day, even though their desks were in the same room. Ellis's office was an annex to her house. The previous owner had been a psychiatrist whose therapy and waiting rooms had a separate entrance off the front yard. It was the bungalow's main selling point, although the trendy West Hollywood neighborhood hadn't hurt.

"Not yet. You know he's old school, and he'll call back when he's good and ready."

Ellis gave a weary sigh and picked up her phone. "I'll call him myself."

Thanks to a volatile, twenty-four-hour media culture, the internet had exploded with London and Maya's hookup over the last thirty-six hours:

"London Green Moves on Quickly after Breakup with Victoria's Secret Model."

"London Green's Revealing Lyft Ride with Bartender."

"London Green's Revolving Romance Door."

The articles, dropping all over the internet, had different titles but shared a similar spin. London had broken up with poor, unsuspecting Shannon outside a bar and then minutes later, pounced on the bartender. They had shared several long, hot kisses outside her Hollywood Hills mansion, captured by the Lyft driver who, as luck would have it, was also an unemployed documentary filmmaker. London was trending as a skirt chaser who blew wherever her sexual desire took her. It didn't matter that most of the stories were overflowing with lies, the perception seemed a hundred percent true.

"Gardner Public Relations," the receptionist said with false cheer.

"Ellis Turner for Mark Gardner, please."

A moment later, Mark's assistant picked up. "I'm sorry Ellis, Mark's in a meeting. It—"

"Portia, I know he's avoiding my calls. But we need to talk. You can throw me under the bus. Tell him I went ballistic and didn't give you any choice."

"Okay. Thanks."

She sat on hold for over three minutes, and then finally, a deep voice said, "I don't work for you, Ellis."

"I know. We both work for London, and now we need to work together to get through this shitstorm. The only thing Prodigy Entertainment asked was for her to keep a low profile in the dating arena. They want her to be a princess offscreen too. The only thing. They're okay with her being gay as long as she doesn't come off as loose."

"I know. I've been doing this since before you were born. Prodigy wants wholesome. I want wholesome. That's fucking easier to market. You need to keep your girl on a tighter leash. You think I want to stand in the shitstorm you created?"

"I didn't create it," she pushed back.

"You might as well have. I've told you a million times that you're her agent, and a truly excellent one, but she needs a real manager. You can't do both. She's too much for you to handle."

"I know exactly where you stand on that."

She could hear him grinding his teeth on the other end of the line. She understood why he was frustrated. It wasn't enough anymore for a PR firm to book glossy magazine articles or block tabloid gossip. In this new global, web-driven world, he had to contend with any Lyft driver or bargoer who had a cell phone and an itchy posting finger.

"Do you have a plan, Mark?"

"Inspired. If I do say so myself. We're going to market this new relationship as the soulmate crap from *Dazzled*. London has finally found true love with a humble bartender who she can't live without. It will be life and art coming together in the most transformative way. Is she smoking hot in real life too?"

"Yes, Maya is very attractive," Ellis said.

"Good. That fucking helps. By the time we're done with them, everyone who has ever dreamed about falling in love, straight or gay or anything else, will want what they have."

Ellis cocked her head back and forth and then nodded. It was a good strategy to show London connected to her character before filming started, if they could get her and Prodigy on board. If Maya didn't screw things up. If London's libido didn't wander. In Mark's words, there were a lot of fucking ifs.

"We've created a content calendar," he broke into her thoughts, "for all the social media platforms and a few choice appearances for the happy couple. We just need the green light."

"You haven't spoken to London?"

"No. It goes straight to fucking voice mail."

She almost sighed before she sucked it back. "I'll make sure she gets back to you."

"Good. Now your real job is to make sure they stay together until principal photography starts on *Dazzled*. A couple of months, Ellis. You have to keep them together for a couple of fucking months. Can you do that? Otherwise, we've made a bad gamble, and everything goes to hell in a handbasket."

"I don't work for you either, Mark. Send me a copy of all content before you post. And I'll need the list of her appearances ASAP." She hung up and clenched a fist. She always felt like she needed to jump in the shower after talking to Mark and wash his bad energy off.

"It's okay not to like him," Yolie said and gave her a thumbs-up when she came back into the office.

"He's an asshole. God help me, he's also good at his job. London's lucky to have him." She filled Yolie in on the strategy for London and Maya.

"And if they break up?" Yolie asked.

"That's the million-dollar question. Mark's right. If we can get London on set without any heartbreak, we'll be good. Then, the PR machine of the movie will take over, thank goodness, and even if they do split, she'll be out of the public eye. I'll call London. You call Shannon's agent and remind her that she signed an NDA. No interviews about London in any shape or form and make it very clear no more meat curtain comments."

Yolie nodded.

"Then, could you call Tisha and give her a pep talk about the *Greenlot* audition? She's going to nail it. She needs to believe that."

"I'm on it. All of it."

Ellis grabbed a jacket and went outside to sit on the bench under the jacaranda tree in the front yard. A tall wooden fence ran the length of her property and kept the lot private from dog walkers and lookie-loos. The lush canopy from the tree made it almost like a second office. She pulled up London's number and hit FaceTime.

After many rings, Maya's grinning face appeared on her screen. "London's phone."

In the smaller box, Ellis watched her own mouth twist into a grimace. "Maya, you can't answer her phone."

Maya squealed with laughter. "That's exactly what she said you would say."

Somewhere in the background out of sight, London also howled. Were they drunk? Or high? Shit, it was only ten in the morning.

"Put London on please." She rubbed the back of her neck, trying to squeeze the tension out of her muscles.

"She's in the other room," Maya said.

Shuffling noises, more laughing, and various angles of London's bedroom flashed on the phone. They'd been in bed when she called, and London sat like a goddess in a cloud of a white duvet.

"Hi, Ellis." The words were drawn out, long and slow, and her pupils were huge.

For Christ's sake. They were high. Times like this, Ellis wondered why she hadn't become an accountant as her mother had told her to. Financial records and numbers would have never popped the pot gummies that she clearly spied on a nightstand in the background.

"Hi, London." She tamped down her irritation, and her tone remained calm. "Can you focus on what I'm saying?"

"Ab-so-lutely." She patted the covers beside her, and Maya bounded onto the screen.

"No, no—"

"Hi, Ellis."

"Hi, Maya." She needed to switch tactics, quick. "I'm glad that you're both there. This concerns you too, Maya. London, can you call Mark back and agree to the new social media campaign? He wants to tell the world the truth. That you and Maya have a once-in-a-lifetime connection."

Pausing, she let this fact sink in. *Buy into it. Please.* With a little luck, she could control the next few months.

"Yes!" London nodded with her whole body, and Maya's grin stretched from ear to ear. Maybe she was lucky they were wasted.

"And Mark has content he wants to get out and some personal appearances for both of you."

Maya squealed and bounced on her knees. "Me too?"

"We'll see," Ellis said.

"That means yes to me." She flung her arms around London and kissed her deeply on the mouth.

Ellis cast her glance away from the screen. "Wait. For now, you have to keep this out of the public eye. Leave them wondering what exactly this is, and then, we'll blind them with the truth."

London came up for air and switched the phone to her other hand. The lower angle focused perfectly on Maya trailing kisses down London's neck.

"Good," Ellis said, "and when you...get out of bed, give the campaign the once-over to see what you think."

"Make sure that show is on it." London moaned and dropped the phone on the bed. Thankfully, only the ceiling was now in the frame.

"What show?"

"You know, the one with Norah," London answered off camera after a long beat of them doing God knew what.

"You mean the cooking show? *Guess Who's Coming to Dinner?*" Damn. She had hoped that London had forgotten about that ridiculous idea.

"Yeah, I want to be on it."

"Why? The show's ratings barely tip the Neilsen ratings. There are many other—"

"Maya thinks it's a good idea."

Maya's face hovered over the screen, filling the frame completely. "My first good idea for London." Her dilated pupils, big as saucers, stared right at Ellis.

Who the hell did this woman think she was? Ellis shivered, not from the cool January air but from a premonition raking through her. *Careful. Maya wants more than London's love. Much more.*

Maya hung over the phone, clearly waiting for an answer.

"I'll look into it. We don't even know if they're in production."

A hand, she couldn't tell whose, flipped the phone over, and the screen went black against the duvet.

"Oh God," someone moaned after a beat.

"No phones in the bedroom," Ellis shouted to the dark screen. "Take it out."

This scenario was exactly what terrified her: sex, drugs, and an upgraded seven-lens camera with an ultrawide angle and digital zoom. Oh, and no NDA from Maya. Mark would quadruple his fee if there was a sex tape.

No reply came except for a sucking noise she didn't want to identify. Tapping on the red X on her screen, Ellis hung up.

First, a power struggle with Mark and now live audio porn streaming from London's phone: a one-two punch, typical for any morning at Ellis Turner Agency. Usually, she could handle it. Today, for some reason, she was pushed out of her comfort zone.

Ellis yawned deeply, the kind of yawn where her jaw almost unhinged. Shit, yawning was sometimes a pre-headache symptom. She stood, placed a flat palm under her belly button, and drew in a slow, rhythmic breath. As she inhaled, her chest, ribs, and diaphragm inflated like a balloon. She held the air for a long count of three and then pushed it out. Like her instructor promised, oxygen primed her brain, and some of the tension drained from her body. Her mind cleared several exhales later.

What caused her migraines, no one knew. Not the slew of high-priced doctors at multiple clinics or the million medical articles she had read online. She had tried everything from popping pills to aromatherapy and acupuncture to orgasms at onset for the endorphins. Nothing had worked. As a child, her mother had sent her to her bedroom for their durations. She would give literally anything to find a cure.

When she stepped back into the office, the warmth of the room enveloped her. Yolie sat, shoulders back, chatting easily on the phone. Laughter spilled out from Tisha's end. Ellis hung her jacket on the antique coatrack and slid behind her own desk.

Perennially upbeat and detail oriented, Yolie was a natural at the job. What was more, she truly cared about ETA's clients.

"You will. Break a leg." Yolie dropped the phone back into its cradle.

"That sounded like it went well," Ellis said.

"I think it did. You were right. She was way nervous. Now she feels better knowing we're behind her."

"We were always behind her, but you made her believe in herself. That was all you."

"Thanks for trusting me. I love it when I get to interact with the clients."

There were days when she wouldn't wish this job on her worst enemy, but Yolie could decide for herself. "Would you like Tisha as a client?"

Yolie's jaw dropped. For once, she had nothing to say.

"You have a good rapport with her. I mean, let her know that I'm still one hundred percent on board, and we think so highly of her that we want to give her double the personal attention. Of course, we should talk strategy before you implement any changes with her career. Tisha's going places, and you should jump on that ride. What do you think?"

Yolie pressed a hand to her chest. "Do you really think I'm ready?"

"I do. And I'm not sending you out there all alone. You're still part of the Ellis Turner Agency. A big part."

Yolie leaped from her chair, dashed across the room, and threw her arms around her. "Thank you!"

"You earned it." She hugged her back. Hard. Yolie was going places too, and both Yolie's and Tisha's places needed to be on the ETA map.

Yolie pumped her arms in celebration as she danced back to her desk.

Right here, right now was why Ellis loved being a talent agent. When the job worked—and surprisingly, it often did— she became a fairy godmother granting wishes and dreams to the Cinderellas of the world. Ellis tried to live the moment fully as her meditation coach preached, but her mind circled too quickly away from Yolie's dreams and back to London's demands.

"Hey, do you have any idea who is the executive producer for *Guess Who's Coming to Dinner*? It's on the Food and Flavor Network."

"No. I can find out."

"Thanks. And we should also think about getting an office assistant to free you up some. Especially now with Maya, London's demands are about to explode."

"Where would we put her?" Yolie glanced around the room, large for a home office but not big enough for three.

"We have the waiting room. It's small but big enough for a desk and a phone."

Yolie grinned. "Oh man, this is the best day ever."

Ellis smiled at her. Her positive energy was infectious.

"I'll get that producer's number." Yolie sat in her chair and took a deep breath, as if she couldn't believe her luck.

When Ellis finally had the executive producer on the phone, he clearly couldn't believe his luck, either. "What? Did I hear you right? London Green wants to come on my show?"

"Yes. We need to film now. If you're not in production—"

"No, we are," he shrieked like a preteen at a concert. "You're lucky we're in the middle of our season. It's short, like most cooking shows."

"So lucky." Ellis bit back the sarcasm. "You can accommodate my client?"

"Okay. Sure. Yes, we can bounce our next guest. We film the dinner part on Wednesdays. Will that work? I'll have my assistant contact yours about London's menu choices." He ran the words together as if he was afraid she'd change her mind, and in what must have been a Hollywood speed record, the deal was sealed.

As she pushed the landline back to the side of the desk, the thought unfurled like a banner in her mind: *Rory will be there.*

Ellis folded the realization up tight, almost before she could acknowledge it. The words burst through again and fanned out to the corners of her mind.

Rory. Will. Be. There.

She hadn't thought once about Rory since she'd sped away from her apartment, red as a beet, the day before. Returning Maya's things—she hadn't been happy about their jumbled state—and over one hundred emails to answer had consumed her afternoon and evening. Running her own agency was a twenty-five-eight enterprise.

She was thinking about her now, though. The woman who had potentially put her work life into a tailspin and then whose strong arms had caught her as she'd fallen. How had she tripped, anyway?

She had been picking up the hamper, and then the room had spun, and she had been tumbling to the ground. And yet, she hadn't crashed. One moment, everything had been out of control, and the next, thanks to Rory, she was still and safe.

Those two moments had turned her into the most common cliché in any rom-com. If she'd seen that meet-cute in a script, she would have gagged, but it had played out for real in Rory's living room. She had the sore ankle to prove it.

Sitting at her desk now, she cringed over how long she had lingered in Rory's arms. The truth was, she hadn't wanted to step away from the protective embrace and back into her crazy, frenetic world. The strength, the warmth, the connection of that hug had been wonderful. Did it have anything to do with Rory? Or just her own situation?

She couldn't remember the last time she had leaned on someone, either literally or figuratively. She didn't have much contact with her parents, who lived in a retirement community in Texas. Her mother, distant and perennially disappointed in her life choices, had made it clear that a lesbian who did something unquantifiable in Hollywood was both baffling and deficient. And girlfriends never stayed long once they realized that London and ETA came before everything.

There wasn't a whole lot of work-life balance because all her energy went to building the Ellis Turner Agency into the top boutique firm in Los Angeles. And London was at the center of that equation. When *Dazzled* became the next billion-dollar blockbuster, as it was surely destined to be, ETA would launch into the stratosphere. She and Yolie would be sitting pretty, maybe even in separate offices. But not if she spent her time thinking about women she couldn't send out for auditions.

Yolie broke into her thoughts. "What's she like?"

"She's…she's…" Heat spun in her chest when she realized that Yolie was talking about Maya, not Rory. She sucked a breath in. This was exactly what she had to guard against. She leaned against her desk and met Yolie's gaze head-on. "She's trouble. Believe me, Maya's big trouble. We've got our work cut out for us. In a huge way."

❖

Wednesday morning came early for Rory. Phone pressed to her ear, she walked into the back kitchen for *Guess Who's Coming to Dinner* just after the sun rose.

"I'm glad Meadow went with you to drop off the deposit for the kiln."

"They are very nice people. Thank you for negotiating the payment deal. We'll find a way for the second and third one, right?" The question was perfunctory. Her mom lived in a world that was almost always sunny. For her, the kiln was already paid for.

"Yes." Rory felt herself being dragged into that sunshine. "I'm on Norah's show until next week, and then, I'm free. I'll find the money. I've got a few things in the works," she lied. Before the kiln disaster, she had intended to explore her options. Slicing and dicing in a prep kitchen had never been her culinary dream, and she hated working for someone else. She was more of a realist than her mom or her sister. Someone had to be in the Hatten family, yet a deep streak of independence ran through her too.

Lately, she had been flirting with how to showcase her talents to a wider audience. A pop-up restaurant, a niche cookbook for the foodie culture in LA, or maybe even her own cooking demonstrations on YouTube. All of them sounded appealing…and expensive to fund. She would give her mom her last dime. The wad of cash she had withdrawn for the down payment on the kiln had dropped her bank balance perilously low. Now she would be forced to accept the next job that came along if she expected to make rent. Especially since, for all intents and purposes, Maya had moved out.

Rory sighed and studied the two-car garage in front of her. High-end commercial kitchen appliances and prep spaces filled every available corner. The production rented a ranch house in the trendy Sherman Oaks neighborhood of the Valley. The family moved out for a couple of months, pocketing the substantial location fees, and the show moved in for thirteen episodes. In this configuration, the show could qualify for nonunion status and keep costs down. Rory could swear to that truth with every measly paycheck.

"Thank God you're here" The culinary producer rushed up to take her arm. "Norah wants to see you as soon as she comes in. She's nervous about the pie crust. Can you make an extra set of ingredients so she can practice before we shoot?"

Everyone on set knew that Norah Gallagher couldn't cook her way out of a paper bag. She was a down-on-her-luck comedian who, if the rumor mill was right, had somehow blackmailed her way onto the show. Rory spent a lot of her time teaching Norah recipes that she, herself, had created.

"Of course." Rory tried to swallow the sour taste flooding her mouth. She had rubbed this producer the wrong way last time she'd offered a different solution for Norah's problems. Her mom was right: she needed to feel, *think*, and then speak.

"Thanks. You know, no one's happy about this revised menu, least of all Norah. I mean, roast chicken, citrus salad, and apple pie would be an easy change for most." The producer leaned in. "Believe me. This surprise guest star is totally worth the trouble she's causing."

Ms. Tight-Ass-Bun-Head had worked her magic fast, although why she had booked London at all was anyone's guess. Maya no longer needed the chance encounter to get with London. And this show was rinky-dink compared to the publicity London usually got. Whatever. Not her problem.

She might not even come with London. Somewhere deep inside, Rory knew she would. Her heart beat a little faster as the knowledge rolled over her.

Rory walked to her station and pulled on her chef's jacket emblazoned with the name of the show. This jacket was a cheap version of the iconic uniform worn in Michelin Star restaurants, but Rory never tired of slipping into the sturdy cotton of any chef's coat.

Time to get cooking. She chopped butter into pretty cubes, measured water and vinegar into tiny pitchers, and arranged the shortening and flour artistically in glass bowls.

The show was strictly *dump and stir*, which meant that Norah had everything prepped for her, and all she had to do was combine ingredients. Rory, on the other hand, would make eight pies by wrap time. Four in various stages of completion for the shoot, one for the beauty shots, one for the actual dinner, and two backups just in case.

She started on the edible ones first since they were shooting the dinner before lunchtime, something about the lighting in the backyard and the mystery guest's availability. People were grumbling about changing the traditional schedule. She knew all would be forgiven when London appeared. She would have Norah and the crew eating out of her hand long before the director called action.

For her part, Rory assembled the dough quickly. The trick was keeping the ingredients as cold as possible and rolling the dough out on a marble pastry board. Cooking for Rory had always been about the deep connection between her hands and her heart, and she applied light pressure with a rolling pin. When the dough was a perfect circle, she eased it into a pie tin, letting the dough fall into the corners rather than stretching it.

Next came the blind bake where the crust baked without the filling. While the empty pie was in the oven, she cut more dough for the top. When Norah eventually brought the pie to the table, the vent that allowed steam to escape would be transformed into a vine bursting with delicate flowers and leaves.

Four hours and three pies later, a production assistant rushed into the back kitchen and cried, "Oh my God. It's London Green. She's the mystery guest."

"No fucking way," a prep chef to Rory's left said. "How did Norah get her?"

"Who cares? It's London Green." The PA grinned ear to ear. "To think, I almost called in sick today. You guys ready?" She gave the cooking crew two thumbs-up and rushed back to the set.

"Shit. I'm not ready. Rory, can you help me with the chicken?" her colleague asked. "I can never make them look appetizing. You're the master."

"Kiss up." Rory laughed and moved to his station.

Four chickens in roasting pans sat on the counter in a neat row. Only one was fully cooked. The others hadn't spent nearly enough time in the oven. He held out a butane cooking torch and a tin of brown shoe polish. "Thanks. I appreciate that you're always willing to jump in to help."

"Of course."

She took the shoe polish and stood back as he fired up the torch. The flame licked the chicken, crisping its edges and finishing off the meat, at least on the outside. As he moved to the next, Rory dipped a small cloth in the shoe polish. Rubbing the breasts and the legs with the polish browned the chicken up nicely, as if it had roasted in the oven for hours. She planted a small bottle of baby oil in the bottom of the pan for later. When the heat of the lights began to dry out the meat, the food stylist could brush a little oil on the chicken, and it would look good enough to eat. No one would, of course. Rory shuddered to think how much food this production and every other cooking show trashed with every taping.

"Rory?" The production assistant stuck her head through the door from the house. "You're wanted on set. Can you bring the pie, please?"

Normally, the cooking crew didn't go anywhere near the principal players. They were hired guns. Rory grabbed an edible pie from the nearby cooling rack, stepped through the house, and out into the backyard, the real reason the production had chosen this house. Bright green grass, which had been reseeded at the beginning of the production, surrounded a sparkling blue pool. A wooden table, decked out with linen, flowers, and china, sat center stage on the patio.

London relaxed on one side while a gaffer adjusted a LED light on her. Not that she needed it. The day was slightly overcast, and the light fell evenly over London's skin and face. She was stunning in bright colors, and everyone couldn't keep their eyes off her.

Norah sat on the other side of the table, fighting between a scowl and a smile. Rory knew she liked to pretend that she was still at the top of her game. Scoring a guest like London was living proof. But London was upstaging her with every smile.

"Hi, Rory." London waved as soon as Rory entered the set. "Maya said your apple pies were to die for. That's why I ordered one for the show."

"Good to see you again." She tipped the pie to Norah, who grudgingly nodded her approval and then deposited it on a pie stand in the middle of the table. An engraved wooden sign, *Made by Norah with Love*, hung below the stand.

Rory adjusted the pie so its best side faced the camera. "I hope they're as good as Maya remembers. Winter's not the season for apple pies."

"No worries. You'll work your magic." Maya materialized out of nowhere. Clothed far more expensively than London and from nothing Rory had ever seen in her closet, she bestowed her blessing on Rory like a queen on a commoner. She had come a long way in four days. Dressed to the nines, hanging out with the VIPs, Maya had sprinted with the chance she had been given. Like, Olympic-record sprinting.

"You three know each other?" The executive producer studied Rory with new interest.

"A little." Rory shrugged and tried to step back into the relative obscurity of the crew.

"No. Stay with me." Maya laced her arm through Rory's and dragged her to where the video assist was set up. Three monitors, one for each camera, sat in a small bank off to the side of the set.

They would be able to watch every angle as it was shot. Maya turned to the producer. "Is that okay?"

"Sure. Great. Yeah," he said. "She's our best cook."

Rory choked back a laugh. He had never spoken to her before. Obviously, he was trying to get in good with anyone connected to London. To prove her point, the producer leered at Maya with an oily smile.

The irony was, the compliment was true. She was by far the best chef on set. Not that it got her anywhere. For here she was, standing on the sidelines watching…again.

As the crew scurried around, making last-minute adjustments to the table and the three-camera setup, the director called London to position one. She stood at the door to the backyard, waiting to make her entrance.

"Action," the director called.

Norah looked straight at the A Camera and said in singsong, "Guess who's coming to dinner?"

The director waved his hand in a silent cue to London. As if someone had flipped a switch, her face lit up, and she started forward. On the B monitor of the video assist, Rory witnessed the transformation. London's presence filled the frame. Everything else, the table, the food, and especially Norah, seemed to fade away. No wonder she was a superstar.

"It's my good friend, London Green!" Norah jumped up from the table and brought London into a tight embrace. On the video assist, her smile looked genuine, and Rory gathered, for the moment, she had won the battle with herself.

"Norah." London squeezed back with more enthusiasm. "It's wonderful to see you after all these years."

"Sit, please." Norah waved to the empty seat.

"Let's start with the pie." London clapped her hands in delight. "What do they say? Life's uncertain, eat dessert first?"

Norah froze. London had gone off script, and clearly, Norah didn't know how to answer. Rory thought a comedian would be better at improv. The moment hadn't been about comedy. It had been about power, and like most people in Hollywood, Norah didn't like anyone stealing her thunder.

"Cut!" The director put Norah out of her misery and pointed at London. "That's a fantastic idea. We'll highlight the pie this show. Cindy"—he spun to a woman next to him—"put the beauty shots of the pie to the top of the list this evening. Norah, we'll need a pickup shot of you agreeing to the dessert suggestion. React like it's the second coming."

A sour expression flashed on Norah's face and then disappeared just as quickly. Rory almost felt sorry for her. No one liked to be kicked down the ladder. At the same time, pride bubbled up in her. Her pie was now center stage. Pies. There was a thought. Maybe she could do something more with pies.

"Action," the director called.

"That's a great idea," Norah said to the A Camera that was focused on her in a flattering close-up.

"Again. With more excitement," the director said.

"That's a great idea."

"Come on. Even more, Norah."

"That's a great idea."

"Cut." The director shook his head slightly at the center monitor. Rory was no editor, but even she saw that with each take, Norah had tightened up.

"Let's move on to the meal. I need a wide and two close-ups on either side of the table.

As the crew rolled cameras and lights around the backyard, a controlled voice behind Rory asked, "How's the show going?"

She pivoted toward the sound like a compass needle finding true north. Ellis stood barely a foot away. When on earth had she gotten there? She thought she would have noticed. Observing as well as she did, people didn't usually sneak up on her.

Yet, there Ellis was, leaning into the producer with her usual intensity. Dressed as if she had stepped out of a magazine, Ellis screamed style in all black: pants, an expensive T-shirt, and a high-end jacket. Today, she had pulled her copper hair back into a tight ponytail that swung around her head freely and popped against her monochromatic outfit. Copper bangles, the exact same color as her hair, jangled on her wrist. How long did it take her to get dressed in the morning?

When he saw Ellis, the executive producer lit up like a Roman candle. "Excellent. Fantastic. She's doing great." He pumped her hand with every answer. "I'm glad to meet you, and I'm even happier that this worked out."

"You should be thanking her." Ellis identified Rory with a nod, although she didn't glance her way. "She set the whole thing in motion."

The producer whipped toward Rory. "You should have told me that you knew London Green."

Rory shrugged and returned her focus to Ellis. As they both knew, her last comment about Rory being the linchpin in this operation was untrue. Maya, ever the opportunist, had made it happen. What exactly had Ellis meant by saying Rory was responsible? Was it a dig to put her in her place or a compliment to promote her to the executive producer? Shit, this woman was completely unreadable.

Ellis's phone buzzed, and she motioned to someone by the firepit. A small plump woman with dark eyes and hair trotted over. "This is Yolie, my colleague. She'll watch the monitor and London while I step away." She held up her phone. "I need to take this call."

Rory's gaze followed Ellis as she slipped beyond the edge of the set and then turned to the woman beside her. "You work with Ellis?"

Yolie nodded. "It's more for her, though. I'm her assistant."

The one whose weekend Ellis had preserved when she'd showed up on Rory's doorstep the other day. Ellis had called her a colleague. Like the delicious coffee, another contradiction dropped on the list of who Ellis was.

"What's she like to work for?" Rory couldn't help herself.

"Amazing." Yolie grinned. "She hired me as an assistant, and right from the beginning, she started teaching me the business. I mean, she's a crazy good agent, and I would have learned a lot from just watching her in action. But she wants me to succeed for myself. And two days ago, she gave me my first client."

Rory's head spun. Ellis was quickly becoming a puzzle that she wanted to piece together. Had she completely misjudged her in London's kitchen?

"Yep," Yolie began as if answering Rory's silent question. "She—"

"Quiet on the set." The first assistant director called and killed whatever Yolie was about to reveal.

Everyone focused on the dinner party, either in real life or the monitors. Everyone except Rory. She turned slowly, looking for the only production she wanted to watch. The Ellis Turner Show. Namely, the episode where Rory got to dig around that cool, controlled exterior to discover who Ellis really was.

Chapter Five

"That's very good news." Ellis stood in the driveway of the production house, far enough away from the set that she could speak at normal volumes. "We'll give her the notes, and she'll see you on Friday. Thanks. Bye."

She darted back inside, eager to find Yolie when she was distracted by two people standing over a prep counter in the back kitchen. "She's a true artist." A man in a chef's jacket said to a woman next to him.

Natural curiosity made Ellis glance over. Two pies, breathtaking in their intricate crust work, sat on the stainless steel top. A flowering vine climbed up the center of each pie, so lifelike that if they hadn't been golden brown, Ellis would have sworn they were real. Then she realized they were talking about Rory. She had made those pies.

Ellis pulled out her phone and pretended to be engrossed in a text.

"She's too good for this show."

"A fast-food cook is too good for this show,"

The woman laughed appreciatively. "I know, but seriously, why is she still here? She could totally be a culinary producer. She knows all the tricks."

Ellis's finger froze above the screen. She wanted to know the answer herself.

"Not the one trick she needs. She doesn't mince words. I mean, you know her. She's helped me out of more kitchen disasters than I can count without asking for anything in return. But sometimes…"

"She calls it like it is?"

Ellis strained to hear what came next.

"Yeah, I heard she told the network that Norah needed cooking lessons if they wanted the show to be even remotely authentic."

"That doesn't sound too bad. It's true."

"She did it in front of Norah."

Ellis grimaced. That totally sounded like the Rory she had met in London's kitchen. She flipped the leather case over her phone. If the pie was half as good as it looked, Rory should shut her mouth and be doing more than cooking in a garage.

Not Ellis's problem.

A production assistant guarded the sliding glass door to the backyard. "They're shooting," she mouthed silently and held up her palm.

Ellis nodded and peeked around her. At the table, London was laughing, and Norah waved in animated conversation. Yolie hovered by the video assist, right where Ellis had left her. Then, almost of its own accord, Ellis's gaze drifted off Yolie and landed to the right.

Rory.

She had tried not to look at her when she was talking to that strange producer who gave three of the exact same answers to every question. Now she couldn't tear her gaze away. Rory towered over both Yolie to her left and Maya to her right. Her black chef coat and pants added to the whole statuesque vibe. Her trim, lithe shape shone through the baggy outfit created for comfort in the kitchen. Her hair, freshly washed today, was tousled and perfect. Ellis had always had a thing for a woman in a uniform.

Did a chef's jacket count?

Yes, which was why she needed to keep the distractions that Rory offered at arm's length.

"They've cut." The PA slid the door open for her. "You can go out now."

"Thanks." Ellis squeezed through and motioned to Yolie, who scampered over. "The casting associate loved Tisha. She got a callback for the casting director of the movie. For Friday." Excitement ran through Ellis's every word.

Yolie's eyes crinkled, and her forehead rose. Every feature seemed to become part of the widest grin Ellis had ever seen. "No way!" She jumped in happy bursts.

"Yes way." Ellis patted her arm. "They have some notes. I'll send them to you now." She tapped her phone. "I've a good feeling about this. And I'm talking about you and her, not the role. Go out in front of the house and call her."

"Oh my God, Ellis. Thank you." Yolie gave her a brief tight hug and bounced off.

Standing with her back to the production, Ellis felt attention on her rather than saw it. The hairs on the back of her neck stood up. She swiveled and met Rory's gaze. Caught in the act, Rory didn't blush or even react much. She only raised a hand halfway and gave a little wave.

Feeling foolish, like she was in high school again, Ellis waved back.

"We're ready." The AD called loudly. "Quiet on the set."

In the hush that fell over the backyard, Ellis moved next to Rory and into the space that Yolie had vacated. She told herself that it was the best position to see the monitors, even if she was almost touching shoulders with Rory.

"All right, you two," the director began, "walking down memory lane was great. Now, let's get to dinner and the juicy stuff." The director checked each monitor. "A Camera, can you pull back a bit? Yeah, that's it…action."

"Pie first?" Norah flashed a fake smile.

"It's almost too pretty to eat."

"Thank you. We need to seize the day, however. Remember all those women on the *Titanic* who waved off the dessert cart."

London laughed. It seemed natural and at the same time, acknowledged the darkness in the joke. Ellis breathed a quick sigh of relief. London wasn't going to let Norah get the upper hand. Did she know how much Norah hated her now that she was superstar famous? And when had Norah started stealing her jokes? That one about the dessert cart and the *Titanic* had been around for ages. Maybe even since the *Titanic*.

"You know," Norah said at the table, "the recipe for pie crust couldn't be any simpler. It only has three ingredients. Flour, water, and fat. But how you put them together? Chefs like me could debate that question for decades." While she spoke, she sliced two huge pieces from the pie and passed one to London.

On the monitor, the B Camera tilted down to capture the moment in a close-up. At the same time, Rory shuffled. Out of the corner of her eye, Ellis saw she was biting her bottom lip. In a flash of understanding, Ellis knew that Norah had stolen the crust information. Or maybe Rory had freely given it. Whatever the truth, those people in the back kitchen were right. Rory was trapped in a thankless job.

"It's quite a production." Norah threw one arm in the air. "Not as exciting as the new production you're currently in, though."

"Oh, my new movie, *Dazzled*, hasn't started filming yet. I'm very excited to be working with Prodigy Studios."

Ellis pulled in a deep, satisfied breath. London had plugged the movie perfectly.

"Mother of pearl." She waved her fork at Norah. "This is absolutely the best pie I've ever had in my life."

Norah accepted the compliment with a curt nod and pressed her lips together, which sent fine wrinkles down to her chin. Rory also reacted to the praise that was rightfully hers. Her stance softened, and her upper arm fell against Ellis's shoulder.

The touch was slight, but Ellis's arm tingled all the way to her fingers. There was something about contact with Rory that—she wasn't quite sure how to describe it—that grounded her. No, that was too obvious. It was as if Rory was touching a crooked picture on a wall that she was absentmindedly setting straight. There was no real intent, just a natural inclination.

To test her theory, Ellis leaned in. She almost missed the B Camera tilting back up to Norah's close-up. She loomed large when she said, "Not that production. The production in your love life. Don't you have a new leading lady?"

What the fuck? Ellis flinched and jerked away from Rory's shoulder.

At the table, London laughed delightedly. "I sure do. She can join us." She reached off camera with one hand.

Maya leaped forward like a lion on a hunt.

Cut. Cut. Cut. Ellis swallowed the words so they wouldn't burst out. She spun to the producer. Maybe he would do his job and stop this travesty. A new girlfriend had not been on the list of approved topics for discussion.

Nope, no such luck. His beaming face said volumes. Thrilled, euphoric, and overjoyed. And why not? London as a guest star would boost the ratings. London and a new girlfriend would be ratings gold for *Guess Who's Coming to Dinner*.

"Settle quickly," the director said to everyone within earshot.

Doing exactly as she was told, Maya dropped gracefully into the seat next to London, and the C Camera pulled out to create a cozy, romantic two-shot.

Fuck. Fuck. Fuck. This was happening. Ellis jostled the director aside as she centered herself in front of the monitors. Tension pulsed in her temples.

Two minutes in, however, the strain began to recede. To her complete surprise, Maya was utterly charming. She hung on London's every word, and when she did speak, she built London up as the most romantic woman in the world. The interview couldn't have played better if Ellis had written it herself.

Consequently, Norah had been effectively cut from the conversation and was reduced to eating humble and actual pie instead of participating. Finally, Norah weaseled her way back in. "Aw. That story is even sweeter than my pie." She looked directly at the B Camera. "Today's real sweet ending is showing everyone what a wonderful couple you two are. Who knew that London Green could be captured so completely?"

"Everyone." London's voice dripped with honey. "My wonderful agent threw us a coming-out party. I'm sorry you couldn't come."

Ellis smirked. They would have to deal with this coming-out party later. Right now, London had put Norah in her place once and for all. On camera, superstar and has-been eyed each other in silence until the director called cut.

Norah jumped up in such a huff that her chair spun onto the grass. "Excuse me," she said and rushed inside the house.

Oblivious or simply not caring, Ellis couldn't tell, London gathered Maya in her arms and kissed her deeply. "You were amazing."

"I loved being on camera…with you."

Of course, she did. Ellis wanted to roll her eyes.

"Can we do more of it?" Maya wrapped her arms around London's waist. "Show the world what we mean to each other?"

"You betcha." London said. They turned as one to the group at the video assist. "Did you hear that?" London locked gazes with Ellis. "We need a coming-out party for real. Ellis, you'll throw it for us at my mother's beach house. And, Rory, you'll make the pies and get to stand in front of your creations rather than behind them."

Maya clapped like a child who had received a puppy for her birthday. "Ooh. We can do it for Valentine's Day."

Ellis nodded slowly. "That's one plan."

"Great. I know you'll make it happen. Nothing big. Like, fifty people at most. You two can work together, right?" London swung from Ellis to Rory.

"I…I…" Rory began.

Maya unhooked herself from London and walked to Rory. At first, Ellis thought she was going to kiss Rory on the cheek. At the last moment, though, she leaned into Rory's ear and whispered something. Curious, Ellis strained her neck but couldn't quite catch what was passing between them. Rory's brow furrowed, and she stepped back as if trying to get away from Maya or what she was saying.

London came over, grabbed Maya's hand, and led her off the set. At the last moment, Maya turned and nodded at Rory. "You know I'm right."

The crew parted like the Red Sea, and as London and Maya reached the house, London announced to no one in particular, "We're going home to work off these calories. Thanks, everyone, for such a great shoot."

Much of the crew applauded, and Ellis thought for a moment that Maya was going to take a bow before her exit. Instead, she pinned her gaze on Ellis and gave her a thumbs-up. From the outside, the gesture was playful, fun, even. To Ellis, it said, *I win.*

Ellis watched them walk out without reacting. She might have lost this second battle, but the war was far from over. One glance at Rory told her that she wasn't the only one observing the drama. Deep in thought, Rory stared at the door long after Maya had disappeared. Ellis stifled the urge to ask what Maya had whispered. It was none of her business. Rory was still pensive. It must have been powerful. Strange how Rory now felt like an ally and not an enemy at all.

Ellis stepped closer and broke the silence. "I guess you and I will be working together."

Rory let out a deep breath. "Do I have a choice?"

"London usually gets what she wants. You can break the mold if you want. You don't have to say yes."

"No. I think I do. This is the last week for *Guess Who's Coming to Dinner*, and I need a new gig."

"Working with London is more than a gig. It's a lifestyle. You're going to have to hold on to your bootstraps." Ellis tried to laugh and lighten the mood. It came out as more of a groan.

"Who's holding on to what?" Yolie appeared at her elbow. "What happened?"

"We're throwing a Valentine's Day party."

"Really?" Yolie asked.

Ellis knew she shouldn't say it out loud in front of everyone, especially Rory. She did anyway. "Afraid so. Trouble is now spelled with a capital M."

CHAPTER SIX

Standing on a dirt pad in the hills of Topanga, Rory watched her sister's new tiny house being delivered. The truck's back-up horn broke the peaceful silence of the canyon and drove the scrub jays to swoop above their heads. This was the kind of chaos her sister always created. Rory thought back to Norah's show the week before. She was surprised that she'd agreed with Ellis about anything. Trouble was, in fact, spelled with a capital M. In her case, the M stood for Meadow.

"If I had known Mom didn't have the money," Meadow said only loud enough for Rory to hear, "I wouldn't have accepted the better kitchen or the other upgrades. Goat cheese brings in more money than milk, and I had to have a place to work."

Rory bit her tongue while thoughts screamed in her head: *One, you can't run a successful business out of a tiny kitchen.* Rory had tried. *Two, other upgrades? And three, did you say accepted? Like a gift?* The truth was probably somewhere in the middle, between her mom's and her sister's stories. Now was not the time to flesh either part out.

She took a step closer to Meadow so their mom wouldn't hear. "You had to know that there was no money in the bank. Look around you. Couldn't you have asked?"

"Mom could have a million dollars, and she wouldn't spend a penny on herself. Besides, when someone gives you a present, you don't ask to see their bank balance before you accept."

"That's what you're going with?"

Meadow threw her a cold glance. "She wouldn't have told me the truth. You know Mom."

Rory did, and Meadow was right. Their mom would give the shirt off her back to anyone in need. She was genuinely kind and wanted people to like her, a deadly combination that had worked to her sister's advantage more than once. In Meadow's defense, however, even in the best of times, their specific mother-daughter dynamics were hard. Ever since their father's death twenty years ago, their mom had always tried hard to pretend that everything was okay. Neither Rory nor Meadow wanted to pull the veil off that lie.

"Stop bickering, you two." Her mom stepped between them, draped her arms over their shoulders, and hugged them close. "We should be celebrating. This is a milestone. Both my daughters have left the nest and are flying solo into their own wonderful lives."

Left the nest by a hundred feet. Rory glanced behind her to her mom's cabin. A tiny house way before they were trendy, this wood and glass structure was the one that needed the upgrades. Rory didn't blame Meadow for wanting to move out. The cabin only had one bedroom. She and her sister had slept in curtained alcoves in the main room as if living in the Middle Ages, and everyone had shared one rustic bathroom with an outside shower. Growing up had been like camping all the time.

However, appreciating why Meadow wanted a place of her own and supporting how she got it were two completely different things.

After Meadow's new home was stabilized and leveled, their mom dragged them into the cabin to celebrate. She poured coffee into lovely handmade mugs with a golden meadow design, created for Meadow's twenty-first birthday. Fresh scones, butter, and jam sat on matching ceramic plates.

"I thought we'd use the plates this morning, and then you can take them to your own place."

"Thanks, Mom." Meadow kissed her cheek. "For everything." And then as she sat, she mouthed to Rory, *I'll pay her back.*

Okay, Rory mouthed back. Meadow was good for the money, just not as soon as their mom was going to need it. That was on Rory.

Over the coffee and scones, they chatted about the goats— Ozma and Auntie Em were pregnant—and of Rory's new windfall.

"Yeah, you say it's only one night," Meadow took the dirty plates to the sink a few steps away. "Think who'll be there, though. If your pies catch on, the sky's the limit." Meadow's positivity came straight from their mom. Every idea in her world was a home run.

"You know"—Rory got up to dry—"I was wondering if you could spare some cheese. Not spare, sell. I'll buy it." She quickly corrected herself. "I'm going to make honey and goat cheese pies with pistachio crusts for the party. Miniature size. One perfect bite."

"Oh, that sounds delicious." Her mom clapped. "I love your nut crust."

"When do you need it by?" Meadow stacked her namesake plates into a pile.

"Three days before Valentine's."

"Plain?"

Rory nodded.

"Yeah, I can totally do that." She paused and held up her index finger. "Only if you tell everyone it comes from Gold Meadow Cheese?"

"If the pies turn out, absolutely. Otherwise, I'll tell them that the cheese came from the market down the street."

Meadow chuckled, and the tension of their earlier conversation dissipated. For the moment. "Oh, they're going to love the pies," Meadow said. "We can even put them on one of Mom's bigger golden meadow plates and give her pottery a plug." She tapped her temple with her index finger. "I'm always thinking."

"That you are, honey. That you are," her mom said.

"Thanks. I got to go." Meadow gathered her booty of plates and mugs. "The goats are calling. I'll be in touch, sis."

Rory sighed deeply as the front door clicked shut.

"You're too hard on her," her mom said when they were alone.

"Am I? She could have had that bigger kitchen ages ago if she had taken that ceramics teaching job at Calmont Prep. That was a bimonthly paycheck, good insurance, and a 403B." She clenched a hand in her lap. "I'm not saying she can't make cheese but maybe as a hobby? And then, she can afford her own upgrades."

"If I remember correctly," her mom said, not unkindly, "you turned down that chichi restaurant as a line cook with all the same benefits. What's the difference?"

Rory shrugged and looked at her lap. "None, except that affected just me. This affects all of us. We're both coming to her rescue, and I guess what annoys me is that she kind of expects it."

"Of course she does. That's what families do. And you can expect it too if you need her. Sometimes, you're too quick to voice your opinions. There's an art to defusing tense situations."

Knowing it was childish, Rory rolled her eyes. She had heard this before, a thousand times. It wasn't only the money that irked her. Sometimes, shit had to be said. There were times when a person couldn't let something go.

"You know, none of this," her mom said brightly, "would have been a problem if the kiln hadn't broken. And this pie party thing came out of nowhere, thank goodness. A godsend, really. It's wonderful where Fate pushes you. What's with the face?"

"What face?"

"That one." Her mom pointed at her. "You're all smushed up."

"Am I?" Rory forced her muscles to relax and dug around in her mind to figure out exactly what was wrong. Surprisingly, she found it quickly. It had been at the edge of her thoughts all week. "I think I'm having second thoughts about the pie party."

"Why?"

"They're paying me too much. I don't want to take advantage of London."

"Oh, sweetie, that's silly. You're such a talented chef. Your pies will be worth every penny. Why on earth would you think that?"

"Okay, maybe it's not that. Or all that. Last time I saw Maya, she said something to me that I'm not sure how to process." Even now, as Maya's words drifted into her head, she pushed them out again. She was not the opportunist that Maya was, was she?

"And all this circles back to the party how?"

Here they were at the crossroads of the matter. Rory should have come clean about how she had stopped Ellis from protecting London that first morning in the kitchen. She had been indignant, and as her mom had said, too quick to voice her opinion. She was beginning to wonder if she hadn't done London, and Ellis, a terrible disservice. They needed to know who Maya really was. But if Ellis lumped her and Maya together, she could easily lose the *godsend* that was paying for the new kiln. She felt like a fly trapped in a Hollywood web. At one point, she had thought Ellis was the spider. Now, she wasn't sure.

Her mom sat across the tiny table waiting for her answer. Her irises twinkled with hope. She only had two gears: positivity and worry. She had cycled back into affirmation with the arrival of Meadow's tiny house, and Rory couldn't send her tumbling back into uncertainty.

"I don't know, Mom. This stroke of good feels more like a test somehow."

"That's silly, sweetie. Have a good time making your pies. Decorate them like the works of art they are, and how can you go wrong?"

Rory turned the conversation over in her mind as she drove down Topanga Canyon Boulevard until she hit the beach. The spot where the mountains met the sea always took her breath away. And today, luckily, it took her sour thoughts away too. Even in midwinter, the ocean sparkled a deep sapphire blue in the noon sunlight. A few surfers caught the rolling waves right offshore.

Living deep in the Valley, she didn't get to the ocean as often as she liked or needed to. The water and sand had been a fixture in her childhood. And a wonderful escape when she'd needed it. Only a five-minute walk to catch an eleven-minute bus ride and the pounding waves of the Pacific Ocean had welcomed her. Swimming into its depths, she had embraced both its power and peace as she had grown up.

Even with the chilly February air, Rory was sorry she didn't have time to stop and jump in the ocean before she turned right onto Pacific Coast Highway. She had misplaced her wet suit ages ago, but the bracing water might've knocked some sense into her. Was it a coincidence that her troubles had started when she had moved away from the ocean? Or was that called growing up?

She made the hard right and drove straight into the heart of Malibu, one of the wealthiest zip codes in the state. The houses here fell into two categories: those right on the beach, crammed together so tightly, residents could dangle their arms out a side window and fist bump their neighbors. The others, built into the hills above the ocean, had space and views to die for but no beach access. Rory had always preferred the houses on PCH. In her book, being able to walk onto the beach outweighed every possible con, and unbelievably, her phone's GPS directed her to a house that had escaped the equation altogether. The ultramodern steel and glass mansion sat on two, maybe three lots right on the beach. There was plenty of space for parking, side yards, and private alcoves that neighboring properties didn't have.

Rory double-checked the address and pulled her trusty Kia through an open gate into the large driveway. Yolie was clearly expecting her, and the gate rolled closed after she eased her car onto the property. They had chatted a few times during the week when Rory had confessed that she couldn't cook out of her apartment. She worried that news would kill the gig. Instead, Yolie had suggested the venue. After the third call hammering out the details, Rory had found she was utterly sold on Ellis's assistant. She was upbeat and kind and always complimentary of her boss.

Rory was looking forward to visiting with her. Besides, it would be far easier to tell Yolie about Maya and let her do the dirty work with Ellis. What did Meadow always say? When in doubt, chicken out and find another way?

Which was exactly what she wanted to do when the frosted glass door opened to reveal not Yolie, but Ellis. She stood framed by the doorjamb and in the distance, by the deep blue of the Pacific Ocean.

"Oh," Rory said as soon as she registered Ellis on the doorstep.

"Sorry. Just me," Ellis said as if she got that a lot. "Yolie had to accompany a client to a third, and I hope, final callback."

"No. It isn't that." Rory made a show of shifting her backpack to give her time to think. "I was just surprised." And she was but not in the bad way that Ellis obviously assumed. Since the taping, she had been thinking about Ellis more than she would like to admit and had sort of changed her tune. Ellis might be wound tight, but she might not be the she-devil of that first meeting.

"Come on in. Let's start with the kitchen and see if it will work." She waved Rory inside. Once again, she was dressed to the nines in a stiff cotton blouse, an A-line skirt, and leather boots. Her copper hair was pulled back into her usual high bun, although this time, a fine braid was wrapped decoratively around the base. It looked complicated. Rory hadn't a clue about hairstyles. She had worn her hair short since she was five and had cut off her own braids with kitchen scissors. She had thrown them over the balcony at the Topanga house with a guttural whoop that had brought her mom running in terror.

Ellis took Rory through the house, passing a kitchen that would give a Michelin chef pangs of envy and into the backyard. A wide swath of grass ran to the sand, interrupted only by a lap pool and bocce ball court. To their left, under a pergola, was another cooking space created for outdoor entertaining. A full bar ran down one side, and on the other was a custom grill, an artisanal pizza oven, and a second full kitchen.

"Wow." Rory spun in a circle to take it in. "This is London's mother's house?"

"Yeah, lately, though, she's based out of England. London can use it when she wants. And you too, I hope. Yolie said you need space and heat. We can give you the use of the ovens down here and all the prep space. Will this work?"

"This is much nicer than my usual garage." She laughed at the truth of it and then rubbed her chin. "But..." She fell silent, not knowing how to broach the next subject. Her stomach swirled painfully.

"But what?" Ellis asked.

Rory pulled her shoulders back. *Fuck it.* She would tell her what Maya had said, even if it killed this gig. Who cared how she came off? This was the exact shit that needed to be said. Being true to herself was more important. "You see—"

Ellis tightened before her, literally shrinking as if Rory was an animal ready to pounce. "I'm not giving you more money," she said quickly.

"No. It's not that." Even she heard the hurt tone in her own voice. "Jesus. I already think you're overpaying me. Is that what people usually want?"

Ellis nodded. "Everyone wants to negotiate a new deal when they see how much money London and her family have. She's the goose who lays the golden egg."

Rory nodded, happy to take this little detour. "And you would be who in that fairy tale?"

"I don't know. Maybe the evil giant?" Ellis blew out a breath that was short of a chuckle. "No. I guess I'm the beanstalk. All I want to do is support London's universe, and all people want to do is chop me down to get to her."

"Well," Rory took a deep breath and looked out to the ocean for comfort. "I don't want to take an ax to you, but I think Maya might."

"Tell me."

"When we were at the show last week, she said something that I think you should know." She turned back and met Ellis's hard stare.

Curiosity sparked in Ellis's irises, and Rory knew that she had been thinking about her too. Or more accurately, wondering what Maya had whispered to her. Strange that they spent tons of time in each other's heads over the last week and were just realizing it.

"What'd she say?" Ellis's voice was low and almost gentle.

Rory's heartbeat thudded loudly in her chest. She didn't let it drown out her conviction. "Maya told me to hijack this gravy train and take what I wanted. We shouldn't care about you or London. A once-in-a-lifetime chance, she'd called it.

Rory paused to see how Ellis was taking this confession. She couldn't tell. Her eyes, her mouth, the tilt of her chin came together in their usual impenetrable mask.

"And that you were the enemy and would try to stop us. Funny. She didn't use those words, but, yeah, she's absolutely going to chop you down. Well, she's going to try."

Ellis's eyes remained cool. Rory wasn't sure what she had expected. Maybe thinking about it now, she had hoped, in part, to tear off the cool mask Ellis always wore. She realized with a start that she wanted to see what was underneath.

❖

Ellis's throat went dry as a band of tension squeezed her temples. She fought to keep her exterior calm. She had already known Maya's real nature, but hearing it out loud had sent it home. Shit, shit, shit. She needed to be one jump ahead of Maya and not be nipping at her heels.

"I think"—Rory brought her back to the conversation—"she was talking more about her than me."

"I suspect you're right."

Rory had taken a big chance coming clean. And with the way she had told her, slow at first and then rushing back to the beanstalk, this woman had real integrity. And if Ellis was being completely honest, she'd been adorable as she'd said it.

"Maya, for sure, has her own agenda," Ellis added.

"And you knew that from the beginning, didn't you?"

"I hoped I was wrong. Actually, I'm beginning to think I may have underestimated her. Most women grab hold of London for the lifestyle bump. She's very generous. The clothes alone are enough to keep anyone hanging on for as long as they can. Maya's different. She wants London like everyone else. She may honestly like her. But she wants to conquer her, not be with her." Ellis frowned as a thought ran through her mind. "Maya said all that to you at the taping?" Playing it back, it seemed as if Maya had leaned in only for a moment.

"Mostly. I may have put my spin and words on it. I mean, I've been thinking about it all week. I knew Maya was a hustler. This, though, seemed truly calculated in a way that surprised me. The words aren't so bad, but the subtext is, I think."

"And London's oblivious to that for sure. So many people want so many things from her that she's developed a fatal flaw. She figures that if she doesn't acknowledge it, she doesn't have to deal with it. She can—" Ellis stopped short and screwed her mouth shut. What the hell was she doing? Why was she revealing anything about London? Rory had come clean about Maya, but that didn't mean she was on Team London.

"And you want to protect her." Rory finished her thought.

Or maybe she was. Arms hanging stiffly by her side, Rory looked forlorn. Ellis had lumped her in with Maya from the start. Maybe she had misjudged her. Her gut was usually right, and now it was telling her that Rory was genuinely upset.

Ellis decided to put her out of her misery. "I do want to protect her. And I will. Don't worry."

Rory dropped her chin to her chest. "I made that much harder for you. With no NDA and all. I'm really sorry."

"Harder maybe. Not impossible." Ellis screwed her feet into the ground. "Maya doesn't know who she's up against."

Rory raised her head. "Let me help."

Ellis stared into her eyes. She had noticed the color back when they'd first met at London's, but not the warmth. After drinking in the blue green of London's irises in print and in person for so long, brown, the most common color on earth, felt realer and more authentic.

"Or I can walk away," Rory said. "I totally get if you want to replace me. I can recommend someone else. I've got a bunch of friends who are great pastry chefs and would jump at a chance like this."

Trying to untangle her burgeoning personal feelings from her professional ones, Ellis shook her head. "I'm not sure how I would explain it to London without tipping our hand to Maya." She rotated her shoulders, trying to loosen them. "Besides, I had a piece of that apple pie. You'll be the hit of the party."

Rory let out a breath. "Good, because I need this job."

She had risked a job she *needed* to tell Ellis about Maya. When was the last time someone in Hollywood had put doing what was right ahead of their own self-interest? That was the point, though. Rory wasn't Hollywood, not really.

A feeling Ellis couldn't quite identify started to circle in her.

"And what's more, I want this job too." Rory unhitched the backpack from her shoulder and motioned to the tiled bar. "I've made a few potential designs for the pies. Can I run them by you?"

"Please." Ellis waved to the stools, and they both climbed up. This time, Ellis deliberately chose the one right next to Rory, unlike in London's kitchen weeks ago.

Rory pulled a leather notebook out of the backpack, flipped to a section marked by a black ribbon, and smoothed out the pages.

Ellis took one glance and gasped.

On either side of the crease were delicate pen and ink drawings so lovely that they could have easily graced a fine arts portfolio. Except they were pictures of pies in every shape and size. The views, mostly top-down, highlighted intricate designs. On the left-hand side was a pie with a stunning combination of pastry roses along the edge and lifelike tulips and daisies layered two to three deep in the interior. On paper, it looked more like a basket of flowers from a farmers market than a dessert. Underneath was another work of art. This one was a riff on a stained glass window with cutout hearts and different shades of red flooding the empty space.

"Wow." Ellis's voice radiated delight and surprise. "Did you go to art school too?"

"Nope. All self-taught."

"They're gorgeous."

"Wait." Rory hurriedly turned the page. "I got cute too."

The rectangle shape of an envelope sat front and center. *TRUE LOVE* in big block letters was cut into the envelope's face, and the stamp was a raised heart. The back had a circle of pastry that looked like an old-fashioned sealing wax with $L+M$ on it.

"That works too."

"And dirty if the party wants to go that way." Rory flipped the page quickly as her enthusiasm took over. Over a dozen hand pies in the shape of the iconic heart candy filled the space. One dirty phrase after another was etched into their middles: *EAT ME. TWO FINGERS IN. LICK FASTER.*

"Ooh." Ellis sat back in her chair as the sexual images jumped off the page and straight into her mind. The temperature in the empty space between Rory and her skyrocketed. She wasn't a prude. She just hadn't expected to think about slipping two fingers in anywhere this afternoon and certainly not with Rory sitting so close by.

"And they'll be different colors like the real hearts." Rory pointed at a blue one that read *SCISSOR!* "This is blueberry dough. And the others, like the pink, the orange, and the green, are gel food colorings. Organic and allergy free. No one has to worry."

Ellis was having a hard time focusing. She pressed a hand to her cheek that felt a little flushed.

"We don't have to use those if you don't want." Rory grabbed the edge of the notebook to flick it closed. "I've other ideas that aren't as crude. They—"

"No." Ellis wrapped her fingers around Rory's hand to keep the book open. "London will love them, and they'll be the hit of the party, especially with her friends. Make as many as you can."

Rory nodded. "I will."

With those words, serenity swept over Ellis, grounding her both to the chair and the moment. She thought it was the satisfaction of a deal well done. Surprisingly, Rory had proven both honorable and talented. And even more, Ellis was beginning to feel very comfortable in her company.

She glanced at the book. Her fingers still rested on Rory's, light as feathers. What the hell? Normally, she didn't like to be touched by people she didn't know extremely well and hated initiating the contact even more. Surprisingly, she didn't want to lift up her hand. As it was, she had lingered too long.

Move it.

She forced her hand to the counter. The second she broke the connection, the usual frenetic energy whirled inside her again like a storm.

She furrowed her brow. Had touching Rory stilled the usual commotion that roiled deep in her? That would be insane. Although...

That day in her apartment, in Rory's arms, she had felt the same tranquility, maybe even more so.

"You okay?" Rory asked.

Ellis squeezed her eyes shut and opened them again to see Rory looking at her full of concern. "Yes." She slid her hand under her thigh to kill the impulse of reaching out for Rory to test this new, surprising theory. "Your pies are breathtaking and absolutely adorable. If they taste half as good as they look..."

"I don't mean to sound full of it." Rory raised her chin. "I'm going for one hundred percent in both categories."

"You're halfway there, for sure."

"Thanks." Her posture softened. "My mom always says that desserts are the real magic of any meal. The sweet, happy ever after that comes no matter how bad dinner was."

"She's right. You want to create your own fairy tale?"

"I don't believe in fairy tales. Both life and making pies takes a lot of hard work." Rory's lips turned up into a smile. "Although, as a beanstalk, you just have to stand strong and tall, right?"

"Believe me, it's much harder than it looks."

❖

"You're not getting a migraine, are you?" Yolie asked Ellis later that afternoon.

She rubbed the back of her neck to see. No familiar stiffness. No yawning. No pounding that started in her temples and radiated out. Surprisingly, she felt pretty good. "No. Why do you ask?"

"I don't know." Yolie sat back in her chair and considered her. "Usually, you're tapping your fingers or twirling a pen. I've never seen you this quiet before. You sure you're okay?"

"Yes." She had been back at her desk for over an hour and still couldn't push Rory and that odd, wonderful stillness from her mind. "It was a long drive back from the beach house. Traffic was bad, and I'm just tired," she lied. Not that Rory's magic touch was any of Yolie's business, but why was she not telling her?

"London called while you were out." Yolie brought her back to the office.

"She called here and not on my cell?"

Yolie nodded.

Ellis closed her eyes and sighed. The encounter with Rory suddenly seemed very far away. "What does she want now?"

"To go on a date. She says they're bored sitting at home and waiting for the party. She wants to go out to dinner."

"Dinner's not so bad."

"And she also wants to hit up the Normandie."

"Of course she does." Ellis rocked her head back and forth. "She'll have to have a chaperone."

Yolie threw her finger to the tip of her nose. "Not it."

"No fair. I wasn't ready."

"I'd do almost anything for you Ellis, but I can't go out with London anymore. First, she doesn't play by the rules. Second, she doesn't listen to me. And third, last time I went out with her, we almost got arrested."

"I know. I'm sorry."

"What you don't know is that when my mother found out, she almost made me quit."

"I thought your mother loves me."

"She does. But she already thinks the hours are insane, and she said she'd draw the line at visiting me in jail."

"Okay. Okay. I'll go. I don't want to be a third wheel, though." She cocked her head in thought. "Try to get someone else. Maybe that producer from *Dazzled*, Francie Winters. We can make it a working evening."

"I'll call her right now." Yolie picked up her cell and headed to the waiting room. Not even a few minutes later, she stepped back in shaking her head. "Francie's on location in Hungary, scouting for castles or something."

"She can't make it?" Ellis stated the obvious.

"What about Maya's roommate? I liked her a lot when we were trading phone calls about the pies for the party."

"You mean Rory?" Ellis asked as if they both didn't know exactly whom they were talking about.

"Yeah, she seems nice. She knows Maya, and you could spin it as a bunch of new friends just hanging out."

At the thought of an evening with Rory, a shiver traveled down her spine.

"It went fine out in Malibu, right?"

"Yeah," Ellis tried to seem nonchalant.

"Should I call her?"

"Sure. See if she wants to join us." *It's not too weird or anything, is it? She did offer to help. The suggestion did come from her first.* Ellis quickly added, "Please make it very clear that it's only four friends getting together and that she'd be doing us a huge favor. It's not a double date or anything."

Yolie chuckled. "I think she already knows that, but I'll make it very clear." She gave Ellis a long, pointed look. "Wait a second. Is there something you're not telling me?"

"No."

"Then why are you fretting?"

"I'm not fretting, and who uses a word like fretting nowadays?"

"My mother. Sometimes, I think her sewing room may be a time machine."

Yolie was right. She was fretting. At least a little. And for the first time in a long while, her apprehension didn't center around London, although who knew how this evening would play out? She was nervous about something else entirely.

Somewhere inside, so deep that it was almost hidden from herself, Ellis was afraid that Rory would say no.

CHAPTER SEVEN

W hy hadn't she said no?
When Yolie had called and asked for *a huge, huge favor*, no was on the tip of Rory's tongue, bursting to escape. A glitzy evening on the town, hanging with celebrities, paparazzi stalking their every move had never been her idea of helping out. She had meant something more behind the scenes, where she could slide into the background unnoticed.

Then, Yolie had mentioned the Garlic Bistro, an upscale Vietnamese restaurant in the heart of Beverly Hills, a place she never could've afforded on her own, and Rory, much to her shame, had heard herself say yes. It was her own fault. She had offered to help.

Now, as she got out of the town car that Yolie had sent, her heart beat a mile a minute. The Garlic Bistro was right off Rodeo Drive in the heart of the Golden Triangle, where gorgeous clothes, delicious food, and opulent jewels collided in a one-stop experience. She didn't belong there. Had she really sold a little piece of her soul for good garlic noodles?

Apparently.

She was no better than the celebrities she criticized.

No one noticed her as she slid through the glitzy crowd assembled at the restaurant's front door. Last year, Chef Dahn, the celebrity chef-owner of the Garlic Bistro, had spent ten million dollars on a lavish remodel. Rory could see where the money had gone. A glowing, U-shaped bar peeked around the corner, and the world-famous river of koi flowed through the main dining room like the real thing. Rory had only read about it online. Chef Dahn, or her famous architects, had built an aquarium into the floor, complete with river rocks on the bottom and colorful fish swimming in the waters. Customers walked over the fish on their way to the tables.

"May I help you?" One of the hostesses looked down her nose at Rory.

"Um, I'm here with the Turner party?" She hadn't meant it to sound like a question. She was out of her element, and these weren't her people.

The hostess looked at her with surprise. "Ellis Turner?"

Rory nodded, then added firmly, "Yes."

The hostess bowed her head slightly. "Right this way." She led Rory through the soft tones of gray and pink, past the open kitchen, to a private room at the back. Floating walls had been pushed together around a large booth to create an intimate, and more importantly, private, dining space for four.

London and Maya sat in the middle as if it was a joint throne. They were dressed regally enough. Big diamond earrings that Rory had never seen before sparkled in Maya's ears. And London just sparkled. A silver sequined tank shimmered under a black jacket, yet it was more than that. London radiated screen presence. She was larger than life. Ellis, looking like the proverbial third wheel, perched next to her.

"Ms. Turner," the hostess asked, "is this woman in your party?"

Ellis waved to welcome Rory. "She is."

Another slight bow, and the hostess closed the door.

"Sorry." Rory looked at the cocktails already two deep on the table. "There was traffic."

"No problem, roomie." Maya turned to her. "We'll catch you up in no time."

"I'm not much of a drinker." Rory slid into the booth opposite Ellis, surprised, although she didn't know why, that Maya knew so little about her.

As if she hadn't heard, Maya held up something red and frothy with skewers of plump blackberries plunged into the crystal glass. "This is delicious. Waitress?" She called.

Magically, a server opened the door. Maya pointed to her drink with the other hand. "We'll have two more of these." After a slight pause, she added, "London, you want another?"

"Yes."

"No."

London and Ellis answered at the same time. London gave Ellis a pointed look until Ellis sat back against the plush booth in defeat.

"I'll have one more." London gifted the server with her thousand-watt smile.

Like almost everyone, the server melted. She stammered out an answer and rushed from the room.

London raised her half-empty drink and clinked it against Maya's. "To a wonderful evening."

"That's already happening. We should toast to something else." Maya said lightly and bit into one of the blackberries.

Rory noticed more than Maya's words, though. A shadow passed over her face as she rolled the fruit around in her mouth without chewing. Rory, on the other hand, did know something about her roommate. She was quietly steaming. She had been in complete control of the room, and with four words and a stunning smile, London had stolen all her thunder.

Rory was confused.. It was not the reaction of someone deeply in love. Rory glanced at Ellis. Had she noticed Maya's power play?

Giving nothing away, Ellis raised her water glass. "Then let's toast to decorum and getting out of this evening with the least amount of publicity possible."

"Jesus, Ellis." London rolled her eyes like a four-year-old. "Can you say buzzkill? I'm going to need three more of these if you keep it up."

"Don't you dare. You can't do anything that will trigger your morality clause."

London's only answer was a deep sigh.

"Do morality clauses even exist anymore?" Rory heard herself say.

"Unfortunately." London pushed her drink back into the center of the table.

"Really?" Rory started up again. "I thought it was okay to be gay. I mean, isn't the moral climate these days much more lenient?"

"Oh, it's not that," Ellis said. "I would never let her sign a contract like that. No, Prodigy is worried about other types of behavior, like multiple partners or crazy nights out at clubs"—she gave London a pained look—"that will tarnish its brand."

"Oh my God, Rory. Don't get her started," London said with a light laugh.

"Too late." Ellis shook her finger at London. "You may already know this. Prodigy started out as a kid's television network, and they depended on advertisers buying their squeaky-clean image. As they start to make movies, they're still demanding no risks and no controversy. They don't want to alienate their target audience, females under age eleven. Those little girls have made Prodigy a boatload of money, and quite honestly, I get it. They're handing London the keys to the kingdom. A worldwide platform of sequels and merchandise and who knows what else now that streaming is in the mix. And in an industry where so few films are female driven. She can't afford to mess up."

"I'm not going to mess up," London said and bit her bottom lip in a pout. "I know how important this is. But I can't stay cooped up in the house day and night, either. I need to blow off some steam."

"Ellis doesn't trust her. That's why"—Maya waved to the closed door—"we are stuck in this tiny little room instead of out there in the heart of the action."

"You're wrong. I do trust her." Ellis picked up a menu. "I always have been completely on her side from the very beginning."

"I know you have. It would be a whole lot nicer, though, if you could let your hair down and relax for once." London threw out the words as much a challenge as a concession and picked up her own menu with a snap.

Rory glanced around the silent table. Were they always like this? Acting more like siblings than professionals? In a flash, she understood how exhausting Ellis's job must have been. London needed to be managed, desperately wanted to be on some level, but resented Ellis every time she did.

"Good. Are we ordering individually or for the table?" Ellis asked without a trace of annoyance and tried, as far as Rory could see, to put the evening back on track.

Rory smoothed her cloth napkin across her lap. Without knowing it, she had wrapped it tightly around one hand during the exchange. Despite her recent interactions with her sister, she hated drama. Now, with both hands free, she also picked up the menu and read through the entries.

"Let's order for the table," London answered easily. "It'll be more fun that way. Although, I think we should get garlic noodles for each of us. They're way too good to share."

"Absolutely." Ellis nodded. "Rory, have you had the garlic noodles here?"

She glanced up to meet Ellis's gaze and shook her head.

"Oh, you're in for a real treat." Ellis smiled and gave her a knowing look. A shiver traveled down her spine. Whether from the garlic noodles or Ellis's soft gaze, she couldn't say.

"You know," Maya began and waited until everyone had turned to her before she continued. "I've never seen you with your hair down, Ellis. Do you always wear it up?" The tone was light, however, there was something darker underneath.

"Ha." London fought back a grin, clearly only hearing the surface question. "Very rarely. She even braids it at night before she goes to sleep."

Maya's eyes widened with an unspoken question.

"No, of course not. We have never slept together. Jesus, that would be like fucking your sister. We've spent a lot of downtime together. I love that you're jealous, though." London bent over and kissed Maya on the lips, lingering long enough to make Rory glance at the door to make sure their privacy held.

After a long beat, London swiveled toward Ellis. "You know, she's right."

"Right about what?" Ellis's eyes narrowed slightly.

"About letting your hair down. That would be the perfect way to show you're not just a chaperone."

Rory twisted the napkin around her fingers once more. She hadn't thought Maya would throw down a challenge so soon. Had she known that London would take the bait, or had she just gotten lucky? Not that it mattered. This was why Rory was here. She needed to earn her garlic noodles.

"Not at the table. Maybe later. At the Normandie."

"I bet it's pretty," Maya said in that same low voice.

"It is. Why don't you show her?" Without waiting for an answer, London reached over to pluck the gold hairpin from the middle of Ellis's fist-tight bun. Ellis veered away, and London lunged, jostling the table with her movement

At the same time, Rory calculated quickly and reached for her water glass. The table seemingly shifted at the wrong moment, and Rory struck the glass with a clang. Water exploded and poured between London and Ellis in a steady stream. They bolted from each other as if there had been a small detonation.

"Oh shit." Rory scrambled for the glass and pulled it upright. "I'm so sorry." The water pooled on the table, and she flung her napkin on it. "Are you wet?"

"No." London, practically sitting in Maya's lap, patted herself all over to make sure.

"Did it miss you?" Rory asked gathering more napkins.

"Yes, perfectly." Ellis threw her a strange look.

"Shit," she lied. "I'm so sorry. I honestly have no idea what happened."

The server opened the door with their drinks on a silver tray, saw the aftermath, and launched into action. In no time at all, she had a new tablecloth and place settings on the table and soft bar towels to wipe up the water that had missed London and Ellis with true precision.

The server, apologizing repeatedly as if the spill had been her fault, brought them a wooden cigar box and placed it front and center to London. It was such a quick response, Rory wondered whose table they'd stolen it from.

"Please accept this with our compliments and remorse." She opened it, and fragrant smoke curled out of the box, revealing four tuna cigars: long egg rolls filled with tuna sashimi. Tiny black caviar dappled the ends like real ash.

Maya clapped at the culinary magic and reached for one. "Oh my God," she said and bit into it with gusto. "This is to die for."

Rory sank back into the booth. Success. Certain disaster had been averted, and luckily, the top-drawer service kicked in. The dishes came one right after another, each one better than the one before. Rory hoped that Maya had forgotten her power play. She certainly ate as if she had.

Soon, their bellies were full of garlic noodles and lobster with a delectable scallion ginger sauce and tiger prawns so big that the word colossal didn't do them justice. At the end of the meal, London waved away the dessert menu. "No, just the check, please. We need to start working all this off."

Rory looked at her empty plate and wondered where they were going next. Yolie had mentioned a place called the Normandie, and Rory hadn't bothered to look it up. She had assumed it was a high-tech dance club, with hip-hop blaring so loudly, she wouldn't be able to hear herself think. She would put even money on whether it was lesbian or not. She knew London had chosen the Honey Pot. Tonight, she might want more attention than a girl bar would create. Whatever. Neither one was Rory's scene. She glanced at Ellis, who was taking care of the bill with a black credit card. She couldn't imagine this was her idea of a perfect night out, either.

What would she like? Something quieter. A place with a great view, big comfy chairs, and craft cocktails with clever names. With a start, Rory realized in this mental image that she sat across from Ellis, as if the perfect night included her too. *I shouldn't go there.*

"Ellis, what's taking so long?" London tossed her napkin onto the table with a huff. "We'll miss our reservation."

"Don't worry. We have three hours booked," Ellis said, although she did pick up speed a little.

"Reservation?" Rory whispered to Maya as they climbed out of the booth. "Where are we going?"

Maya shrugged. "Don't know. She said it was a surprise, and I was going to love it. Somewhere we can be seen, I hope."

The limo picked them up at a private side door. Maya went straight for the champagne cooling in an ice bin and poured four flutes. Rory sipped hers slowly as they drove from Beverly Hills into Hollywood. Easing down Santa Monica Boulevard, they passed the weird mishmash that was Los Angeles. Expensive restaurants nestled next to fast food chains and independent soundstages. The Hollywood Forever Cemetery, the eternal home of Rudolph Valentino, George Harrison, and Toto, the dog, came up on the right. Past the 101 Freeway, the limo stopped at a three-story industrial warehouse with no signage.

Even worse than she had thought. Rory took a deep breath and climbed out of the car behind the group. A dilapidated building in the middle of nowhere could only mean one thing: a rave with pounding music and a crush of sweaty people.

London was already at the door. When she opened it, an oldie but a goodie, instantly recognizable, drifted over their heads. There were other noises too. Laughter, mechanical sounds, and wood hitting wood that Rory couldn't quite place. It wasn't until Ellis joined them, holding bright red leather bags did Rory put two and two together.

"Oh my God. We're bowling?" Even as she said it, she thought she was wrong. Surely, London Green wouldn't be caught dead in a bowling alley.

"London fell in love with the sport when she was on location with her mom as a kid. Apparently, there was nothing else to do in Nebraska. It was good for both of them. Charlotte got an Oscar, and London nearly became a scratch bowler." Ellis held out one of the bags. "Would you mind? They're a little heavy."

"Oh, of course."

Ellis rubbed the back of her neck with her free hand. "I gather Yolie didn't tell you about our after-dinner entertainment?"

"She told me the name, and I assumed it was a club."

"London is a woman of many talents and moods. Come on. Let's see how Maya's taking it." She bit back a smile. "I believe London was saving the Normandie as a surprise."

Just inside the door, Maya's face had dropped about a foot, and the grin she had tried to plaster on was also slipping. Seemingly too excited to notice, London pointed to the ceiling.

"Over there in 1927, there were doctors' offices upstairs. During prohibition, they would write prescriptions for medical whiskey, and then everyone would come down here to get them filled at the pharmacy." She swiveled and pointed to an old sign hanging at the far end of the hallway. It read: *THE NORMANDIE*, and underneath, *Clinical Pharmacy since 1927*. "They would get their whiskey and come in here." She grabbed Maya by the arm and dragged her through old-fashioned double doors.

Rory followed and entered a different era. The hall was true to its speakeasy roots. Ten gleaming bowling alleys ran the length of the building, original league pennants adorned the walls, and tufted leather sofas sat at the end of the lanes. Scores were kept old-school style on chalkboards at every station, and on the lanes, the original pin mechanisms were left exposed. Every rerack was a visual steampunk treat.

Rory stood, mouth agape, and took in the little details. The rest of the group had made its way to a lane on the far end, and when she noticed, she trotted after them. "This is amazing," Rory said as soon as she caught up to Ellis. "I have to tell you, I can't bowl."

Ellis snorted. "Oh, don't worry. We're only here as supporting cast. We cheer them on and run interference when fans come over. Although, we booked the two lanes next to us to cut down on that possibility." She met Rory's gaze. "Hope you're okay with that?"

"Very okay." She plunked down on one of the leather sofas as relief spun through her body. All her life, she had fought her visual stereotype. She looked sporty but wasn't.

"Ellis?" London held out her hand and took the bag that Ellis immediately offered. Unzipping it, she pulled out some of the most beautiful shoes Rory had ever seen. She was not a clotheshorse. She believed clothes were to be comfortable and cover her in the right places so she wouldn't be arrested. As London held the shoes in her hand, she began to see the other side.

They were black leather, with one wide metallic gold stripe that ran at a diagonal across both shoes. "These are mine," London said to Maya. She dropped them to the floor with a soft clatter and dug back into the bag. "And these are yours." She pulled out the mirror image of hers, gold with one black stripe.

Maya leaped to them as if they were a fine meal, and she hadn't eaten for days. "Ooh, I love them," she squealed.

"She should." Ellis came over and sat next to Rory, positioning herself in the corner of the sofa so she could see the entire alley. "They cost over seven hundred bucks."

"You're kidding?"

Ellis shook her head. "I told you. London likes to spoil her girlfriends. And look. They're gold. Coincidence? I think not."

"She knows she's the golden egg?"

"It's worse than that. She craves it. Watch."

Still performing, London pushed Maya playfully down onto the sofa opposite them and squatted to her level. She raised Maya's foot onto her lap and ran a hand tenderly down her calf, stopping to cup her heel. With a gentle tug, she pulled off Maya's shoe. A quiet groan of pleasure came from their side of the alley. Everything London did had sex at its center. It was her superpower. It was what made her shine on the screen and here with an audience of two. And Rory also recognized that she and Ellis were united by the simple fact that they both enjoyed the show.

London slid the golden shoe onto Maya's foot.

"Oh, London. I love it." Maya sighed and stuck her leg out to admire the shoe gleaming in the lights from above. "It fits perfectly."

"And now, we're in a different fairy tale," Ellis said for only Rory to hear.

Rory whipped her head around to look at Ellis in delight. "That's exactly what I was thinking. Maya's no Cinderella, though."

❖

Ellis chuckled. "No, she's not. That's London's role."

Across the lane, Maya jumped up and twirled on one heel. London clapped at the performance and then got down to business. She shrugged off her jacket, draped it over the arm of the sofa, and swung her arms in big circles. Everyone in the bowling alley looked her way. The silver tank was skimpy at best; thin straps slid around her shoulders. As she warmed up, they threatened to slip completely off.

Like a watchdog, Ellis scanned the warehouse for potential risks, anyone who might dart over or shoot a video with their phone. Not that a bowling video would be that bad. If London put her jacket back on, Prodigy Studio would eat good clean fun like this right up.

At the moment, people were behaving themselves and keeping to their own lanes, literally. Satisfied that London's reputation or future was not in immediate danger, she scooted back into the couch and smiled at Rory.

For the first time that evening, Rory seemed relaxed. Her hands rested open on her lap, and the fine, nervous lines that had surrounded her eyes at dinner had faded.

"So." Ellis leaned in slightly. "How did you get the water to go between us when you knocked the glass over?"

Rory's body went taut. "I… I…"

"Don't try to deny it. I'm thanking you. You took a crazy, intense moment and defused it completely. And on top of that, no one got wet. How did you do it?"

A ghost of a smile crept to Rory's lips. "A little bit of intent and a lot of luck."

"Ha. It's a standby move of yours?"

"God, no. I took a huge chance. I mean, if either you or London had gotten soaked, the evening would have taken a very different turn. I had to do something. Maya wasn't letting it go."

"And it wasn't about me taking my hair down like Rapunzel, was it?"

"Nice. Fairy tale number three," Rory acknowledged. "Nope. That was a full-on challenge if I've ever seen one."

"She was asking London to side with her. Against me." Ellis swallowed hard. If Rory hadn't knocked that glass over, Maya might have gotten the upper hand. And once she did, the dynamic between Ellis and London would have changed, maybe for good. She patted Rory right above her knee. "Thanks."

Rory nodded. "I'm glad it worked out. As we said, both the water and the evening could've gone wrong in so many ways." She chuckled, and Ellis, a little to her surprise, joined in.

After they sat for a moment in silence, Rory shifted in her seat and asked, "Are you an agent or talent manager or only a manager? I mean, I have none of those. I don't even know what the difference is."

"We don't have to make small talk if you don't want to."

"No, I want to know. What exactly do you do?"

Ellis shifted her gaze to London and Maya both laughing loudly on the lane. London draped her arms around Maya, showing her how to grip and throw the ball. Even though London's hands were everywhere, it was PG and instructional and very sweet. A man three lanes over had his cell phone out and focused in their direction. He smiled good-naturedly while he shot, and Ellis nodded to herself. She was right. It was great PR even if London hadn't put her jacket back on. Just what Prodigy had ordered.

Satisfied for the moment, Ellis returned to Rory. She got personal questions like this one a lot, usually when people wanted to butter her up to get to London or get their own representation. Rory didn't seem to have that agenda. Only curiosity, not greed or ambition, swirled in her irises.

Ellis sat up straighter. "For ninety-nine percent of my clients, I'm a licensed agent. I hone their acting skills and connect them with productions or casting directors and get them jobs. ETA works with a few law firms to negotiate their contracts. If they want personal attention outside of securing acting roles, they usually hire managers, personal assistants, and public relations firms."

"And the other one percent?"

"She's standing right there." Ellis cocked her head to the bowling alley. "London hired me on a whim. We were at the same party, and when she found out I was gay, she said she wanted me."

Rory's eyes widened.

"Oh, not like that." Ellis smiled to herself. Strange, she normally hated evenings like this, where she was the third wheel on London's romantic bicycle for two. Tonight, however, felt very different.

"Seriously," Ellis said, "London told the absolute truth at dinner. We've never been together. I'm the only lesbian on earth who doesn't have designs on her."

"Not the only one." Rory met her gaze, then looked away.

Ellis's heart skipped a beat. What did that mean?

She rushed back to the comfortable side of the conversation. "What London wanted was for me to make her famous, and I was so grateful to have her as a client. I mean, she was already getting a lot of play because of her mother, who had just won her third Academy Award. But London wanted fame on her own terms. Unbelievably, she invited me into that world."

"That must've been amazing."

"It was...and it still is."

"But?" Rory asked gently.

Ellis shrugged. "I was so excited to sign her, we never defined what our professional relationship would be. I never put limits on what I would do for her. The list gets bigger as her career grows. Fact is, once you jump into the deep end, it's hard to get out." She glanced at Rory to see how she was taking it. The conversation had gotten heavy, fast. If Rory was here for underhanded reasons, she would push the London angle now to see what else she could get.

"I'm sorry. That must be difficult," was all Rory said.

Ellis's chest expanded with relief. It was nice to be seen and heard. London had a way of making people around her invisible.

"How does someone become an agent?" Rory asked.

"I kind of fell into it by accident. You see, there was this girl."

Rory pulled one leg up and under her as she settled in. "That's how every good story should start."

"Agreed." Ellis laughed softly. "There was this girl in high school, and she was super talented. A real triple threat: she sang, danced, and acted. Of course, Kira was gorgeous too. And keeping to the script, I was head over heels for her."

Rory nodded her encouragement.

"She was the star in all the school plays, dramas, and musicals and every choral performance. Then one day, I'll never forget, she was telling a friend in the hallway that she wanted to try her hand at Hollywood but had no idea how to make that happen. I saw my opening and grabbed it. I told her I would do it for her. I wanted to be the one who made her dreams come true. And then, I hoped she would make my dreams come true, if you know what I mean." Ellis warmed to the subject.

"I do. I had one of those in high school. Becky."

"I was in heaven. We spent every day after classes together. I found out everything I could about casting calls, went with her to her auditions, and fell so hard that the gravity around her seemed to double. The night she booked her first commercial was the best day in high school for me. We were giddy with excitement. She swiped a bottle of her parents' champagne, and we celebrated in her bedroom. First time I ever got drunk."

She bit her bottom lip. It had been a long time since she had thought about Kira or that night. They'd sat for hours on her bed, wrapped in her pink bedspread. They'd talked and talked and created a fantastical future where Kira would accept her Academy Award at twenty-six and thank Ellis on stage. She had also spent the whole night trying to gather the courage to tell Kira how she felt. The words had frozen deep in her throat. Finally, she had left and had walked home only to throw up in her mother's rhododendrons. The alcohol? The half-mile walk? Or the fear that she would surely disappoint Kira somehow? It could have been any of them. Or maybe all three.

Rory was looking at her expectantly, and she realized that she hadn't finished the story.

"She did the shoot, and as it turned out, hated everything about production: the downtime on the set, the long hours, and to top it off, the director tried to hit on her. At school the next day, she thanked me and said that was it. She didn't need me anymore. She was going to Broadway to do theater."

"She just dropped you?"

"Like a hot potato."

"That's not cool."

"That's high school."

"Nope. That's harsh at any age."

Rory didn't know how right she was. A horrible migraine had descended almost immediately. Ellis had lain in her darkened bedroom for two days, an invisible jackhammer attacking both her head and heart. Her mother had just closed the door and told her to come out when she was feeling better. She shook the black memory from her head. "To be fair, we weren't really friends to begin with. I was only a means to an end for her. And when she didn't need me anymore…"

"I'm sticking with harsh. I got to call it like I see it."

"I know. I like that about you."

"Do you really?"

Ellis nodded. "Yeah, I think I do."

"Can you please tell my mom that it's not an inherent character flaw?"

Nice, someone who talks to their mother. "Sure. Anytime." Ellis took a deep breath and relaxed into the moment. "Sometimes, I think I should find Kira and thank her. I found that I was good at the organizational part, and what's more, I love it. My job is like putting together the most complex puzzle, and then I get to see the lines between the pieces disappear."

"Still."

"Don't worry. It was a long time ago." She glanced over Rory's shoulder to her present. London danced on the blond wood of the lane. Even subconsciously, she called attention to herself. Were there always going to be difficult women in Ellis's life? Had she traded up with London in this respect? She had no romantic feelings for her, although it occurred to her in a flash that London pushed her emotional buttons the same way Kira had. Even now, Ellis was afraid that somehow, someway, London would become dissatisfied with her, and that would be it.

On the lane, Maya rolled a gutter ball and spun on her heel to make sure the whole alley was looking. When she saw they were, she stuck her bottom lip out in a pout that even Ellis had to admit was adorable. London rushed over to comfort her, to the collective sigh of the room. A sweet kiss to the head, like a mother would give to a child, and the performance was complete.

Ellis returned her attention to Rory. She was still looking at her and hadn't shifted to the production behind her. Man, it was nice to be the center of attention for once. Their gazes met again, and Ellis, much to her surprise, dropped her head first. "Did you always want to be a chef?" she asked as she picked an imaginary piece of lint off her skirt.

Rory sighed. "I don't think working in the back kitchen on a reality show is really being a chef."

"What about making the pies for the party? That's being a chef, right?" She met Rory's gaze.

"I'll let you know." Rory cocked her head in a cute, self-deprecating way. "Or rather, your guests will."

"They're another group who doesn't hold its tongue. What is it about cooking that you like?"

She lifted a shoulder in a half-hearted shrug. "I don't know. I like to eat. I like the way ordinary tastes can slide together to create something new and unexpected. I like making pretty things. For a while, I thought maybe I wanted to be an illustrator. Then, I realized pies and desserts can also be little works of art."

"All good reasons."

"At the center, I guess it's about connecting to other people. My mom bakes almost every day. She's a potter by trade, and when she sells a mug or a set of plates, they always come with a tasty treat wrapped up in colored cellophane. It's good marketing, and my best childhood memories were coming home from school and being met by the smell of fresh chocolate chip cookies. She always made extra for me and my sister."

"That sounds idyllic." Her own mother had never greeted her with baked goods or even a smile when she'd come home.

"That part was, absolutely. There was a lot of love and cookies in our house. That's where the abundance ran out. It was only the three of us, not a lot of money, and a handful of hopes and goodwill tying it together." A faint blush crept over her cheeks. "Sorry, TMI. I know I'm just here for the ride tonight."

"Maybe that's how it started, but I haven't had a real conversation like this in a long time."

"I'm having fun too." Rory smiled, revealing a tiny chip in her front tooth.

Ellis's lips curved up. She couldn't help it, and she realized that Rory had called it correctly. They *were* having fun. Somewhere between the water maneuver at the Garlic Bistro and Rory's cute, chipped smile, the evening had shifted. To what, though? Friends? She wasn't exactly sure. It had been a long time since she'd had a real friend. Her professional life had consumed all other aspects of her existence.

"What happened to your dad?" When Rory said nothing, Ellis bit her lip. "Oh God, too personal?"

"I don't mind answering. My father died when I was young, right after my sister was born. Car accident."

"I'm so sorry."

"Thanks." Rory shrugged again. "I don't really remember him or how it was before. My mom missed him terribly, though, and I think she baked in part to instill happiness in the house. You should taste her cookies. There are little pieces of joy with every bite."

"Now I think I'm being taken for a ride." She chuckled as she realized she didn't mind.

"You are a little bit. Joy is her actual name. The way she creams the butter and sugar longer than most recipes call for, that's her real secret. But I'll bring you some, and you tell me it's not true joy."

"I would like that."

And just as Ellis was thinking that she would brave chocolate and a possible migraine to try one of these magic cookies, someone two lanes over cried out. "Oh my God. Look."

Ellis jerked her head to the right. A man, the same one who had been good-naturedly filming London earlier, was again holding out his phone. This time, his whole body shook. Clearly, he was excited. She followed his focus.

A sharp bolt of panic hit her like a spear right in her gut. London stood in the center of the bowling lane, bending down to retie her shoe. Her glittery tank slid up and down in all the wrong places.

Stand up. Stand up, Ellis willed. She didn't want the man with the phone to get a free show.

London stood, and her top, all knotted up, slid off her one shoulder and then dropped completely to her waist. Of course, she was not wearing a bra, and her perfect breasts were on full display.

Beside her, Maya dropped her ball to the floor with a loud crack and threw both of her hands over London's front, one crushing each breast. They were covered, but to any outsider, it now looked like London was exposing herself in public, and Maya was copping a feel. The PG fun had twisted into an NC-17 video.

In a flash, Ellis flew to them and swung them around to the wall so that any new video would reveal nothing.

"Holy shit, London." A sharp pain shot up the right side of her neck.

"Oops," London said with no trace of embarrassment in her voice.

Ellis grabbed the tank and tried to yank it back in place. Maya wasn't letting go, and the gyrations of three people and six hands, all having minds of their own, presented like slapstick comedy.

"Jesus," Ellis hissed at Maya, who only hugged London's breasts tighter. "Get out of my way.

"You wish," Maya wheezed back.

Fuck me. Was this the final play of the power struggle started at dinner?

Ellis couldn't let Maya win because she didn't trust Maya to do the right thing if she backed off. She was the only one who had London's best interests at heart.

They were at a stalemate and yet, still moving as if they were in a dance contest. Neither was giving in.

"Here," Rory said.

London's jacket, the one she had discarded on the couch, dropped almost by magic in front of them. It covered her and Maya's hands. Rory had appeared like a fairy godmother and had changed the narrative.

"Thanks, Rory." London pulled the jacket around her. She shrugged off both Ellis and Maya and pulled the tank top back up.

The moment was over.

But the damage was done.

❖

The next morning, the online tabloid platforms ran close-ups of Maya's hands cradling London's breasts. Prodigy had logged several calls that Ellis hadn't answered since she sat at her desk with a full-blown migraine. It was as if someone was inside her head pounding to get out with a hammer. She felt it along her right side: her eye, her neck, even her teeth pulsated with an unholy beat.

Yolie stuck her head into the darkened room and held out Ellis's cell. "Mark Gardner. He wants a word," she whispered. She crept into the room and slid the phone onto the desk.

Ellis reached to punch the speaker button. With the simple movement, nausea rolled in her stomach. "Mark," she began. Her voice sounded weak, and she cleared her throat to start again. "This is what we're going to do. We're going to tell the truth. London was bowling. She was on her way to a perfect game." She had learned that fact in the limo on the way home as London's main concern was leaving pins on the lane. "Her top fell off. You can say a strap broke, and Maya, like a knight in shining armor, rushed to her rescue."

"You're spinning it as a wardrobe malfunction?"

"That's exactly what it was."

"If I look at the complete video, I'll see the top breaking?"

"Yes." Ellis had no idea what he'd see. She hadn't been doing her job. She could barely admit that to herself, let alone Mark.

"And there are no pictures of her naked."

"No. From what I gather, the man who took the video was shaking too much at that point."

"Wardrobe malfunction. It's a little tired. It might work, though. Especially if we emphasize how Maya saved the day." Mark's normal voice, loud and booming, assaulted her. "She would have to give some interviews."

"I know." It was the worst part of the plan. Ellis had searched for another solution since she didn't want to give Maya any type of stage, but nothing else had come to mind. "I think she'd be amenable to it."

Mark scoffed. "She'll jump at the chance."

At least Mark had her number. "Can you make that happen?"

"Give me a couple hours. Tell her to get to my office at…let's say eleven-thirty." He hung up without waiting for an answer.

"Yolie? You still there?" Ellis asked without moving her head.

"Yes. I'll take care of everything." Quiet as a mouse, she exited the room and closed the door.

Ellis rubbed her forehead with the heels of her palms. She had taken her migraine cocktail of pills the second they'd gotten into the limo, had gulped them down without water. The migraine had still crept in in the middle of the night, clinching her head in a vise. Now, sitting at the desk, she felt a stabbing pain with every heartbeat.

As usual, she didn't know what had set it off. It could've been lugging those bowling bags around. They had tweaked her neck a little when she had pulled them out of the trunk. Or the pain when she'd jerked her head later. Her neck tightening like that usually spelled trouble.

Maybe it was the stress of the bad publicity? But she had been here so often with London, it seemed unlikely. This time, however, Prodigy was breathing down their necks. Maya would have to deliver. Fact was, Maya's impulses were a new headache waiting to happen.

Ellis pulled on her hair to relieve the pressure on her scalp. For once, it fell freely down her back, its weight making the headache worse.

No, it wasn't Maya. Ellis was up to the challenge of this woman for now, and historically, London would sour on her soon enough.

Could it be…

…Rory?

Their conversation last night had grabbed her. She had felt calm and safe when they were talking. So secure, she'd shared a memory that she had told two people, total. There was something about Rory that pulled her in deep and also pulled down her guard. She had lost track of London, who always circled her like a hurricane.

Not that she would have been able to stop the tank top tumbling off London's shoulders from thirty feet away, but she would've seen it coming, and perhaps if she hadn't been charmed by magic cookies and a chipped tooth, she could've prevented the moment before it happened. She should have told London to put her jacket back on when she thought about it, before they'd started bowling.

Rory was far too distracting in a million different ways. Ellis was so close to her career prize. All she had to do was get London to Hungary.

Problem solved.

Stay away from Rory, do her job, and get London to the set unscathed.

She could shut her feelings off.

She had done it a thousand times before.

CHAPTER EIGHT

H ere's another one." Meadow stood in the center of her kitchen a few days after Rory's night out. She was glued to her phone and gave no space to Rory, who inspected the goat cheese on her counter.

"Another one of what?" Rory asked absently and untied the butter muslin to reveal a big ball of white cheese in the middle. "These look good."

In her mind's eye, she could already see the sweet tartlets they'd become. For the first time, she was beginning to believe she could pull the party off. If the little pies tasted as good as they would look, the bite-size beauties would be the hit of the night.

"A story about Maya. It's on *Hollywood, Now*." She turned the phone around so Rory could see.

On the tiny screen, Maya stood in a two-piece bathing suit that covered very little. She looked younger, clearly pre-London. The headline underneath read: "Sexy Savior: Who is this New Princess in London Green's Kingdom?"

"Please tell me you don't read garbage like this." Rory pushed the phone back toward Meadow.

"I don't usually, but you know these people. You were there. It's like two degrees of separation from Hollywood royalty. I can't believe you're not reading it."

"I've got a lot on my mind lately." Rory wasn't going to admit that she had read the first few interviews when they'd popped up.

They, like this one, had made Maya sound like the hero of the evening. That London Green had finally found her protector. Maya Layton was trending everywhere.

Not only was Ellis giving Maya the spotlight, exactly what she wanted, but Ellis, not Maya, was London's true protector. What was she thinking? In Rory's opinion, Ellis gave in too quickly to London's needs, and she wondered just how far Ellis would go.

Rory had called ETA with questions about the party and had asked for Ellis, hoping to broach the subject. Yolie had answered and seemed, for reasons Rory couldn't grasp, to be running interference for Ellis. They hadn't talked since their night out. Rory had to admit that she was more than a little disappointed. They seemed to have clicked on that couch in the bowling alley. Had she read the moment wrong?

Meadow broke into her thoughts. "Let me ask you this, what's the point of the party now that the whole world knows about them?"

"I don't know." She had wondered that too. "London still wants it. Maybe it's a Valentine's Day party. It doesn't matter. I've only been hired to make the pies. Can I taste the cheese? It looks good."

Meadow edged around her to get a spoon and open the fridge. Inside were little jars of creamy goat cheese waiting for their culinary future. "Here," she said handing one to Rory.

She rolled a small amount of the cheese over her tongue. Flavors burst in her mouth—tangy and somehow still slightly sweet, earthy, and unbelievably fresh.

"Holy shit, Meadow. This is incredible."

"For real?"

"Seriously, the best I've ever tasted." Rory dropped the spoon in the tiny sink and took her sister's hand. "You should be super proud."

"I separated the males from the females this time to get rid of the hormones. I guess it worked."

Rory squeezed her hand and met her gaze. "You did good. I should say it more often. I will be proud to serve this on Saturday."

Meadow's lips curved up in a slow smile. "Thanks, Rory. That means a lot coming from you."

They stood, hands clasped, both basking in the moment. This was what their mom was talking about. She could very easily support her sister. They had rounded a corner.

"Can I come to the party?"

Rory dropped her hand and pulled back. "No."

"Come on. You said it was great. I think I should be there to hear what people say about my cheese."

"Jesus, I can't imagine anything less professional than bringing my sister to work."

Meadow stomped her foot like a child. "Do you know how hard it is to build a business at farmers markets? Getting up at four a.m. every morning, carting goat cheese all over the Southland, handing out samples to people who've no intention of buying. I just need one little break." She took a step closer as a challenge. "Please?"

Rory sighed. "Okay, if people like it, I will try my hardest to arrange for London and Maya to endorse it somehow. Will that work?"

She could almost hear the different answers whirring around in her sister's head before she finally spoke. "You promise?"

"I do."

Meadow nodded several times as if convincing herself. "I really need a break."

"I know." She reached out for her hand again. "We all could use one."

Later that evening, with several rounds of goat cheese tucked neatly in her fridge at home, Rory tugged open the door to the Honey Pot. Looking inside, she stopped dead in her tracks. Dozens and dozens of people milled in the bar. The counter was full, and every table in the back had several drinks on it. Almost as one, the crowd whipped their heads around to see who it was. Rory felt their disappointment rolling over her like a tidal wave.

Sack of shit. They're waiting for London and Maya.

She stood right inside the door, unsure if she wanted to go any farther. She hadn't been here since the fateful night when Maya had quit. Terri, the usually frazzled manager, waved to her from behind the bar. "Rory. Rory! Come here."

Terri had to be furious with Maya and Rory. If she was tending bar, clearly, she hadn't found a replacement. Rory threaded between the crowd to squeeze up to the counter. Most people were dressed for a night out and were a much higher clientele than the bar usually got. Even Terri had a trendy new hairdo. "Wow, Terri. This place is packed."

"I know." Terri grinned and pulled back the tap on Rory's favorite draft beer. "Where have you been?" She placed the overflowing glass on a brand-spanking-new Honey Pot coaster.

Rory shrugged. "I wasn't sure I'd be welcome with what Maya did."

"Are you kidding me? Maya ditching us for London was the best thing that ever happened to this place. I do have a favor if you don't mind. Could you maybe…get her to come back for a night?" She slid the beer toward Rory and hastily added, "As a customer, of course. With London."

"I don't know when I'd get the chance to ask," she said, imagining cornering her at the party and demanding she return to the Honey Pot.

Was this the way it was going to be now? People asking her for favors because she kind of, sort of knew London Green?

"There's no way people are going to keep coming here if London never comes back." She tapped the counter next to the beer. "That's on the house."

"Thanks." Rory pulled cash out of her pocket anyway. She sipped the beer. It was cold and fizzy like always, but now, there was a bitterness to it. This was no longer her quiet neighborhood bar. A brunette to her side swung her arm widely as she laughed and threw it into Rory's shoulder. The beer splashed over her hand and dripped onto the counter.

"Sorry," the brunette said without even bothering to look around.

Yep, she was going to have to find a new dive to call home. She took one more sip for old times' sake and was turning for the door when a hand grabbed her other shoulder.

"Rory? I was hoping we'd run into each other."

At her side was a second brunette. This one, however, was grinning up at her and rose to her tiptoes and kissed Rory on the lips.

"Alejandra?" She broke from the kiss and took a step back. "I thought you said you were done with the Honey Pot."

The woman crossed her arms. "Never. This is sacred ground. Where we met. Although, like everyone else, I'm here waiting for nothing. There was a rumor that London Green was coming." She tilted her head to the left. "Started by Terri, I think."

"You're here for your podcast, I gather?" Like everyone these days, Alejandra was taking her shot at fame.

"I am, Trying to get *Fresh Beginnings* off and running. I still think it's a great idea, but the stars who have made it don't want to talk about their big breaks with a nobody like me, and the actors who haven't don't have anything to say.

"That's a real issue." Rory wasn't sure why Alejandra was pursuing this. She had a very lucrative job as a video effects editor.

"I don't want to sit in front of a screen anymore," she said as if she had heard Rory's thoughts. "I want to dish on celebrity lives. But it's a spectator sport if there ever was one."

Rory chuckled. Alejandra had always made her laugh, more now as friends than when they'd been dating.

"Grab your drink and join me. I've got a table in the back."

"Maya's never coming back here. You're wasting your time."

"Time with you is never wasted. Come on. We haven't seen each other in a while. Grab your drink, join me, and let's catch up."

"Okay."

Rory didn't want to get back with Alejandra, but she was fun and hot and being next to that heat tonight was what the doctor ordered. Since they'd broken up, Alejandra had texted her a few times suggesting a *friends with benefits* evening. Unlike someone else she could think of, she always knew where she stood with Alejandra, who was now dragging her to the back of the bar.

They chatted amiably, and one drink led to two. Just after the clock struck ten, Alejandra slid a hand up her thigh and said, "*Mi amor*, you know that I've always had a soft place in my heart for you."

A jolt hit Rory below her stomach, and she wondered if a flirtation-ship, as Alejandra had called it in one text last year, was possible.

"So much so"—the hand moved a little higher—"that I know that I can ask you…if you would ever consider…" She tilted her head and smiled, letting the sentence trail off while hunger flickered in her eyes.

Rory licked her lips. Shit, was she actually considering this? Alejandra had always been exciting in bed. God, it had been a while and was more than a little tempting.

But she wanted someone to look at her with more than sexual hunger. The mental revelation hit Rory harder than the physical jolt had earlier. She wanted what she had seen in Ellis's eyes at the bowling alley when she had covered London with her jacket. Gratitude.

Gratitude…and trust.

"Would you ever consider," Alejandra started up again.

Rory would have to let her down easily.

"Introducing me to Maya or London, even, for an interview for my podcast?"

"What?" Rory pushed Alejandra's hand off her thigh. "This is about an interview?"

"What did you think it was about?" Understanding flashed in her face. "Oh, we can have that too. I would never turn that down. They're not contingent on each other."

Rory jumped up quickly and hit the table with her knee. The remaining beer sloshed around in the glasses. "No. Absolutely not. I'm not a fan of Maya's. However, she deserves her privacy."

"Are you kidding? She's giving interviews to practically anyone who asks."

"Then ask her. Reach out in an official channel. I'm not going to help you get to her."

"In celebrity gossip, this is an official channel."

Rory grabbed her backpack off the chair. "Good-bye, Alejandra."

"Think about it. I could really use a break. I'll text you."

"Please don't." She stomped off.

"What about the other offer?" Alejandra called after her. "That's always on the table."

Rory let the door slam behind her and stood for a long time in the chilly night air. As it pooled around her, she took a deep breath, trying to find her usual calm. "Fuck me," she said out loud to no one.

In a million years, that was not how she'd thought the evening would go. Two different people asking her for favors in the space of two hours? Three, if she counted Meadow.

How on earth did Ellis put up with it? Rory had thought she had chosen to be the beanstalk because it suited her buttoned-up nature. Maybe her only option was to stand tall and strong against the many favors people wanted.

Maybe Rory should climb up there with her.

Early the next morning, on a raised triangular stage in Prodigy Studio's grandest fitting room, London stared at her reflection in several huge mirrors. She wore the skeleton of what would become her signature costume on *Dazzled*. Long petticoats hung under a tight corset, and the dress itself was a muslin mock-up of the final piece. The initial fitting had arrived, and the production, since it had real money to throw at costumes, was trying out designs in the cheaper fabric before creating the real thing.

Ellis had told London that she didn't have time to stop by Prodigy this morning. She had recovered from the migraine after two long days in the dark and had to reschedule appointments and activities, not to mention the miracles she had wrought to rehab the bowling alley debacle. The Prodigy executive had admitted that the press campaign was working.

They'd dodged a bullet.

This time.

London, however, had insisted she show up, and here she stood next to Maya and Paulette de Sande, Academy Award-winning costume designer. They watched London slip into critical actor mode.

She appraised the dress from every angle in the articulating mirrors. Even in a dress the color of dirty bathwater, London looked stunning, regal, even. She would be a phenomenal Princess Carina.

"How does it feel?" Maya asked, leaning in, her eyes widening. Clearly, she was asking about the whole experience: star treatment at a costume fitting at a top studio on the way to a blockbuster success. People had flitted around London like worker bees to the queen since the moment they'd arrived.

"This corset is unbelievably uncomfortable," London answered, the only question that mattered to her. "I can barely breathe. What's this, Paulette?" She tugged at her waist. "Real whalebone?"

"You know Anthony. He's the kind of director who wants to be as authentic as possible."

"Authentic to what?" Ellis put down her espresso with a soft clink on a nearby table. "Isn't this a made-up fairy tale in a fictional kingdom, out of time and place?"

"Exactly. This is why I need you here, Ellis."

Paulette waved them both off. "Anthony is channeling Gustave Dore and his illustrations of the nineteenth century. He wants everybody's waist to be inhumanly thin."

Ellis pursed her lips and then said, "Does he also know he's channeling body shaming of the twenty-first century?"

Paulette didn't answer, made a note on the drawing, and directed her next statement to her assistant. "We can let out the zipper a bit. No one has to know."

"Good." London tugged again at the corset. "I feel like I'm just sipping air here."

"Anything else?" Paulette asked.

London cupped her breasts. "It's also pushing me up. It looks like my boobs are growing out of my chin."

"Anthony—"

"I don't care what Anthony wants." London swiveled in the mirrors. "This is absurd. My character doesn't lead with her tits. She's an innocent from the forest."

"True," Paulette said noncommittally, though there was a slight head tilt to an assistant that was full of judgment.

"Okay. Noted." Ellis tried to catch London's eye. She needed to take this up with the director. "Should we move on? Are there more dresses?"

"Yes. Let's get the next one on her," Paulette said.

Two assistants surged forward to help London and the dress off the stage and into a small curtained room nearby. Maya tried to follow, but Paulette held her back. Ellis pulled her phone out to see several texts from Yolie giving her directions to her first and second lunch meeting.

Her finger was poised over one link when London stuck her head around the curtain. "Ellis? Can I see you for a sec?" Inside the fitting room, London stood naked except for a pair of bikini briefs that hugged her body like a lover. One end of the scar from her childhood injury, ugly and puckered, spread out from under the elastic band. Her hand rested over the scar as if trying to cover it up.

Two assistants flittered around her, slipping one dress off and another on. The dresses were cumbersome, even in these early stages. London would give up all independence for this role.

Going to the bathroom on set would involve two PAs and four yoga poses.

"Look," London said as soon as Ellis stepped through the curtain. "Maya and I have been thinking…"

Ellis's stomach clenched. No good could come from a sentence that started that way.

"Maybe you could talk to Anthony or Francie and ask if he could find a role for Maya somewhere in the production."

"I think everything's already been cast," Ellis said as evenly as she could manage.

"Get them to come up with something for her," London said. "It doesn't have to be big. She wants to come to Hungary with me, but she doesn't want to be a third wheel on set."

One assistant scooted in front of Ellis and dropped the new dress over London's head. She reached down to quickly cup London's bare breast to adjust it into the built-in corset that already had room for the harness that would allow her to fly. London didn't flinch at the touch. It was almost as if the assistants weren't even there.

"Sorry," Ellis said to them. She knew this conversation was making their job much harder. Actors had to stay on the good side of the wardrobe department. If they didn't, Ellis had heard tales of assistants taking in costumes a little at a time to make the actors think they were gaining weight.

"No worries," one assistant said in the most neutral tone possible. Paulette and her team must have practiced their calm inflections around the Prodigy water cooler.

"Still sorry. London, she doesn't have to stay on set," Ellis offered. "She could go sailing on the Danube or visit the thermal baths in Lake Héviz. You know, there's a reason they call Budapest the city of lights."

"She's not interested in a trip to Europe, although I'm thinking we'll stay for a while after the shoot's over. She feels that if she disappears for months, people will forget about her. This way, we can do joint interviews like all couples do about working together during the publicity tour."

"Is this her idea or yours?"

"I don't know. I think she brought it up, but I totally agree."

Ellis pinched the bridge of her nose. She had only herself to blame. Her idea to give Maya her own publicity had let this monster out of its cage.

"You'll make that happen?" London asked, less of a question than a demand.

Ellis glanced at the assistants, hanging on every word even though their expressions were blank. "I'm sorry. Is there any way you can give us a minute?"

"I'll make a call to the producers," she said when they were alone. "Are you certain about this? You know Princess Carina doesn't have a girlfriend. You called it. She's the innocent in the film. It might be hard to have Maya there and give your best to the part." Ellis knew with one hundred percent certainty that a small role wouldn't be enough for Maya, and London tipped for greatness, needed to be in the game even when the cameras weren't rolling.

"Trust me. I know what I'm doing. I want her there." London's face grew serious and even more lovely, if that was possible. "I think she may be the one."

"The one?" Surely, she had misheard. "You've only known each other for, like, a few months."

London raised and dropped her shoulders. "When you know, you know. Honestly, I think I loved her from the first moment in the bar." She clapped her hands in delight. "Oh my God, that's the first time I've said it out loud. Please, please call them. I can't live without her."

Love? London had enjoyed each one of her relationships fully, yet this was the first time she had ever used the L word. And she did look like a kid on Christmas Day who'd just unwrapped a shiny new bike.

Fuck. "I'll reach out. But I'm not guaranteeing anything."

"You'll make it happen. You always do. And by the way, Maya doesn't have a passport."

"You should ask Gina to help you with that. That's what personal assistants do."

"Oh, I had to let her go."

"Are you kidding? Why?"

"Maya didn't like her. She said that she would help me in that regard until we found someone new."

"Great, then she can help herself with her own passport." It wasn't like Ellis to be uncharitable, but Maya was a piece of work, and London had stopped listening anyway.

Ellis was still grumbling to herself when she pulled her BMW out of the Prodigy lot onto the Burbank surface streets. *I don't work for Maya.* The thought marched through her mind like a small army. And yet, here she was, calling Yolie to set in motion a series of favors that weren't going to end well for anyone.

"Hey, boss." Yolie's cheery voice poured out of the car's speakers. "Please tell me you're on your way to your first lunch meeting?"

"I am. And now I'm apologizing in advance for what I'm about to ask."

"Uh-oh. What?"

"Can you please call Francie Winters in Hungary and set up a FaceTime or Zoom meeting for tomorrow morning if possible? Work it around her schedule." She explained the reason, including the juicy details. Yolie was a great audience, sucking in her breath with London's confession of love and blowing it out in a huff when she heard that London had fired her latest assistant.

"Shit. No more Gina? She was the best by far. That's going to be a nightmare for us." Yolie's frustration was almost palatable.

"I know." Ellis took one hand off the wheel to rub her forehead. "We should talk to her about the new office assistant position. What do you think?"

"That's a great idea." And then, after a beat, "Do you think that maybe you should also talk to London?"

"I don't think she was the one behind letting Gina go."

"That's not what I meant. Ellis, I don't want to overstep here, but ever since you gave me Tisha as a client, she and I have been talking about the industry."

"That's good. You should make a real connection with her."

"I think I am, and it's got me thinking about other things as well."

"Good. Let's hear it. I truly want your input, Yolie." And she did. Maybe not on a day when London was pushing all her buttons. Yolie, however, deserved her full attention. She cleared her head and tried to give it to her.

"When I first joined ETA, I couldn't believe London was a client. And now I've seen your influence firsthand. *Dazzled* could be a real game changer for her and hopefully, for women in the industry. I mean, it's female driven. The director, the producer, and forty-two percent of the crew are women too. I looked it up. And you were the one who got London that job. Because of that, she's now part of this new female-centric movement in Hollywood."

"Thank you. That was always my goal."

On the other side of the call, Yolie took a deep breath. "I know, and that's great for London. I mean, you've told me you want to build careers for all sorts of women in this male-dominated industry. Look at me. I'm living proof. And maybe now's the time ETA got into the fight in a more visible way. We got Tisha, Anna, and Morgan all making career changing deals. Let's totally jump on it. ETA can become a real player for social change in Hollywood."

Yolie's passion poured out of the speakers and landed squarely on Ellis. She was deeply touched that Yolie had dreams for ETA and that she had gone from "ETA" to "we" in a heartbeat.

Yolie took another deep breath before she added, "We just need a little more time in the day."

Ah, there was the crux of the matter. Yolie wasn't going to say it. Managing London was all-consuming. And she wasn't wrong. Every little whim of hers took time and energy away from this bigger dream that Ellis had had from the beginning. And Yolie was saying it with love, unlike Mark.

There was, however, no way she could have this conversation with London. She would totally flip. And without London, would they even get traction in other deals around town?

She didn't think so. *Sometimes, you just can't say shit.* Especially if that something would cloud London's lovely face with disappointment. "All excellent points. And I think we should talk about this more when London's on location."

"And not talk to her now?"

"Let her get to Hungary." She kicked the can down the road and into a different country. Silence filled the car's cabin, and then Ellis added, "Thank you for bringing this up. I really value your input, and please know, this conversation isn't over."

"Okay," Yolie said.

"Are you good with the party?" Ellis quickly found another topic. She hated upsetting Yolie as well. "No surprises there, I hope."

A true professional, Yolie pivoted with her. "No, I'm good, and thanks for getting me the stipend for putting it together."

"God, no one deserves it more. Seriously, though, no worries?"

"Rory has called a couple times. Her questions are more nervousness on her end rather than ones that make me nervous on mine. She's never done this before and wants everything to be just right. She kind of reminds me of you in that way. If you have a second, you might want to call and reassure her."

"She's a professional. She'll be fine."

"I know. She's texted me pictures of the test pies. They look amazing. I thought maybe you might want to touch base with her and put her at ease. Didn't you guys sort of connect during your night out?"

"What gave you that impression?"

"I don't know. Something Maya said, maybe when she was giving me the menu for the party. And Rory sounded a bit disappointed when you weren't around. She seems nice."

Ellis pinched her lips. She didn't want to bang up against Rory in her mind again. Despite what she had vowed during her migraine, she had thought about several moments on the couch during the past week. Not what was said but the feeling, that wonderful calmness, that had circled them while they talked. It was kind of addictive. Yet, it came with a huge price.

No, she wasn't going to talk to her now, and she would avoid her at the party. She would pack up all her pie tins, London would leave for Europe, and then she and Yolie could figure out the next step for ETA.

"You going to call her?" Yolie asked.

"Sure, sure," Ellis said to get Yolie off her back. "When I get a second. I'll give her a call."

"Oh my God. You're lying. Your agent mind games don't work with me."

For a moment, Ellis had forgotten whom she was dealing with.

"Call her or don't call her." Ellis could see Yolie's raised eyebrows twenty miles away. "It's up to you. I think she's great. Just saying."

Damn. Work life or personal life, Yolie always knew what was up.

❖

A few days later, with music blasting in her kitchen, Rory dropped a bright blue N onto the crust of a hand pie with a pair of long, delicate food tweezers. She held up the giant conversation heart in pie form and admired her work. "Perfect," she said smiling and then read the word out loud, "STRAP-ON."

"Strap-on?" A clear voice startled her from the living room. "Please tell me you're having crazy sex in the kitchen."

Dropping the pie and clutching the tweezers like a tiny, culinary weapon, Rory scooted around the kitchen countertop to confront whoever was in the apartment.

It was only Maya, resting against the front door with her new, easy confidence and her keys swinging off one finger.

"What are you doing here?" Rory asked. Truth be told, she almost hadn't recognized her. Her hair was cut shorter in a new style that softened the angles of her face, and another brand-new outfit hugged her curves and gave the impression of elegance.

"I still live here, you know." She tossed her hair, and the new highlights shimmered. "Sorry to barge in. I've one or two things I still need to pick up and…" She dug into the back pocket of her trousers. "And I wanted to give you this."

She held out a fat white envelope. Rory plucked it from her hand and juggling the tweezers, peered inside. A neat bundle of fifty-dollar bills, fresh from the bank. "What's this for?"

"Rent, silly. I told you, I still live here."

"You never pay your rent early."

"It's a new me." She ran an open palm down her body like a hostess on a game show.

"I can see that. You look great."

Maya's smile brimmed with self-satisfaction. "Thanks. You going to be here for a sec? I need to get those things."

Rory nodded as Maya disappeared into her room and shut the door. Rory had been panicking about the rent for over a week and hadn't wanted to dip into her ever-dwindling savings to come up with Maya's share. Her plan had been to corner her at the party and bring it up. A solution that was tacky beyond belief and sure to have a low success rate, but she hadn't seen another choice.

"Hey!" Maya came into the kitchen. Her purse now bulged in places it hadn't before, and she carried a book with marketing in the title. "I should tell you that I'm going to move out. At some point, I hope."

"I thought as much." Rory leaned heavily against the sink. At least she had next month's rent in hand.

"I'll give one month's notice before I do. I promise." Her forehead crinkled in a deep frown. "After today, I think I should keep a backup place for a little while, just in case."

"What happened today?" Rory couldn't help herself.

Maya sighed deeply. "We had our first fight. Maybe fight isn't the right word. London and I had a discussion where for the first time, we weren't on the same page." Tiny pinpricks of red rose on her cheeks. Clearly, she was mad, and in a flash of understanding, Rory knew she had come over to get someone on her side.

Sure enough, Maya leaned in conspiratorially and said, "You know she's going to Hungary for the movie, and she wants me to come with her."

"Oh my God. That's amazing."

"Totally. However, it seems like the wrong time."

"You're going to have to explain that to me." There was something very appealing about flying first class away from all her problems.

"Last week," Maya started, "I got a call from a producer who wanted me for a part in his web series. Amazon Prime was looking at it. He said he had seen me in an interview, and I would be perfect for the part. Can you believe it?"

"I can. You came off nicely on camera."

"I did, right?" She paused until Rory nodded several times. "London said I should turn it down. She said it was small potatoes, and I couldn't shoot it when I was overseas."

"That last part's true."

"And she suggested instead that I could have a speaking part on *Dazzled*. I told the producer, thank you, but no, thank you. Then, I found out that there isn't going to be a speaking part on *Dazzled*. Ellis had a bunch of meetings, at least she said she did. In the end, they offered me only a featured extra role in a few crowd scenes with no lines." She clutched the book until her fingers turned white. "The worst part is, London seemed totally okay with that. She said we could bring it up again when we got over there, but it was like she had forgotten about the other offer from the web series. Like, she had no idea what I gave up for her. It could have been a big move for me. It seems like her career is the only thing that matters."

"This is a breakout role for her."

Maya's spots of anger spread across the bridge of her nose and merged. "She's not the only one in this relationship, Rory," she said as if scolding a child.

"True." Rory nodded. "Have you told her that?"

"No." Maya dropped her head to stare at the scuffed linoleum floor. "How could I? She told me she loved me. She said that she had never told anyone that before. And I think I love her too."

"Oh my God."

"I know." Maya lifted her head and stared. "If only we could stay in LA, everything would be perfect."

"I guess you need to decide whether you're in this for love or fortune."

"I want both." Maya shrugged, trying to be cute.

"You're not in control here. You're going to have to choose." The second the words came out, she wanted to bite them back. It wasn't her call, and as usual, she hadn't been able to keep the judgment out of her voice. It was a fair statement, though.

One that apparently pushed Maya too far. Her irises went hard and cold, and her face closed up completely. Instead of answering, she picked up the blue conversation heart and traced the S with her forefinger.

"What do you think?" Rory asked. "It's a test pie for the party."

"Cute," Maya said through pursed lips.

Clearly, the conversation was over.

❖

The next night, Ellis climbed into bed and pulled a new weighted blanket up to her chin. The packaging promised that lying under it would release serotonin and other hormones for a great night's sleep. Ellis knew she was a sucker, but it hadn't been too expensive, and she had done far dumber things to banish her migraines.

Of course, sleep didn't come. Too many things raced in her mind. The party the next day was the least of her worries. Yolie totally had it covered. She could organize goldfish to parade in their tank two by two if she put her mind to it.

Maya, however, was a different story.

Ever since Ellis had broken the bad news about the speaking role in *Dazzled*, Maya had been strangely absent in her dealings with London. A no-show for expensive sushi in Santa Monica and "too busy" when Ellis had stopped by the house.

Maya had no idea how hard Ellis had pushed for a speaking role. Featured extra, which had no lines but would be recognizable in the final cut, had been a huge concession on Francie's part. The producer's tone had been decidedly frosty when she'd ended their last Zoom meeting. And now, snuggled under her latest mistake, Ellis couldn't believe she had wasted her goodwill with Francie on Maya.

Shit. She pushed the blanket off. Was Yolie right? Had she left other dreams on the table to manage London? And lately, not only professional ones.

The truth was, she was at a psychological impasse with London.

And the deeper truth was, she was too scared to get beyond it.

CHAPTER NINE

Valentine's Day arrived with the bluster of a full winter's day for Los Angeles, thick ocean fog and temps in the mid-fifties. Not extreme for most of the country in February, but Angelinos were thin-blooded babies. Rory stressed over the weather from the moment she woke up until she handed her car over to the valet at the beach house. As if on cue, when the guests arrived, the ocean fog rolled out, and stars burst to life in the night sky. The full moon, like a key light in a soundstage, hung low above the ocean. Its long silvery reflection stretched to the horizon. No set designer could have done better.

Standing alone in the backyard kitchen, Rory fixated on the first star she saw and whispered, "Star light, star bright. First star I see tonight. I wish I may, I wish I might, have this wish I wish tonight" She licked her lips and added. "Please let tonight be the start of something big for my career."

"Wishing on a star?"

Rory turned to see a woman dressed in the black uniform of the catering staff. She nodded, annoyed at being caught.

"I hope you're asking for more food."

Rory glanced at the decorated tables on one side of the yard. They were full of pies, big and small. In fact, the tables looked like they might buckle under their weight at any moment. "Why?" she asked.

"Delicious Dinner Catering was told fifty people. Were you told fifty?"

Panic rose in Rory's chest. "Yes."

"There's at least twice that. And they're starving. Which is crazy for actors, right? I thought they ate like mice." Without waiting for an answer, she headed to a table to neaten the plates, something Rory had already done a dozen times.

Jesus. Who was this woman? Had she come down to help or stir things up? Or was she just another person who coveted a star's lifestyle? Probably the latter, since she was now staring over the backyard as if studying the various places she would linger if she was a guest.

Heels clicked on the wooden stairs. Rory plastered a smile on her face and hoped she didn't look as nervous as she felt. The smell of buttery crust and fruit fillings, fresh from the oven, wafted across the patio. The pies smelled great, and Rory knew they tasted great too. She also knew the saying: a party without cake is only a meeting. If the guests came down *hangry* because food was scarce upstairs, the reviews on the pies could go either way.

Leading the pack, London jumped the last two steps into the backyard. "Oh my God, Maya, look. This is beautiful." She pointed to the strings of fairy lights running across the porch and to the dessert tables draped in red felt and sparkly hearts. Sectional seating with their own personal firepits peppered the backyard. In the middle, the portable dance floor spread out over the pool and was lit from within. Two bars lay at either end.

Maya grinned as if she, not Yolie, was responsible for the transformation. "Welcome, everyone. Come in. Dessert is from Upper Crust by Rory Hatten. I'm proud to say that I discovered her myself, and she's totally awesome." She waved to the table. "Please, help yourselves."

One woman who Rory recognized from a blockbuster film led the rush to the table like a wild animal. Starving was an understatement. Rory glanced up at her star for luck.

"I didn't know Upper Crust was your company's name." Yolie materialized at her side. "You should have told me."

"I didn't, either. Maya just made it up, I think."

"It's cute. You should totally use it."

"I might." As Yolie turned away, she added, "Hey, is Ellis here? I haven't seen her." Rory could have kicked herself. She had promised she wouldn't seek Ellis out at the party. Truth be told, she also thought she would have run into her by now.

Yolie gave Rory a searching look. "She hasn't come down to check on you?"

"No."

"Mmm." Yolie furrowed her brow as she scanned the backyard and then pointed to the far corner. "Oh, there she is."

She followed Yolie's gaze and found Ellis chatting with another partygoer.

"Excuse me." Yolie put a hand on Rory's arm and gave her the tiniest of pushes toward Ellis. "I have to go and deal with Delicious Dinner. Our numbers were higher than what we told them, but they put out food for, like, half of what we quoted."

Rory took one step and then zeroed in on Ellis, who threw her head back with a loud hoot. This was not an Ellis she knew. She was in her usual costume, elegant pants and a thin cabled sweater, and her hair was in its expected bun. But this was the first time Rory had seen her laugh. Tendrils of hair escaped and fell against her face and neck. They caught the copper color of a firepit nearby, and between that and her grin, she was transformed.

She's lovely. Rory dropped a hand to her stomach in surprise. Butterflies sprang to life and fluttered wildly. *What the fuck?*

When had she fallen for Ellis? A woman who'd wanted to drop-kick her to the curb at their first meeting. A woman who was as tightly wound as they came, and on top of everything, a woman who was kind of her boss.

Across the yard, a completely different woman stood, and now that Rory was really looking, she stood far too comfortably with a smoking hot woman. A girlfriend? *Fuck.*

The mystery woman was tall and lean, with short messy hair that must have taken an hour to style and a natural presence that radiated all the way to Rory. Ellis wasn't immune, either because she reached out and cupped the woman's arm while they chatted.

At the touch, Rory chewed at her bottom lip.

Wait a second.

She ran her tongue over her lip and felt the indentations from her teeth. She recognized this woman. Celebrity chef Scarlett Dorien. She had the number one show on the Food and Flavor Network: *Small Bites with Scarlett*. Rory's old boss, Norah, had pinned a picture of Scarlett to a wall and stuck pencils into her eyes when she had won her fourth Emmy. Unlike Norah, Scarlett was the real deal: a James Beard Award nominee who toured the country looking for that one perfect bite. She found it with every episode, but it was her personality that kept the viewers coming back. She could charm the panties off a nun, and now, damn her, she was turning that well-healed charisma on Ellis.

The butterflies in her stomach became wasps and stung again and again until a leggy blonde rushed over with one of Rory's goat cheese tarts in her hand. She sidled up to Scarlett, who opened her mouth in response to whatever she had said. The blonde slipped the tart inside, and the pains in Rory's stomach flew away.

The action was intimate and sexy. Scarlett and the blonde must be together. Relief and confusion washed over Rory, and before she could tease out her contradictory feelings, Ellis was waving her over.

She wasn't cut out for the limelight, but she wanted to know that there was nothing going on between Ellis and Scarlett. That and the promise she had made to Meadow to promote her goat cheese was pushing her forward faster than her good sense could stop her.

"This is Rory Hatten," Ellis said when she arrived. "She made the pies."

"Oh my God," Scarlett said, still chewing. "They're incredible."

"Told you." The blonde tapped her chest. "I'm Kristina, by the way. And this is my girlfriend, Scarlett."

"I'm a huge fan." Even more so now that she knew Scarlett was taken.

"I'm a huge fan of that tart. Great crust," Scarlett said.

"You're not kidding. I've already had three." Kristina smiled. "They totally overrode my off switch."

"Not just you." Scarlett motioned to a table where people grabbed the tarts with both hands. "Everyone's eating them like they're going to run away. Where do you get the goat cheese?"

"From my sister. She has a tiny goat farm up in Topanga."

"Oh, a family affair." Scarlett nodded. "That's a good story."

"A good story that would make good TV." Kristina poked Scarlett on the shoulder.

"I know." Scarlett grabbed her finger and brought it to her lips for a light kiss. "Great minds think alike."

A burst of adrenaline rushed through Rory's body. *Seriously? Holy Shit!* Meadow would be beyond thrilled. How to answer? As big as her mouth was, she knew nothing about negotiations.

Scarlett looked back and forth between her and Ellis. "You guys together?"

"Oh no. We're not together," Ellis said far too quickly.

"No. Not in that way," Scarlett was the only one laughing at the misunderstanding. "I mean, are you her agent? All I want to know is who does my EP call to talk about an episode on the goat cheese girls?"

"Um." Rory chewed her lip again. Ellis's reaction had been a little too intense. Was she embarrassed to represent a nobody like her?

"We'll have to do interviews and scout the location." Scarlett didn't lose a beat. "Sisters. A goat farm and this tart. It's a slam dunk. You absolutely should have someone representing you."

"I don't know…" This was moving way too fast for Rory. However, Meadow would kill her if she didn't run after this opportunity. "I have no idea how this works."

"She does." Scarlett nodded toward Ellis. "It's what she does for a living."

Ellis's forehead knotted as she said nothing.

What the fuck did that mean? And in a flash, Rory realized that she was far more invested in why Ellis wouldn't represent her than getting a spot on Scarlett's show. The four of them stared at each other, each waiting for someone else to speak. Rory swallowed hard. She had never thought she would be at a loss for words.

"Can I have your attention, please?" London's voice rang out over the party. Everyone swiveled, and the people in front instinctively backed away to give her a makeshift stage. The chatter died quickly. Rory released her breath. She had been saved by the spectacle that was London.

"Thank you for coming." She stretched out a hand for Maya who jumped, lightning fast, into the widening circle. "This shindig was supposed to be my coming-out party where I introduced Maya to my closest friends as my one and only girl." She gave Maya's hand a squeeze. "You guys know me. I came out when I was fourteen. And the whole world knows about Maya, thanks to her daring rescue at the bowling alley." London clapped and bowed her head to Maya in thanks.

Around them, the partygoers joined in, and Maya, drinking the applause in like a fine wine, curtseyed in response.

By Rory's side, Ellis rubbed the back of her neck. They both knew that Maya was not London's savior. People always told themselves the truth they wanted to hear.

"She's one of a kind." London's tone was sultry. "That's why I need to take this to the next level."

The crowd squealed with one voice. Ellis stood out with a soft gasp.

London paused dramatically, and then, as the excitement was about to explode, she scanned the dessert table next to her. She selected one of the conversation heart pies from the front and held it up to the crowd. Spelled out in bright pink letters were the words: TRUE LOVE.

"Ah," the crowd sighed.

And then, unbelievably, London dropped to her knees and offered the pie to Maya with outstretched hands. "You're my true love. Will you marry me?"

"Oh, fuck me," Ellis said so softly that only Rory could hear. Not that anyone else was listening. The guests leaned in to see what would happen next, although none doubted Maya's answer.

"Yes," Maya screamed and jumped up and down, her heels tapping out her happiness against the stone patio. She grabbed the pie and pulled London up in a deep hug. "Oh God, yes!"

Everyone hooted their congratulations and bobbed and weaved closer to be a part of the big moment.

Everyone except Rory and Ellis, who hadn't budged, and now stood off to the side like a frozen mirror image to the happy couple. Rory couldn't tear her eyes away as London cupped Maya's chin and tilted her face upward. And what came next was right out of the movies. With a liquid heat, London lowered her lips to Maya's, hovering over them but not touching. She teased with a nip at her bottom lip and then pulled back. Everyone could see the tremors that raced through Maya's body. Almost in slow motion, Maya slid her fingers up and tugged at the back of London's neck.

"Kiss me," she moaned.

The guests leaned forward in expectation, and a few of them couldn't help calling out encouragement.

"Please."

"Do it."

London didn't leave them hanging for long. She leaned forward and covered Maya's mouth completely. Possessively. The kiss was long and deep and a statement to everyone who stood in the backyard. *She belongs to me.* And when it had run its course, London pulled back only to plunge in again. This time, she took Maya's head in her hands and cradled it tenderly as she explored Maya's lips and mouth.

"Did you know this was going to happen?" Rory asked Ellis without turning her head.

"The kiss or the proposal?"

"Any of it"

"No. You?"

"Uh-uh. She never asked me for a true love pie or anything." Rory shrugged. "Do you think she saw the designs beforehand and planned it? Or was it just a crazy, spontaneous thing?"

"I honestly don't know."

Rory finally glanced to her right. Ellis stared at the happy couple, who'd broken apart and were accepting congratulations and pats on the back like the stars they were. Ellis pinched her lips to the point of them disappearing and carefully twisted the tendrils of hair back into her bun one by one.

At her side, Rory's hand trembled. She longed to reach out and run a comforting touch down Ellis's arm. Instead, she curled her fingers into a fist and let the moment pass. Ellis wasn't a friend. She didn't even want a professional connection, apparently.

The beanstalk would have to stand tall on its own.

❖

Hours later, Ellis dug her fingers, for the millionth time, into the base of her neck and massaged the muscles. The party had wound down, and except for the caterers cleaning up, London and Maya sat alone by a firepit on a rattan couch. Their heads touched, and they spoke in kisses and whispers.

Ellis glanced around the backyard. The dessert tables were picked clean, nothing left but crumbs and the empty ceramic plates of golden meadows. Rory should have been very pleased.

That was where her good thoughts died. London's big moment had created so much extra work that Ellis's head swam.

Yolie trotted down the stairs to her side. "Delicious Dinner finally broke down and said that they would give us a partial refund. They're angry because they didn't put in the surcharge from driving all the way from North Hollywood. It's not like I didn't tell them a million times the party was in Malibu. It was right there on the contract."

"Everything is always about the bottom line."

Yolie tilted her head to the couple on the couch. "Did you know about this particular bottom line?"

"Nope," Ellis admitted for the second time.

"Good. I would've been upset if you had kept something that momentous from me."

"Never." Ellis grabbed her arm and dragged her to a private corner of the outdoor kitchen. "Look," she said after she had made sure they were alone, "I know it's late. Can you both call and email Mark. He won't pick up. Leave him a message. Tell him the bare bones of what happened here tonight. He needs to call me ASAP. There were too many witnesses, and we need to get ahead of this, especially with Prodigy."

Yolie whipped a phone from her back pocket and was already dialing as she scurried back up the stairs for more privacy.

Not for the first time, Ellis watched Yolie jump into work mode and thanked her lucky stars for her assistant. No, she was a full-fledged colleague. Ellis would have to remember to tell her that.

Okay. Here goes nothing. She pumped her fist by her side.

She rounded the corner, intending to march up to London and Maya and lay down the law. Tell them that they were going home and couldn't set one foot outside their house unless Mark had given them the go-ahead. There would be lawyers, NDAs, and prenups now, and God help her, that was only the start.

She took two steps and stopped dead in her tracks.

London still sat facing forward on the couch, her back pressed against the pillows, and Maya stood between her legs and leaned her upper body forward. Her back arched, and her ass shot up in the air. She gyrated her hips, slowly, sexily swaying to music only she could hear.

Ellis froze, dumbstruck, unable to move. How had this happened? She had only left for a few minutes.

Hiking her skirt up to reveal silk panties, Maya climbed on the couch, knees on either side of London, to straddle her. She gripped her shoulders for balance and slid her body back and forth right above London's crotch. On one downward thrust, Maya brushed her breasts against London, who raised her own hips in response. And then, seizing the opportunity, Maya made real contact, grinding into London's soft center. London threw her head back and moaned.

Holy. Fucking. Shit. The guests were gone. However, servers still crisscrossed the outdoor kitchen, tidying up. Were they fucking idiots? Ellis jumped across the patio in huge leaps.

"Hey! What the hell are you doing?"

It hadn't come from her. She swiveled to the opposite corner of the yard.

Not twenty yards away, Rory ripped a phone out of a server's hand. She must have had it focused on the lap dance and was in the absolute perfect position to capture everything. Both London and Maya would've been in full profile, and every NC-17 rated action would've been captured.

"You have no right." The server lunged for the phone "Give it back."

"Fat chance." Rory went onto her toes and held it out of reach as if the server was a child.

"Jesus Christ." Ellis rushed over, fingers outstretched for the phone.

Rory handed it over and stood over her shoulder, close enough that she was touching. Ellis registered her nearness, but her attention was on the screen in her hand. Running on adrenaline, she hit the red square to stop recording, punched the video, and then the trashcan icon.

This video will be deleted from iCloud on all your devices.

Exhaling deeply, she hit the red *delete video*, and disaster was adverted.

"You can't do that," the server cried.

"Too late." Ellis fixed her with a fierce stare. "By the way, California is a two-party consent state."

The server's forehead furrowed with confusion, and she glanced over at Maya and London. Ellis followed her gaze. They had stopped their fun, and Maya, eyes bright, was watching the encounter with interest.

"I wasn't trespassing." The server jerked her head back and forth. "I was invited onto the property."

"California Civil Code 1708.8 says that you can't take photos or make audio recordings of people participating in personal activities."

"They were out in the open. There was no expectation of privacy." Her tone was desperate.

Ellis swallowed hard. This woman had a clear knowledge of California recording laws? Had she come hoping that she might get lucky and record something she could sell? It didn't matter. London couldn't afford whatever this woman had up her sleeve. If this had gone up on social media, the wedding proposal would look tawdry and cheap. Prodigy wouldn't like it, and Mark couldn't sell the true love angle. Time to nip it in the bud.

"We're not unreasonable," Ellis said. "How much is it going to take to make what you saw tonight disappear?" Shit, now she sounded like a typical Hollywood asshole. That was on her. She needed to talk to London about not putting her in this situation again.

A greedy glint popped into the server's pupils. "I'd be willing to discuss that."

London instantly got up. This no longer had anything to do with her. She grabbed Maya's hand and led her up the stairs, taking two at a time, presumably to finish what the lap dance had started.

As soon as they were out of sight, Ellis jumped into warrior mode, and an NDA was secured. Yolie drafted the check, and she signed it. Despite the late hour, the server left with a bounce in her step.

"You going to talk to London now?" Yolie asked when they were alone. "Forget the other stuff. This can't keep happening."

"I know. Can you set up a late lunch at Cat's Corner tomorrow? I'll come back to Malibu." She was already dreading the drive. "And make sure she knows that Maya needs to be there too."

"Will do." Yolie took in a deep breath. "I didn't overstep just now, did I? I mean, last time—"

"No. I needed the push."

"Here's another one, then." Yolie palmed the small of her back and gave her a gentle nudge. "You should thank her." And when Ellis didn't budge, "Okay. I'm going home now if you don't need anything more."

"Good night, Yolie. Thank you"

"Not me. Her." She tilted her head to the far side of the yard on her way out.

Out of earshot, Rory packed up, slipping serving plates into padded slots of a large dish box. Just looking at her simple movements, Ellis felt calmer. Her repetitive motions washed away the frenetic energy of the party and the troublesome greed of the server. Her chest loosened until she remembered she had been rude to her before with Scarlett. And even worse, she didn't quite know why. If tonight proved anything, London and Maya were going to throw curveballs whenever they could, and Rory's keen eyes and quick thinking had rescued them twice now. Maybe it was better to have her around.

Despite the chill of the winter evening, warmth washed over her.

Ellis stepped toward her with a new purpose until Rory faced her with a guarded look and a hand on her hip.

Shit. Ellis stopped dead in her tracks. A thank-you was nothing without an apology first.

"Look, I'm...I'm sorry about earlier." Ellis stumbled for the right words. "Scarlett meant well, but she doesn't really know what I do. I find jobs for my clients. And your pies already did that work for you. For everyone besides London, the rest is taken care of by managers. You don't need me."

"Okay." Rory went back to packing. "I get it."

And, suddenly, Ellis was the one who was hurt. If she was being honest, she wanted Rory to need her on some level. "I can absolutely connect you with our entertainment lawyer who can draw up a contract, and I will look over it afterward." When Rory said nothing, she added, "If you want me to."

"I wouldn't want to be any trouble." Rory cocked her head to the chair and the scene of the infamous lap dance. "It seems like you have plenty of that without me."

"That's where you're wrong. Helping you would be my pleasure, not my trouble. I could do it, let's say, as a friend, and then there wouldn't be any expectations between us." As soon as she said it, she realized that she hoped there would be a few expectations.

Rory bit her lip as she clearly chewed several answers in her head and finally nodded. "Okay, thanks. It wouldn't be for more than the one show. I made a promise to my sister, but I'm not interested in being on-camera talent."

"Then it will be easy to help you." Heat tingled along Ellis's spine.

Had they turned a corner?

Were they friends now?

Was that all she wanted?

Yolie's phantom hand was at her back again, pushing her forward. "And speaking of helping, thank you so much for what you did for London earlier."

Rory shrugged. "I happened to be there. Right place, right time." Of course she would downplay it. That was Rory to the core.

"Yeah, but you did something about it. You didn't stand there and watch it play out. Most people would've."

"I don't like to see people taking advantage of situations when they shouldn't. Besides, that server was kind of a bitch when she first came down."

She took a step closer to Rory. Close enough to see the starlight reflected in Rory's irises. "Whatever the reason, I can't tell you how grateful we are."

Rory didn't back away. "Helping you was my pleasure," she said, the earlier gruffness fading from her voice.

Ellis smiled inwardly at the gift of her own words returned to her. They absolutely had turned a corner, but to where? What if she was wrapped up in the victory of the evening and the soft moonlight around them, and this was nothing more than her being a good Samaritan? She wished she could reach inside Rory's mind to hear what she was thinking.

Rory cleared her throat, stepped away, and all possibilities hovering at the edges of their conversation evaporated. She grabbed a second soft box and unzipped it. Ellis, unable to let the moment go, grabbed a plate and followed her. She handed it to Rory, only to immediately pull it back. A golden meadow, so lifelike it almost moved in the night breeze, rose against a dark background. She traced the grass with a finger. "This is gorgeous."

"Thank you." Rory returned to her side. "My mom made it."

"That's right, she's a potter. Are you all crazy talented? I've never seen anything this delicate."

"She made it for my sister, whose name is Meadow, and she went all out." She pointed to a flower at the edge of the plate. "This she did with a Mason stain before she fired, and this golden pop"—she slid her finger over to where Ellis's still lingered—"she did with an overglaze afterward."

Their fingers touched. A surprising jolt of pleasure flared below Ellis's belly, and she turned to Rory, whose face was now inches away. Warm brown eyes met her gaze, and something Ellis couldn't identify flickered within. Not quite a question. Maybe the beginning of one? They stared at each other in silence for a long moment.

Rory broke contact to glance at Ellis's mouth and lingered there.

Ellis's lips tingled. She felt the look as if it was physical, and her breath hitched, ragged and frayed with sudden emotion. All she wanted to do was raise her head, crush Rory's lips with her own. Kiss and be kissed.

Did Rory want that? Indecision tugged at her. And the understanding of how much courage it took to kiss someone for the first time stopped her dead in her tracks.

Rory's tongue darted along her bottom lip, and she swallowed hard. Her body swayed first toward Ellis and then, as if thinking better of it, spun back to the plates and the box and the easier decision of cleaning up.

If Ellis didn't act now, she might never get another chance. Almost of its own accord, her hand jerked up and caught Rory's arm. She spun Rory back to her, holding her in place. Her heart skipped several beats, and she leaped off the cliff. "May I...Do you...Can we..." Her words trailed off as she lost her nerve.

A soft smile full of understanding curled at the edges of Rory's mouth. "Yes," she said and leaned in.

The kiss was gentle at first, closed mouth and chaste, as if they were both testing the waters. Rory's lips, though, were surprisingly soft and full and completely relaxed as she pressed them against Ellis's. She expected her whole body to burst into passion or lust. Instead, a stillness radiated through her and narrowed her world to only Rory's hand sliding up her back and the heat of her own fingers still clasped tightly around Rory's arm and the caressing touch of Rory's lips on hers.

Surprising.

Delicious.

Intoxicating.

As if the kiss was the first bite of a delicious dessert, Ellis greedily wanted more. She wrapped her free arm around Rory's waist and pulled her closer. Rory had several inches on her; still, somehow, they fit together. Ellis's hips pushed into the lean muscle of Rory's thigh, and their bodies clicked. With Rory's chest resting lightly on hers, they touched from head to toe. It gave the kiss gravity and a true center, pulling them even closer.

Their mouths opened in unison, and the tips of their tongues met and danced together. Rory tasted of apple pie and a sweetness that was just her. The kiss deepened, and Ellis's heart swelled in her chest.

And then, a noise that Ellis had never heard before, a mixture of a low sigh and a high sob, swelled between them. She broke contact and stepped back quickly. Her eyes widened with shock and surprise. "Did that come from me?"

"I think so." Rory laughed and reached to pull her back.

Ellis stood her ground as warmth flooded her cheeks. "Oh my God. That's so embarrassing."

"No, it was adorable."

"Are you kidding?" Ellis took a step away and tugged at her turtleneck. "It sounded like an animal dying."

"No, it didn't. It sounded like someone giving into their feelings in the most wonderful way." Her voice was soft as she leaned in. "To really know, though, maybe we should try again?" And when Ellis said nothing, she added, "I enjoyed that."

Ellis had too, a lot, until she had morphed into some unknown marine species bellowing out a mating call. As good as she was in her professional life, she was plain crap in her dating life. Why even try? Besides, the frenetic energy always churning around her had swirled up again like a tornado, separating them. She glanced at her feet, unable to meet Rory's hopeful gaze. "It's late. We should be getting home."

"Um…okay." Rory sighed deeply.

Ellis responded with a ragged breath of her own. This was fucked-up. Was she going to let a silly embarrassment stop her from grabbing something she wanted? Or was it more than that? She needed to figure out a lot of stuff and not send a million mixed signals.

Rory moved back to her dish box and shoved in the platter that had brought them together. Ellis pursed her lips. They'd had a first kiss that should have led to something more, much more, and instead, they were yards apart, both upset and disappointed. Fuck, here she was again. Disappointment all around.

Ellis watched and did nothing. If this was a movie, the scene would hard cut to a bedroom upstairs or even a chaise lounge by the pool, depending on the rating, and their earlier passion would consume them. There would be no time to think about human whale sounds or how late it was. None of that would matter. If this was a movie, Rory would not be holding up a white plastic trash bag and shaking it at her.

"Do you want me to take this trash home, or is there somewhere I can dump it here?" Her face was blank. No trace of any emotion. Was she as good an actor as London, or had the kiss meant nothing to her?

Ellis pointed to the front of the house. "Garbage cans are around the side. Near the garage in a white shed."

"Thanks," Rory said, hitching the bag up over her shoulder and heading off.

Ellis smoothed back her hair where the kiss had tousled it and glanced around. The backyard was deserted. The moon had dropped beneath the horizon, and the firepits were dark.

The party was most definitely over.

CHAPTER TEN

The next morning, Rory jolted awake to the shrill ringing of her phone. Again? She untangled herself from the blanket and swiped her cell off the nightstand.

Goddammit, Maya. Too early.

The sun's rays cut brightly through the open window, and people chatted loudly in the alley below. It was only early for her. She had pulled into the parking garage around four a.m. after the long drive home, after cleaning up, after that humiliating rejection from Ellis.

Wait a sec. Maya had no reason to call her now. She flipped open her phone, and a frown creased her brow. Not Maya. And not Ellis. It was Meadow. "I was sleeping."

"It's after eleven."

"I got in very late last night."

"That's what I wanted to talk to you about. How was the party?"

"God, Meadow. It was incredible. They covered the pool with a dance floor and firepits, and I met all sorts of people—"

"The pies! Did people like them?"

"Yeah, they did. The apple pie was a big hit," Rory said offhandedly, knowing that she was pushing her sister's buttons.

"Rory!"

She would put Meadow out of her misery. "They loved the tartlets, and your cheese was the hit of the party."

Meadow squeaked with happiness.

"Don't overreact to this. You know who especially loved your cheese?"

"Who?"

"Scarlett Dorien."

"Who does *Small Bites with Scarlett*? The number one show on the Food and Flavor Network?"

"The one and only." Rory relaxed against her pillows. This was fun. She was beginning to see the appeal of Ellis's job. "And." She paused for the drama. "This is what I don't want you to overreact to. She's thinking about doing a show on the tarts. Actually, on both the pies and the cheese. Coming out to Topanga to highlight you and the farm."

"Holy shit." Meadow drew the words out into one long breath. "Seriously?"

"It could be something you say at a party to make conversation. We'll see if it comes to anything."

"It will. It has to."

"If it does, London's agent...my friend...said she would help us with lawyers and stuff." Rory shifted against the pillows. Would she still? She had seen a lot of different Ellises last night. Which one would wake up today?

"Oh my God," Meadow shrieked. "This could push me to the next level. The next five levels." She, much like their mom, lived only in the extremes.

"Even if nothing comes of it, you should be happy that everyone loved the cheese."

A soft plopping noise came across the line as Meadow must have dropped into a chair. "Tell me everything. Nothing's too small. If it's about my cheese." She giggled with pure delight.

Laughing with her, Rory pulled the covers up, snuggled into the bed, and drew out every detail she could remember. How Scarlett had chewed thoughtfully and had immediately asked where the goat cheese had come from. How the pies had sat front and center on the heart decorated table as if on an altar. How the women had pushed each other out of the way for a second and third helping.

"And when they came back," Rory continued, "the table seemed to magically refill itself. Just as people reached out, another appeared beneath their fingers."

"Now you're making things up." Meadow sighed happily.

Rory rewound the image backward in her mind. "No. I'm not." Strangely her mom's ceramic, two-tiered pie pedestal had always seemed to be full.

She caught her breath in a startled gasp. It wasn't magic; it was that catering woman. The angry one who'd come down early. The full memory flooded her mind. That woman had been hanging around the table all evening. Starting with tidying up an already neat table, making sure the pie stands were never bare, and then cleaning up that one table when the party was over, even though she was with the catering company that did not include Rory. Now that she focused on the memory, she always seemed to be looking at the firepit and whoever was lounging around it. Standing by the goat cheese tarts gave her a perfect view to—

"Fuck me," she said, barely a whisper.

"What?"

"Meadow, I got to go."

"What's wrong?"

"I'm not sure. I'll call you back. Oh, and tell Mom that everyone loved her plates too."

Rory hung up before Meadow could protest. Had that woman been casing the joint? Figuring out the perfect angle to shoot, say, a lap dance?

Rory bolted out of bed and started pacing her bedroom. That was a big accusation. Huge, in fact. Was she remembering the authentic moment, or had she conjured a more exciting drama in her mind? She had thought it strange that the woman had the presence to pull out her phone and record the lap dance. While lots of people were opportunists, her actions had been very calculated. Too calculated?

Still clutching her phone, she swiped it open only for her finger to freeze in midair. What was she going to say to Ellis? She had no proof of her suspicions, and after the way the kiss had ended last night, would she seem desperate? Or even worse, someone who saw conspiracies in every corner? This would be the second piece of bad news she had brought to Ellis about someone.

Shit. No matter how she came off, she had to call. Her finger dropped to her phone. The kiss had most likely been a one-off anyway.

When the call went straight to voice mail at the ETA office, her heart beat in double time. Why hadn't she prepared a message? She swallowed hard at the beep.

"Um, hi. It's me. Rory. Rory Hatten." Fuck, a horrible way to start. "I don't want to bother you, but I was telling my sister about last night, and it occurred to me that the woman from the catering company, the one who filmed the lap dance, might have been looking for it before it happened. Not sure what that means. Or if I saw it right." She paused and searched for a way to end. "Call me back if you want to unpack it more." She gave her number.

Hanging up, Rory looked at her phone as if it was the offending party. That was terrible. But there was nothing she could do about it now. Maybe Ellis would hear the urgency in her words and not the stumbling way she had said it.

She headed into the kitchen, pulled the coffee supplies from the cupboard, and tried to push Ellis from her thoughts. It didn't work. As the beans whirled in the grinder, all she saw was Ellis's face moving closer for the kiss. That vulnerable look in her eyes and that unearthly moan, which even now set her insides shivering.

Fuck this. She grabbed her favorite travel mug out of the dish rack. Usually, making coffee was almost a spiritual experience full of timing, patience, and reward. Today, dammit, Ellis had her off her game. She splashed too much water into the pourover dripper and rushed the "bloom" of the grounds. Her first sip was both thin and bitter. She palmed the travel mug anyway and within minutes, had thrown on sweats and was locking the front door of her apartment behind her.

Walking was second fiddle to swimming when it came to clearing her mind, but she needed help now. She marched out of her complex and into the eclectic urban village that was North Hollywood. Focusing only on her sneakers hitting the pavement, she strode past the huge, neon clown on the corner that stood guard over the liquor store and the seven-hundred and fifty varieties of beer. She passed mini-malls with prepaid cleaners and doughnut shops and the commuter parking lot for the local Metro station. She stopped, as she always did, to marvel at the apartment building painted by French artist Thierry Noir. His giant, colorful heads, made famous by the Berlin Wall, covered the complex in sanctioned street art.

The winter sun warmed the streets, and people milled about, enjoying the weekend afternoon. Laughter and chatter in various languages, accented and not, drifted around her, and for the first time since Ellis had told her she would rather go home than kiss her again, her chest loosened. The walk in her neighborhood had done the trick. She opened her travel mug and poured the rest of her weak coffee into the gutter.

When she hit Magnolia Boulevard, she headed left into the heart of the NoHo art district. Immediately, the vibe changed. Cafés and themed restaurants sat next to vintage shops and theaters advertising homegrown plays and music. She strolled now, peering at the classic purses in one store window and the life-size cow statue in another. Happy cheering poured out of the sports bar next door, and she stopped to watch the television replay of an NBA star slamming the ball into the net.

In her back pocket, her phone pinged. Her chest tightening, she slid it out, swiveled away from the sun only to see Meadow's face and the beginning of a message on the lock screen. Not Ellis. Was she happy or upset?

Hey Sis! The message read. *Give me your friend's number? I want to set a date for Small Bites with Scarlett ASAP. Strike while the iron is hot. I want...*

Jesus. Meadow never knew when to quit. *You don't jump in to manage something this big before you're asked. Shit, is this how I sounded in my voice mail earlier? No wonder she's not calling me back.*

She flipped the cover over her cell with a snap and jammed the phone back into her pocket. Meadow was unbelievable. She was pushy. She bent the world to her wishes. She was…no, it couldn't be…right? Maybe Rory shouldn't wait for Ellis to get back to her. Maybe she should take the bull by the horns and work out what had happened last night on her own.

She yanked her phone out again and tapped on the screen. Delicious Dinner's website popped to life. The address in bright green was only five blocks away from where she stood. Wasn't this the place Ellis had been meeting with that first day when she had just shown up at Rory's apartment?

Delicious Dinner: Catering and Classes was a brick and mirrored glass storefront in a small industrial park. Rory shielded her eyes with a hand and peered inside. Two full kitchens sat inside a large warehouse-type room, and on a Sunday, couples stood around a marble island pulling pasta through big silver machines. A cooking class was in full swing.

"*Ciao*, are you here for the class?" the instructor called as soon as Rory opened the door. "I can get you some chianti and an apron, and you can jump right in."

"Actually, I was hoping that Corrine was here?" It was a big chance she would be.

The instructor glanced hesitantly to the back and a closed office door. "She is. Today's her day off, though."

"It's all right." Rory nodded and tried not to let the relief show. "We met last night at the London Green event. She said to stop by."

"Oh, okay." She sounded both impressed and unconvinced at the same time but pointed at the door she had been eyeing.

"Come in," a muffled voice said when Rory knocked.

She opened the door to the woman from last night sitting behind a mountain of paperwork on her desk. "Hi," Rory said with forced cheer as she entered the small office. "I'm Rory Hatten. I made the pies for the London Green party last night, and I was wondering if you needed a pastry chef." She bit her bottom lip. "I can do more than pies. I have experience with cake and chocolate showpieces." She had practiced on the way over, down to the nervous pause.

"You made the pies? Then you came from ETA, didn't you?" ETA sounded like a swear word in her mouth.

Rory nodded. "I'm a friend of a friend, and they were doing me a favor." Rory took in the sneer on Corrine's lips and pushed the boat out even farther. "Last night was kind of a shit show, wasn't it, and I like things to be more professional. I mean, that whole thing with the server with the phone who stayed afterward. They said that was you. That you had somehow organized it."

"That's fucking total bullshit." Corrine clenched her fists in anger. "I only found out about it this morning. From the very person who demanded we hire her."

"Excuse me?"

"Yeah, Julie or Yolie or whatever her name is. She's left a dozen messages. Told me what happened. And then demanded that I take responsibility. I don't know what the fuck she's talking about. She was the one who called me last week and demanded I hire her for the party."

Rory furrowed her brow. "Let me get this straight. Yolie, personally, told you to hire that specific woman?"

"She talked to one of the assistants. We accommodated her, and now she's all up in my business this morning when things didn't go right? Fuck that and fuck her. I'm letting her calls go to voice mail." Corrine threw her pen onto the desk. It hit the papers with a slap.

"I can see I came at a bad time." Rory floundered for a way out. All she could think of was to pull her business card and drop it on the desk. "I'm going to leave this for now. If you think you can use me for another event, give me a call. If not, that's okay." She backed out of the office clutching her newfound knowledge like a winning lottery ticket. Hopefully, Corrine was too angry to put two and two together. Before she cleared the parking lot, however, her phone was pinging.

Son of a bitch. The business card had been the perfect exit ticket, but she had left her contact information. Stupid.

Rory darted around the corner in case Corrine thought about it more and came after her instead. Pursing her lips, she tapped the text that was identified only by a number, steadying herself for whatever Corrine was going to throw at her.

I would very much like to unpack your thoughts. Maybe over dinner?

Three gray dots rolled and then, *This is Ellis*, popped on the screen.

Rory's mouth went dry, and she sagged against the brick wall at her back. The surprise of how much she wanted to see Ellis hit her. Mostly because she wanted to fall into her exciting energy, but dammit, she also wanted to ask what the fuck had happened last night.

When and where? she typed.

The answer was almost instantaneous. *Tonight? You like burritos?*

❖

Burrito Bonanza was a surprising Los Angeles oddity: truly amazing Mexican food in the middle of a gas station. People ordered at the tiny grill at the far side of the on-site convenience store and took the food to picnic tables out back.

Standing by a sunglasses rack near the grill, Ellis pushed one arm behind her back and stretched her neck in the opposite direction. She was exhausted, and the usual muscles on her right side tightened from her neck to her hip. She had gotten very little sleep the night before, the lunch meeting with London and Maya had been a disaster, and she had spent way too much time hunched in her car. Now, she stood under bright florescent lights for possibly the worst encounter of the day.

She needed to know what Rory had seen. A phone call or a text would have been easier. Especially since the way she had ended things last night would hang over their meeting like storm clouds. This wasn't a date. This was a mistake.

A digital bell rang out, and Rory stepped through the door. Starting with the opposite end, she scanned the store, giving Ellis plenty of time to study her. Skinny jeans hugged her long legs, and a man's V-neck sweater fell from her broad shoulders. She had taken time with her appearance tonight. Her brown hair popped against the green of the sweater and swept back from her face in thick, textured layers.

She wasn't classically pretty by Hollywood standards, too long and lean, with too little cleavage. Walking in with her wide, confident steps and her chin held high, she was better than pretty. She was comfortable both in her body and in the space around her, and that was very sexy. Ellis took a quick breath with the realization. Goddammit, she wanted to trust this woman. And now she worried that she had already fucked everything up.

Rory waved as soon as she saw her and headed right over. Happily, she stopped a couple feet away and took away the awkwardness of how they were going to greet, either by a handshake or a kiss. "What is this place?" Rory considered the grill behind a solid sheet of Plexiglass.

"Only the best burrito you'll ever have."

"Wow. I'm surprised."

"Why? Because you didn't think gas stations could have fine dining?"

She shook her head

"Oh, you expected me to choose some overly cute place that sitcom characters go to at the end of an episode?" *Stop talking. You're nervous.*

Thankfully, Rory chuckled. She had taken it as a joke. "No, it's not the place. I love Mexican food, and this smells amazing. It's the fact you asked at all." She met Ellis's gaze in a bit of a challenge. "To be honest, there were a lot of mixed signals last night."

Ellis shifted her weight and fought hard to keep her eyes fixed on Rory's. "I know."

Rory nodded. "Cut a girl a break. What's my takeaway from last night?"

Ellis swallowed hard. "We're…we're doing this now?"

"If you don't mind. I know we're here to talk about the party. But I need to understand the way it ended first. So I know where I stand." Her breath hitched slightly. "Is that okay?"

Ellis chewed her lip and finally nodded. She had wanted to talk about it too. Maybe it was better to rip the Band-Aid off quickly. "Okay."

"Good. I don't like to play games. Fact is, I'm terrible at them. They say games are how all relationships start. People are too afraid of rejection. I get it, I don't want to be hurt, either, but games don't work for me. I'm going to come right out and say it. I enjoyed our kiss last night."

Ellis's heart skipped a beat. Jumping in with her feelings was way out of her comfort zone. She opened her mouth. Nothing came out.

"Did you?" Rory asked.

She was making this easy for her. Ellis could shake her head, and this would be over. She would return to the part she was good at, finding out what Rory had seen at the party and building London's star. But, no, she wanted to audition for another role: WOMAN WITH FEELINGS.

"I did too," she said so softly, she wasn't entirely sure she had said it out loud.

"What happened?"

Heat flushed her face. "I got embarrassed. I made that noise, and something almost magical became very real."

"And that's a bad thing? Being real?"

"I don't know. It kind of felt like it messed things up. Like at your place when I tripped." She cupped her cheek with her hand. Shit, it was five-alarm hot.

Rory's eyes sparkled and softened at the edges. She reached up to grab Ellis's hand and took it off her cheek. "Not for me. When things get messy, I think that's how you know you're doing it right." She gave her hand a gentle squeeze.

Once again, Ellis's focus narrowed to Rory's touch, her fingers firmly cupping her hand. With the awareness, calmness flowed through her body, pooling in her feet and connecting her to the ground and space around her. She laughed with delight. She had no idea how Rory did it. Unlike last night, she wasn't going to question it.

"Well, if you like messy"—she returned the squeeze and luxuriated in the feeling—"then you're going to love these burritos."

As she studied the menu Rory nodded repeatedly as if she and it were having a conversation. She selected chicken al pastor and chose chili lime corn, cilantro, and pico de gallo from the "customize your meal" board. The burritos, the size of overinflated footballs, came wrapped in tinfoil and crammed into red plastic baskets. They carried them, a mountain of chips, and two drinks—a Diet Coke for Ellis and an horchata for Rory—out back. Several patio heaters glowed red against the night sky and gave the enclosure a comforting vibe.

They made small talk as they ate, mostly about how truly delicious the burritos were. How the chicken was both seared on the outside and juicy on the inside. How the tomatillo salsa had both tang and heat. And how the layers of beans, rice, and meat were a lesson in flavor explosion.

Rory wrapped almost half of her burrito up in the extra foil that was thoughtfully tucked under the basket and said, "I'm stuffed, and I'm going to have lunch for days."

"I know. And it only gets better tomorrow."

"I'm going to come back until I try the entire menu. I don't know if I love you or hate you for introducing me to this place."

"Love me, I hope," Ellis said without thinking and then tried to bite the statement back. Too late, the words were out there, circling the table like vultures, threatening to dive between them and attack. "I didn't mean that," she blurted before Rory could respond. "I meant—"

Rory laughed gently. "I know what you meant. And to be clear, I'm on the same page." She slid her basket to the side of the table. "Here it is. I was talking to my sister this morning, and it occurred to me that the serving person, the one who filmed London and Maya, was lurking around the space all night."

Quick on the uptake, Ellis said, "Like she was scoping it out."

Rory nodded. "Exactly."

"You're saying that she knew the lap dance was coming?"

"What do you think? I know how crazy that sounds. She was there the entire night, as if she was staking out her territory. I was just so thankful to have help that I didn't give it much thought until this morning. And I should tell you something else." Rory licked her lips and paused. "Something that you may not like. I went out for a walk after I texted you, and I kind of went by the catering place. To see if I could get any more information. It's close to my apartment, as it turns out."

"You did?"

Rory pushed her hands on the table as if to brace herself. "I know, I had no right, but I couldn't let it lie."

Ellis reached over to touch a finger on one hand. "I actually like that you took the initiative." And she did. It was what she would have done herself if she hadn't been troubleshooting with London and Maya. "What'd you find out?" When she saw Rory's frown, she added, "Bad news?"

"I don't know. You tell me. They said that Yolie had called the office last week and told them to hire that particular server."

"Yolie?" Ellis couldn't believe her ears.

"That's what she said. Yolie had left a message with an assistant."

"Impossible. There's no way Yolie would ask them to hire her." She wasn't going to go there even in her head.

"You're sure Yolie isn't…"

"What? Involved?"

Rory shrugged, clearly not able to put words to the accusation. Her meaning was clear, though.

Ellis shook her head vehemently. "I'm sure." And she was. There was no fucking way that Yolie had set it up. If there was anyone's integrity she was one hundred percent certain of, it was Yolie's.

"Good, I like Yolie," Rory said with relief. "But someone did. And I don't think it was the catering company. She was mad as a hive of hornets about last night."

"And it would kill their business if they did."

"Then, who?" Rory wondered out loud.

Their gazes locked, and at the exact same time, they said. "Maya."

"Son of a gun." Ellis curled her fist against the table.

Rory mulled it over. "She was the one who started the lap dance. I saw it. She obviously knew it was coming."

"And you think the server knew it too? Had her phone out and ready before it started?"

"That makes sense if she was invited to the party through Maya for that reason."

"She did know an awful lot about California recording laws." Ellis nodded. Pieces of the puzzle slid together in her head. "Maya also knew who we were using for the catering. She was at the office several times last week. She could have easily called them from there and set it up. They would have seen ETA on the caller ID. Clever."

"But why?" Rory asked the only question Ellis couldn't figure out.

"I don't know. Money is the obvious answer. We had to pay…" She hesitated. Rule number one: never air a client's dirty laundry in public. Rory wasn't public anymore…but she also wasn't part of ETA.

Ellis took a deep breath and leaped. "We had to pay high five figures to make it go away. And when I told London that this afternoon at lunch, she laughed and said that the lap dance had been worth every penny."

"What did Maya say?"

Ellis took a pull from her Diet Coke and rattled the ice in her cup. "Not much. Come to think of it, she was quiet for once."

"Quiet like, I'm super tired after the party, or quiet like, my crazy plan worked, and I just made a shitload of money?"

Ellis raised her hands to the sky. "I've no idea. The thing I'm wondering about now is how'd she know you'd be there to see her filming it? How did she know her plan would work?"

"That's the million dollar question, isn't it, or at least one worth another five figures."

Ellis smiled thinly at the joke. "God, I hope not. The goose has to lay the golden eggs before she can spend them."

❖

Her back against the driver's door, Rory leaned against Ellis's BMW, taking in the cars and people milling around. She could imagine an infinite number of more romantic places for a good night kiss than a gas station parking lot. However, she wasn't going to let the opportunity pass her by.

"I had fun again tonight." And she had. The conversation had been surprisingly easy once they'd shelved Maya and her motives.

"Again?" Ellis asked.

"I'm sort of counting this as our third date. The bowling alley, the party, and here."

"We need a better quality of dates." Ellis shifted to her side. "One where we're not piggybacking on someone else's evening or obsessing over other women."

"Agreed." Rory turned as well. The car's door was cold against her side, but the heat between them kept her warm. They were less than two feet away. Just a step would close the distance. "We'll do it again?" She scraped a hand through her hair as she waited for the answer.

"I'd like that," Ellis said softly.

Rory didn't know what else she was waiting for. She inched in until their lips were only inches apart. "And this? Would you like this too?"

"Yes." The answer was more of a shaky exhale.

Rory felt the pull and gave in. Ellis met her halfway with lips that were soft and insistent, as if she was trying to right the wrong from the night before. Hoping to show that there was nothing to make up for, Rory slid her hands down Ellis's arms. Ellis's whole body softened, and the kiss deepened. Rory felt the connection to her toes. She gave her forearms a squeeze and pulled away. They were in public, after all.

The kiss in Malibu had been a question. Did they like each other? Would a physical touch be exciting? This kiss was a promise. Yes, they definitely liked each other. And, *yes*, there were sparks. Her toes still tingling in her boots settled that debate.

Rory smiled. "I'll see you soon?"

All Ellis could seemingly do was nod.

"Good night." Rory kissed her cheek and lingered against her warm skin.

"Night," Ellis said.

Rory had to tear herself away, and the cool winter night swirled around her. "Let me know what you find out about Maya," she said taking one more look over her shoulder as she walked to her car.

CHAPTER ELEVEN

Ellis practically floated into the office the next morning while carrying a take-out container from Burrito Bonanza. She had woken up without a headache and with a surplus of energy.

Yolie already sat at her desk, multitasking with her computer screen open and several teleplays and headshots on her desk. Science needed to study Yolie when they claimed that no one could juggle several tasks at once. She smiled. "Hey. Happy Monday. You want the good news or the bad news?"

"Why can't it just be a wonderful Monday morning, where all news is good?" She placed the white take-out box on the desk. "I'll start. I was at your favorite burrito restaurant last night, and I got you a carne asada."

"Ooh, thank you." Yolie squcaled in delight. "I love that place."

"You're welcome. Now, your turn. Good news, please."

"I talked to Portia, and she said that Mark is thrilled with London's marriage proposal. He's already hired some influencer to direct three videos for social media. Oh, by the way, he's going to need three more of those hand pies that Rory made. The true love ones. Someone put them up on Instagram. and they're trending. London's already called. They're all in. Do you want to make an appearance?"

"Where?"

"That's part of the bad news. Back in Malibu."

"I should drop by," she said, already dreading the twenty-six-mile drive in traffic.

Yolie glanced at a list on her desk. "Don't stress out. Marta from *Happy at Home* left a message and wants to talk about both Sharon and Brenda for reoccurring roles on the show."

"Oh, that *is* good news."

"And Gina's coming in at one for an interview. She's super excited."

"We'd be lucky to have her." Ellis tapped her desk. "Hey, why don't you take her out to lunch and explain what the job is, tell her the things you wished you had known about working here, good and bad, and see what you think? If you like her, I can talk money with her later today."

Yolie sat up straighter in her chair. "My first lunch meeting?"

"But not your last." She waited until Yolie's smile had faded. "What's the bad news?"

Yolie sighed. "I've gotten nowhere with Delicious Dinner. I think I might have to drive out there to find out what we need to know about the server."

"Hah. I'm way ahead of you on that. And it's not exactly bad news. It's more a mystery. You want coffee?" She crossed to the office espresso machine, telling Yolie what Rory had uncovered as she brewed two cups.

Afterward, Yolie accepted the coffee and deep in thought, laced her hands around the mug. "And you really think it's Maya?"

"I do. We need to figure out what's up her sleeve before she makes her next move."

"We will," Yolie said with such certainty that it washed over Ellis. They would figure this out. Maya was tricky and maybe even clever, but she was young and very new to a world that Ellis had navigated for a long time. With Yolie in Ellis's corner, there was no way Maya would get the better of ETA.

"You want me to call Rory about the pies? Or do you want to do it?"

Ellis tried to shrug as if she didn't care. "I can do it. You have a lot on your plate."

Yolie gave her a pointed look. "Is there something else you want to tell me?"

Damn. Yolie knew her too well. "I don't know yet," she said, coming clean.

"Okay. I'll totally accept that." She grabbed the burrito and took it to the fridge in the outer office. She called from the other room, "Just to let you know, I really like Rory."

"Me too," Ellis answered, thankful Yolie couldn't see her blush.

Putting distance between her embarrassment and reaching out to Rory, she instead called a big-time casting director who had a leading role on a new TV show and wanted London. Not today's London, she was quick to clarify. London ten years ago. And not gay. Ellis ended the call with a sigh and moved on to the PR firm to get the lowdown on the shoot the next day. Finally, she spoke to an actor who'd been passed over for a hot new historical drama. Ellis broke the news gently, and by the end of the call, had suggested two more auditions that she would be great for. The bad news in Hollywood always outweighed the good by a hundred to one, and any agent worth their salt had to navigate it carefully with actors.

Ellis was in full work mode when she finally dialed Rory's number.

"Hey." Rory picked up on the second ring. "Good morning. I didn't think I'd hear from you so soon."

"Unfortunately, this is work and not pleasure."

"Oh." She sounded disappointed, and maybe...a little irritated?

Ellis plowed ahead anyway. "Yeah, sorry. London and Maya are shooting promotional videos about their new relationship status, and the PR firm is requesting three true love pies. Exactly like the ones you made at the party. Can we count on you for that?"

Shit. I'm sounding like an asshole, again. She didn't know how to do this. Be professional with Rory when all she wanted to do was talk about how good it felt to be in her arms last night and when they would see each other again.

"Ah...yeah, I can do that. I have no other commitments today." Rory mimicked the businesslike tone.

"I'm not asking a favor. We would pay you, of course."

Silence greeted her on the other end. She had fucking made it worse. "You don't have to," Rory said finally. "I got leftover ingredients, and no one's going to eat them, correct?"

"Yes."

"Then it's easy. We can count it as part of the original contract. Like I said, you overpaid me for the party anyway."

"This is a different deal. Gardner Public Relations is footing this bill...although, like everything else, it comes from London in the end."

Silence again. Ellis's shoulders tensed. They seemed to be taking one step forward and two steps back with every encounter. "You could..." Ellis began, "I mean, if you wanted to...drop them by the shoot tomorrow and stay and watch a little. It's at London's mother's house." Rory still said nothing. "Only if you wanted to."

"Would that be work or pleasure?" Rory asked after a long beat.

"Let's start with work and then maybe have a pleasurable lunch? There's a good Greek restaurant up the coast a little bit."

"I would like that," Rory said softly after a moment.

"Me too," Ellis said for the second time that morning.

❖

The next day around noon, Rory pulled through the mansion's open gate. The house and the lawn were pristine. No one would have guessed that two days before, there had been a raging party on the grounds. The production was out back. The pool deck was littered with camera rigs and dollies. It made *Guess Who's Coming to Dinner* look like a student film. She had stupidly assumed the shoot would be quick and bare-bones. But this was London. Apparently, nothing in her life was simple.

Maya, however, was the one in deep discussion with the director, who, by Rory's quick reckoning, was also a brand-new adult and far too taken with himself. He stood with a hand on his hip, listening intently to Maya but also sneaking looks at his reflection in one of the mirrored reflectors already set up.

Maya threaded her arm through his and spun him around the pool deck. "Hey," she said, her voice smooth as honey, "in your professional opinion, if you only cared about the light, where's the best place to shoot in the backyard."

"Over there." He pointed to two lounge chairs on the far side of the pool.

Rory also scanned the backyard and found Ellis off to one side, chatting with an older man in a business suit. She looked good. Really good. Her hair was in a high ponytail, and she wore an expensive T-shirt, maybe silk—Rory had no idea—untucked over dark slacks.

Ellis must have sensed her presence, since she waved, excused herself, and walked to Rory's side.

A good sign. Rory had spent most of the ride over wondering what her reception would be. Would it be the exciting energy from the gas station or the weird coldness of the phone call? She liked Ellis, more than anyone in ages, but being yanked around in a relationship wasn't going to work for her especially when, so far, ninety percent of her attention was on another woman. London was her job, but a person could take that commitment too far.

"Oh, I'm glad you're here," Ellis said when she was close enough to whisper. "Thanks for the interruption. If Mark mansplains one more time how to run my business, I might kill him."

Rory pinched her lips together. She had hoped *glad you're here* would end up somewhere else.

Ellis must have heard her thoughts because she quickly added. "I'm also happy to see you personally."

Rory reached out to squeeze her forearm. "It's okay. We're in work mode."

Ellis bowed her head. "I'll get better. I promise."

Rory gave her arm another squeeze and dropped her hand. "We'll get better. There are two of us in this." She purposefully left it vague. She didn't want to scare Ellis off with a label that she wasn't ready for.

"Are those the pies?" Ellis pointed to the box in Rory's other hand.

"Yes."

Ellis passed them over, and soon, the production was under way. First, they set up, lit, and shot dozens of *spontaneous* selfies of the happy couple, all PG and all promoting a wholesome love affair. Rory's pies were featured in several of them and even had their own close-ups. The team then rolled into a lip-dub of an electrified version of the old Bing Crosby song *True Love* for TikTok. London and Maya danced and sang to the beat and pulled off several magical costume changes with the help of trick photography and a bubbly costumer.

Finally, London shot intimate testimonials with the sparkling blue of the Pacific Ocean behind her. Once she had memorized her lines, she opened herself up to the camera and confessed how true love had changed her life. Rory glanced around after the director called cut. Three people were wiping their eyes, and even Ellis's face shone with respect. It totally didn't matter if London meant one word of it; everyone would believe her.

"I think we got everything we need here," the director said.

Maya dashed into the frame and planted a huge kiss on London's lips. "Oh," she cried, "that was wonderful." She paused until everyone's attention landed on her and said again, even more theatrically, "Absolutely wonderful."

"It's easy when your subject is a superstar." The director joined her center stage. "London, you're truly miraculous."

She took the compliment with a slight nod and met his gaze completely. He melted, like everyone at the Honey Pot had months ago. Rory realized inviting people into her world was her superpower whether in person or on screen. It didn't matter. Her looks went everywhere. She gave the gift to anyone who asked.

Rory shifted her gaze to Maya. Deep lines furrowed her brow, and she quickly stepped between the director and London. "Hey, babe. Why don't we drive to Cup or Cone for ice cream?"

"You want to drive all the way to the valley for ice cream?"

"No, silly, I want you to drive all the way to the valley…for me." She emphasized the "for me" so the meaning was clear to everyone.

London rolled her eyes but got up. "Fine, let's go. But I'm not driving. You can drive my car."

Ellis grabbed Rory by the elbow. "This is our time to scoot too."

Once again, Ellis had chosen a delightful place. Calypso's Garden was about a mile inland and nestled into a canyon. Brown and green hills that looked like the pictures Rory had seen of Greece rolled down to a rustic whitewashed building with bright blue trim. Ellis led them to a large patio to one side, an attractive space littered with bright blue tables, white awnings, and red bougainvillea climbing up the walls. Lemon and lamb, oregano, and garlic spiced the air, and Rory's mouth watered. She hadn't realized how hungry she was.

"This place feels like a magic hideaway." Rory pulled out a chair from one side of the table.

Ellis plopped down across from her. "Yolie introduced me to it. Her family's Greek, and they swear by this place."

Rory glanced at the table. Even though it was normal-size, Ellis felt too far away. She pushed back the chair and joined Ellis on her side. "I'll let you order, then." Rory sat and handed control over a meal to someone else. Something she couldn't remember doing for years.

❖

A short while later, Ellis studied the appetizers crowding the table. Baskets of pillowy fresh pita bread surrounded hummus, grilled eggplant, and tzatziki dips. Grape leaves stuffed with meat and rice, fried calamari, and an herb feta baked in a flakey phyllo pastry sat dead center.

She had over-ordered. She had wanted to impress Rory and was hoping, like the saying went, that food might be the way straight to her heart.

"Oh my God." Rory bit into a piece of the feta pie. "This is goddamn amazing." She glanced up. "Oh sorry. You know, I haven't heard you swear—"

"I swear." Ellis frowned. For some reason, she didn't want Rory to think she was a prude. "Maybe not over food, but I swear."

"Food is the only thing to swear over. And this"—she waved a hand over the table—"is fucking amazing."

Ellis laughed. It wasn't that funny, and she realized with a start that she was at that wonderful stage where everything Rory did was charming. She hovered her fork over the calamari, pretending to look for the perfect piece as she let the realization wash over her.

"How do you think the shoot went?" Rory asked.

"Are you asking about the footage or the personalities?"

"I'm asking about Maya, of course."

"I don't know." Ellis speared a ring near the side of the plate. "She seemed fine when she was on camera, but that stunt at the end? That 'for me' thing was flat-out ridiculous."

"It was another power play or test."

"Exactly. Testing how much London loves her seems to be her go-to game."

"And how far is she prepared to go?" Rory asked thoughtfully. "It's like she keeps doing things to see how far she can push the boundary and how much she can demand."

"I've been thinking about that. It's not enough for her to date London or even marry her."

"What do you think will be enough?"

"She wants to be London. She wants to be a superstar."

"That makes sense," Rory sighed. "You know, she was seriously pissed off when you couldn't get her a role in the movie."

"Was she?" Her whole body tensed. "That really grinds my gears. I pretty much ruined my relationship with the producer begging and pleading for a speaking part." She speared another calamari as if it was still wiggling. "You know *Dazzled* is more than London's vehicle. It's ETA's too."

"And she can fuck a lot of things up for you."

"Yes. If the movie's a hit, as we all think it will be, Yolie and I can affect the gender balance in Hollywood."

"Meaning?"

"We want to build ETA into an agency for women of all ages and ethnicities. Women are often cast as stereotypes in films and TV. They're hypersexualized or at best, ancillary to the plot. I mean, things are changing, that's clear. I want ETA to be part of that change and not be known for soliciting roles for women who get or give public lap dances."

"That's wonderful. And amazing. And I hope you totally do that."

Ellis rubbed her forehead, wondering how far she was away from that dream.

"Speaking of lap dances, did you ever talk to London about Maya's part in it?" Rory asked.

"No. I wanted to get through today. Get the PR on social media. She's going to pooh-pooh it, and I have to do it super carefully, or I will drive her away. Or at least down a more destructive path. I'm heading over to her house tomorrow before work. I'll have my shot then."

"It's a wonder you have any time to run ETA at all."

"That's a whole other issue." One she didn't want to get into here or now, but she found herself wondering. "You haven't been talking to Yolie, have you?" She heard the vulnerability about her career and life path in general in her voice and wished she could say it again. This time without the self-judgment.

Rory must have heard the self-reproach too because she laughed gently. Not at her, Ellis realized, but with her. "When I do, I'm going to tell her that this is the best dolmathes I've ever had." Rory picked up a grape leaf roll and popped it into her mouth.

Ellis relaxed against her chair and chuckled too. This was one of the things she liked best about Rory. She didn't invite drama. Ellis pretty much knew where she stood with her, and seemingly, Rory had the almost magical ability to quell the unrest that always spun inside her.

Ellis took a deep breath. Enough about work, wasn't this lunch supposed to be about pleasure? "I will tell her. And maybe I can also tell her that we are... we are..." Shit, now that she had rushed in, she had no idea how to finish.

A heavy silence hung for only a second before Rory once again rescued her. "Spending time together?"

"Spending time together." The perfect way to define it. Ellis gave her a slow smile. They were turning the awkward corners easier, and that was real progress.

"Please do." Rory grinned at her.

"She'll be happy. She likes you."

"I like her too. In fact, it was Yolie who said wonderful things about you on Norah's set. And I started thinking that I might be wrong about you."

"What do you mean, wrong about me?"

"Come on, we didn't get off on the best foot at London's that day."

"True."

"When did it change for you? When did you realize that you no longer wanted to wring my neck?"

Ellis gave the question real thought. Was it at the bowling alley when she'd leaped to everyone's rescue? Or maybe in Malibu when Ellis had seen the gorgeous pen and ink drawings of her pies? No, if she were being honest, it was that first day when Rory had stomped across London's driveway, all riled up from their confrontation in the kitchen. She had been deliciously disheveled, her short hair standing on end, going everywhere, and her sweatshirt so thin, her breasts had been front and center. Not that Ellis had been looking, though in retrospect, perhaps she had. A shiver ran down her spine. Would she see them without the sweatshirt at some point?

"I don't know," she said a little breathlessly. "I think I fell into the understanding slowly."

"Slow can be good," Rory said and without any warning slid a hand onto her upper thigh.

Ellis froze. The hand didn't travel. It stayed put, its warmth radiating through her pants down to her skin.

"Is this okay?"

She liked that Rory kept asking. It made her feel heard and seen, and it kept her in touch with her own feelings which, even at the best of times, had never been good communicators. "Yes," Ellis said and raised her leg into more contact. "You keep surprising me at every turn."

"In a good way, I hope."

"Not every time." And to Ellis's instant relief, they both laughed. "I did totally want to throttle you that first day."

"Yeah, I know. I'm still sorry about that."

"I'm not. It got us here."

"That it did." Without turning to look at her, Rory stretched out her little finger and found her way under Ellis's T-shirt to her stomach. She ran her pinkie across her bare skin right above the pant line. The touch was slow and light and sent a rush of desire through Ellis's body like a shock wave. Yet another wonderful surprise.

At the farthest point, her finger dipped just inside Ellis's pants and lingered for a moment before sliding back. Even though no one could see, being caressed in public was exciting. It made them complicit in a shared secret. Ellis closed her eyes to savor every second of the connection and only opened them when Rory's hand had moved back to her own lap.

"I can't wait to take my mom and sister here," Rory said as if the last minute had never happened. "They're going to love it. And to think, they've never bothered to look into this corner of Topanga."

"They haven't?" Ellis asked lamely. Her head was down. She couldn't focus on anything either of them said. The skin on her stomach still tingled, and every pulse point in her body throbbed with a new awareness.

Beside her, Rory shifted in her seat, and a gentle hand raised her head until their gazes met.

Rory cupped her chin so she couldn't look away. "Sometimes, the best things happen when you look into a different corner of your world. One that you never knew was there."

Ellis knew that Rory wasn't talking about good Greek food anymore. Embracing the moment, she looked deeply into her eyes. Her irises were alive, burning with the things that she would do to Ellis when they were alone.

That was one corner she gladly would peer into.

And sooner rather than later, she hoped.

CHAPTER TWELVE

Early the next morning, Ellis stood on London's balcony, her hands wrapped around a steaming mug of coffee. The hustle and bustle of a city just coming to life drifted up the canyon. London's house was literally above the fray.

Beside her, London took a sip of coffee and tossed her freshly washed hair. It caught the golden rays of the sun peeking over the Santa Monica mountains and shone like a halo. She looked impossibly lovely in the morning light, although every time of night or day was especially kind to London.

"This is nice." She clinked their mugs, toasting the morning. "I almost always drink my first coffee alone. Maya likes to sleep in."

"Really?" Ellis said as if she didn't already know Maya had the sleep schedule of a teenager.

"Yes. She thinks I'm insane that I like to get up early when I don't have to."

"I don't." In truth, it was one of the things Ellis liked best about her. Early morning London was usually calm and easy to deal with and the reason why she had asked for this first coffee meeting. "I'm kind of glad we can speak alone."

"Oh?" London gave Ellis her full attention.

"I know we already talked about this at lunch the other day," Ellis began, "but we are eight weeks away from *Dazzled*, and I want to be clear now that it is just the two of us. If Maya starts anything like another lap dance in public, you must put a stop to it immediately."

"We both heard you at lunch, Ellis. There won't be any more lap dances."

"I don't want there to be any more anything."

"We heard that too. I thought we also agreed that in the end, there wasn't any harm."

"This time." Ellis took a deep breath and dove in. "I'm thinking that Maya might want to take center stage more than she wants to protect you and your career." There, she had finally said it. She dropped her head; she couldn't look at London. *Please, don't let her freak out.*

"Of course she wants to be center stage."

Ellis whipped her head up. Had London agreed with her?

"She always wants to be the principal actor, not the bit player. Everyone who comes to Hollywood does, and she'll fight like a tiger for her dreams." She shook her head as if Ellis couldn't see the obvious right in front of her.

Ellis hadn't expected that reaction. London wasn't wrong. In fact, she was quite perceptive. "And you're okay with that?"

"Yeah. Why wouldn't I be? That's why I love her. She's passionate and full of life and makes me appreciate my own career that much more." Her eyes shimmered with intensity. "She has a way of heightening things. In me and in life. Everything is more exciting when she's around."

"Oh." Ellis rubbed the back of her neck. London's response had taken most of the bite out of her argument.

"And I can give her everything she wants too," London continued. "I told her once we get back from Hungary, I'll get her the part that will make her career. Maybe we can even do something together. How fun would that be?"

After a long beat where several different responses ran a sprint in her head, Ellis said, "That's great, London." And she meant it on some level. She didn't trust Maya as far as she could throw her, but with all her heart, she wanted London to be happy. And if Maya made her happy…dammit, there was no good way out of this.

"I know. I'm really lucky." London grinned at her own good fortune. "I never thought that I'd love someone like this. That I'd be getting married!" She turned back to the view and gazed out as if she was looking at this amazing future playing out in front of her.

Ellis's heart softened. Was London right, and their relationship was destined for the tidy happy ending of all romantic movies? Could she explain away the lap dance? Maybe Maya had wanted to star in her own little London and Maya Show and had asked a friend to film it. Maybe the money had been completely unexpected. Who knew if the server had even shared it?

Or maybe not. Certainty kicked at the pit of her stomach like a wild animal. "I just want everyone around you to have your best interests at heart."

"They do," London said lightly. "And if they don't, that's why you're here." She laughed and pulled her into a side hug.

Ellis laughed too but silently bet her bottom dollar that London wasn't joking.

❖

"Do you mind explaining this?" Meadow had barely let Rory open her car door before she thrust her phone, screen side out, into her face.

"Jesus, can you give me a second?"

Rory had driven out to Topanga under the pretense of checking out the new kiln, but she wanted to tell her mom about Ellis. There wasn't much to talk about. Two kisses and a lunch, but she was happy. And that was plenty to share.

Meadow grabbed her arm and pulled her out of the car. "Seriously, what's going on?"

Rory focused on the small screen and a close-up of the true love pie. It looked fantastic. Flakey and delicious and something she wanted to bite into immediately. "Wow, that's a great picture. Where'd you get that?"

"It's trending all over the internet."

"What?" Rory grabbed her sister's phone. The Twitter page posted the day before was London's and already had 381K hearts. Understanding washed over her. "Oh, this is from the shoot yesterday."

"What shoot?" Meadow snatched her phone back like a selfish toddler. "I thought we agreed. We were going to do something with the goat cheese, not your pies."

Rory sighed. She didn't have the patience today to deal with Meadow's drama. "We are. At least, I think we are. I haven't had a chance to talk to Ellis about it…"

Meadow glared at her.

"A lot's been happening and—" She pinched her lips to stop herself from talking. She was off her game. The last thing she could do was read Meadow in on the Maya mystery.

"Rory, this is important to me."

"I know. There's a lot at stake here for everyone." The image of her hand resting on Ellis's thigh surged into her mind. "You're not the only one in this situation."

Meadow opened her mouth to answer but stopped when their mom appeared at the front door.

Seeing their body language, she raised both her hands, palms out. "What are you two bickering about now?"

"Nothing," Meadow said and stomped off in the direction of her own tiny house.

"What was that about?"

"I think she's annoyed that I haven't had a chance to get that celebrity chef out here to do an episode on her cheese."

"She's always been impatient. Deep down, she knows that you'll help her if and when you can."

Rory nodded. She knew this too.

"You want to see the new kiln?" her mom asked with a grin and led the way to the pottery barn.

After twenty minutes of showing her every bell and whistle, her mom closed the lid. "Thank you for helping me get it and humoring me by listening to me go on and on. Now, tell me why you really drove out here."

Rory didn't bother arguing. She shrugged and said, "I think I've met someone."

"Oh, sweetie." Her mom clapped with delight. "Tell me about her."

"Her name is Ellis. She's smart and pretty. Super serious but she knows how to laugh. She's kind of tough on the outside and mushy on the inside. She cares about the people around her."

"Oh my goodness. You're grinning ear to ear."

"I know. I like her a lot."

"But?"

Her mom knew her. "But I'm scared." Rory raked a hand through her hair. "Remember Maddie? I liked her a lot, and you know how that ended. I—"

"Sweetie, stop. You can't blame yourself for that one. Maddie wasn't right for you. That wasn't your fault."

"You're the one who told me I'm too hard on people. What if I'm myself, say what I think, and get dumped again?"

"You can't judge one relationship by another." She waved to a bisqueware pot the color of red clay on a table beside them. "Relationships are like pottery. You prepare the clay to throw it. You create designs full of wonderful detail. You mix the glaze and painstakingly apply it, and no matter how careful you are, it isn't until you pull the pot from the kiln that you know what you have. It could be a shiny work of art or a cracked mess. It's the heat that transforms the pot from potential to whatever the reality truly is."

Tears welled in Rory's eyes as her mom's kindness washed over her. "You're saying that Maddie and I were never going to work."

Nodding, her mom took her hands. "I know she broke your heart, but her glaze was too thin from the very beginning. Not your fault. She was never going to make it through the firing."

"And how do I know that Ellis and I will?"

"You don't." Her mom squeezed her hands. "That's the beauty of beginnings. You get to live in all that wonderful potential until you turn up the heat to see if that porous clay you started with will transform into a hard ceramic that will last for decades."

Unable to look at her mom's hopeful face any longer, Rory dropped her head. She wanted to believe that when their firing came, this new relationship would come through intact.

"Enjoy molding the clay, sweetie," her mom said with a soft smile. "And don't be afraid to get your hands dirty. It's part of the process."

Over the next few weeks, Rory took her mom's advice, even though she wasn't exactly clear what *getting your hands dirty* meant in a relationship. Instead, she totally leaned into *spending time together*. They ate at a celebrity chef's restaurant in Venice and gorged on fresh pasta and crispy squash blossoms. They watched experimental theatre in East Hollywood when Ellis was invited by the lead actor who hoped Ellis would represent her. The play was baffling beyond measure, and sadly, the acting only mediocre, but they held hands the entire third act. They hiked in Griffith Park and rode the merry-go-round. They both chose jumpers; Ellis's was decorated with sunflowers and Rory's with lion heads. "Look. No hands," Rory cried and held her arms out like a child as her horse glided up and down.

About three weeks in, Rory grabbed Thai takeout from her neighborhood and drove over the hill to ETA. Yolie's entire face brightened when Rory entered the inner office, and she glanced over to Ellis with a happy smirk.

"Yes." Ellis got up from her desk. "We're seeing each other." She took the bags of food off Rory and then leaned in to kiss her lightly on the lips.

Their first kiss in front of people they knew. Rory was relieved how easy it had been for Ellis to confirm their relationship.

"I knew it." Yolie crossed to Rory and pulled her into a quick hug. "This is the beginning of something special. How wonderful."

Rory grinned down at her "If it's half as good as this Thai food usually is, Ellis and I will be very lucky."

"Let's eat before it gets too cold." Ellis headed out of the office with the food. The tips of her ears and the back of her neck were flushed. Maybe revealing their new status hadn't been that easy. Ellis cared what others thought of her, possibly too much. That's part of her job, Rory mused as she followed her into the outer office.

A thin young woman with a flower tattoo crawling up the side of her neck sat up straight when Ellis entered. She seemed ready to jump if Ellis asked. After a brief introduction to Gina, ETA's new assistant, Ellis held up the bags of food. "We're going to have lunch. Let the phones go to voice mail and join us."

"Really?" she asked, eyes wide as if Ellis had just announced tea with the queen.

"Of course. This is for all of us."

Ellis led them through the courtyard, through her front door, and into her own personal kitchen. The rooms ran in clean, uncluttered lines with wooden floors and white walls. Original oils and watercolors of both people and places hung next to old movie posters and black-and-white photos. Not surprisingly, elegance graced every corner. Softness did too. The furniture was the comfortable sort with throws and pillows. Around Rory was also the faint smell of oranges. A diffuser, maybe, in another room.

They unpacked the food on the kitchen table and were soon digging into pad thai and red curry with cheap wooden chopsticks.

"Thank you for including me," Gina said as she helped herself to more curry.

"We try to have company downtime at least once a week to relax and connect as people, not agents," Yolie said. "Usually, it's coffee and breakfast dessert to start the day. Lunches are prime time for meetings."

Gina nodded slowly as if trying to imprint ETA policy permanently in her mind.

"I take it London didn't ask you to lunch often?" Ellis asked casually.

"Never," Gina said. "She did tell me to order lunch for myself when I went to pick hers up, though."

"That's actually thoughtful." Ellis sounded relieved.

Rory studied this woman who, in such a short time, had become important to her and wondered how she was able to navigate such a tricky relationship with London. Rory knew she couldn't have done it for one week. She would have popped off about something, and London would have gone looking for a new agent.

"Speaking of London." Yolie waved her chopsticks in the air. "She's been strangely silent of late. You think we should be concerned?"

"No, I don't think so," Ellis answered. "She's driving to Prodigy every day for meetings and rehearsal, and I take it she and Maya are spending a lot of time at the beach house since it's closer to the studio."

"She is always less demanding when she's working," Yolie said.

Gina quietly scoffed, and Rory was happy to see she had some bite in her.

Yolie's phone pinged several times in a row. "Sorry," she said glancing down.

"What's the emergency now?" Ellis asked.

She swung her screen in Rory's direction. "Diane Cortez wants to stage a gender reveal for her pregnancy."

"The influencer?" Ellis's brows creased. "How does that involve us?"

"It doesn't. She wants Rory."

Rory shifted in her seat. "Me?"

"Yep. She saw London's true love post and wants a pie of her own. She's hoping to track you down through us." The phone pinged again. "And she's desperate too. She needs them Sunday night." She pointed to a text that had appeared on her phone:

I'll pay big $$$

"She can, you know," Gina said. "Diane Cortez has over six million followers."

"Then she's mis-stepped," Ellis said, always the agent. "She's cut out all room for negotiation. You should triple your rate."

"Should I forward them to you?" Yolie asked Rory. "From what I know, she's a real ally to the LGBTQ+ community."

Everyone at the table stared at her. Conflicting thoughts Ping-Ponged around her head, and before she could answer, Ellis jumped in. "Yes. Of course."

And without Rory opening her mouth, it was decided.

Later, when Yolie and Gina had returned to the office and they were cleaning up, Ellis turned to Rory. "You're going to do it, right? Make the pie for Diane Cortez?"

"I don't know." She shifted on her feet. "I don't have a workspace."

"You could do it here. Come over on Sunday and cook them." Her voice was calm and firm. "I mean, it's not a long-term solution or anything. For this one job, why not?"

Rory studied the kitchen with a professional eye. Enough counter space, and a high-end convection wall oven across from the sink. This part of it could work. If she was being honest with herself, however, her issues were more than space.

"To be truthful. I don't have a lot of patience with celebrities or negotiations or anything else that comes up. Ask Norah's producing team. I say what I think." She blew out a short breath. It was too early in their relationship to disclose all her flaws. Although this one, Ellis knew already.

"That's why working for yourself is perfect." She caught Rory's gaze and wouldn't let go. "If you want, ETA will sign your pies as a client, and we'll give the account to Gina. She can do the due diligence to see if this Diane Cortez is someone you want to align your brand with."

"I don't have a brand."

"Not yet. Let Gina see what she can do with it." Ellis nodded rapidly, seemingly as the idea took hold.

"I don't know. You think it will work?"

"I do. If she can manage London, she can handle anything. You'll have to pay the full ten percent, though. There're no discounts for…" She trailed off and rubbed the back of her neck.

Rory now understood she only did that when she was uncertain. She tilted her head and said with quiet confidence, "For girlfriends?"

Ellis's lips parted with a slow smile. "Yes, for girlfriends."

"I wouldn't expect a discount." She held out her arms, and Ellis fell into her embrace.

Nestling into each other felt so right. As right as the first day in Rory's apartment when she had caught Ellis after she'd tripped. The difference was, now they could acknowledge it.

Rory leaned in to brush her neck with her lips and then trailed light kisses up to her ear. "You know, I can do more than cook pies in this kitchen," she said in a low voice.

Ellis moaned in response.

"I could come over Saturday and make you dinner."

"I would like that."

"With a sweet ending?"

"That sounds delicious."

Rory hoped they both knew what she was really talking about. As an answer, Ellis raised her head and found Rory's mouth with her own.

CHAPTER THIRTEEN

On the big day, Ellis changed three times before she settled on brand-new dark jeans and a casual sweater. She pulled her hair back into a messy ponytail at the nape of her neck. She didn't want to look like she was trying too hard, or even worse, expecting too much. Truthfully, she was on both accounts. She liked Rory a lot and was excited…and scared. First times had always been a little awkward for her. In the past, they had gone badly because she'd spent more time in her own head than in bed with her partner. And she was determined not to make that same mistake this time.

Promptly at six, Rory appeared at her door with two big grocery bags, a bouquet of fiery orange tulips, and a huge smile. "Hi," she said, kissing her on the lips before handing her the flowers.

"Hi." A nervous flutter danced in Ellis's stomach. This was really happening.

Ellis detoured into the living room to grab a crystal vase for the tulips and took several deep breaths before joining Rory in the kitchen. She had already tied on an apron that read *bake someone happy* and was unpacking the ingredients for dinner: lemons, fresh artichokes, carrots, chicken breasts, a bottle of white wine.

Ellis picked up a lemon and drank in its fresh, clean scent.

"These are the last of the Meyer lemons from my mom's tree out in Topanga."

"I'm honored. I love lemons." She placed it back on the counter and brushed an artichoke with the tip of her finger. "In fact, I love everything here. How'd you know?"

Rory shrugged. "I may or may not have texted Yolie several times yesterday asking her what you might like for dinner."

Ellis laughed to cover up how touched she was that Rory would go to the trouble. "Is that wine for cooking or drinking?"

"Both."

Ellis pulled two wineglasses from a nearby cupboard, and over the next hour, watched Rory make their meal. She moved around the unfamiliar kitchen with ease and gave Ellis simple tasks to do. With her hands busy, her mind relaxed, and they chatted about all sorts of things. Mostly about Diane Cortez's gender reveal that was going live the next day. Gina had brought it together in a flash, even though she had to meet with Diane's husband in a supermarket parking lot to learn the sex of the baby. No one was supposed to know, and the Cortezes didn't want to take any chances that it would be leaked.

"So what is it?" Ellis asked.

"A boy." Rory covered her mouth in a quick motion. "Oops, I wasn't supposed to say," she said through her fingers.

"You're worried about me? I'm the queen of NDAs, remember?"

"No, I wasn't supposed to tell anyone. Meadow's been trying to get it out of me since I told her about the gig."

"I'm not just anyone."

"No, you're not. And because of that"—Rory's eyes gleamed with excitement—"I'm thinking blueberry with cyan-blue lime curd. The different shades of blues should pop on camera."

"It will. Everything you do is a little work of art."

"Ah, speaking of which," Rory wiped her hands on a dish towel and pulled her portfolio from the other grocery bag. "Do you remember how my mom always bakes cookies to give away with her pottery? She suggested that I do this." She opened her notebook to reveal a smallish watercolor on thick, handmade paper. The picture was a pie in the shape of a baby's rattle with round dumbbells on each end and a raised question mark, half-blue and half-pink, in the middle. One end of the rattle was cut open, and shades of blue flowed from the pie in a clear gender reveal. The visuals were folksy and graphic with bold black outlines emphasizing the saturated blue color. "I thought she could put it in her baby book or frame it for the nursery or, hell, just throw it away if it doesn't work for her."

Ellis studied the watercolor. It was bright and fun and somehow, almost alive. Diane Cortez would be absolutely thrilled. Anyone would.

"What do you think?" Rory broke into her thoughts.

"I think your mother's a genius. Everyone wants to remember a life event. And soon, everyone will want a Rory Hatten original as that memento."

"Good. I'm glad you agree. Because I also made this." She turned a page to reveal another vibrant watercolor. Two *true love* pies in the shape of conversation hearts were drawn with the same bold lines on thick, handmade paper. One was cut in the middle and red filling, the color of passion, spilled out. The other sat on top, its letters etched into the pie. Ellis laughed with delight, and then, her pulse raced. True love. It was quite a statement.

"I thought London might like it," Rory said, unsure. "You know, as a souvenir from the party and the proposal."

Oh my God. A flush swept up her neck and ran across her face. Of course this was not for her. This was not for tonight. "She'll love it," she said and hoped Rory couldn't hear any tinge of embarrassment in her voice. She swallowed hard and pivoted back into business mode. "Seriously, Rory, this is brilliant branding. If we market this right, you could be looking at your new career. Dessert with a side of art."

"I thought it was just a cute gimmick." Now, Rory was the one who sounded unsure.

"Careers have been founded on a lot less. And you don't always make pies? You do other things, like cakes?"

"I do, and you should see my decorated Christmas cookies." She bounced from foot to foot. She looked radiant in her excitement. "I can also do a little chocolate and sugar work. I'm not an expert by any means, though with what Diane Cortez's paying me, I could totally take time off and practice."

"See, it's already working out."

"Hardly, but at least I can see possibilities." She grabbed Ellis's arm. "Is this what you do for all your clients?"

Ellis saw the gratitude swirling in her eyes and melted in response. "If I'm lucky," she said.

"I see why you love it."

Over dinner—grilled artichokes, carrots, and chicken with a lick-your-plate-clean sauce of lemons, wine, and butter—there was much more to talk about. Ellis's mouth seemed more full of words than food. She talked about scoring great roles for two of her other actors that week. "ETA is more than a one-trick pony," she said.

They both laughed when Rory pointed out she had puffed out her chest with the statement.

She also confessed disappointment when she'd asked Gina, after promising herself she would not, to get Maya a passport. "It's weird." She shifted in her seat several times. "London almost seemed more interested in it than Maya was. They only have about a month before they go, and when it came up that she hadn't even started, Maya kind of shrugged it off."

"Maybe she assumed you would do it. Which you have."

"It's strange. I wonder if she even wants to go to Hungary."

"That's crazy. I'll take her place if she doesn't. I've never been out of the country." Rory chuckled. "Do you like to travel?"

"I do. I've been to Europe a few times. Lots of places still on the bucket list, though. Like Germany. I'd like to see the castle that Walt Disney is supposed to have modeled the one at Disneyland on."

"I knew it. You do want to be your own fairy tale. Princess Ellis. I can start calling you that if you want."

"Or maybe, it's because my favorite aunt and uncle took me to Disneyland every year on my birthday. Good memories." She rolled her eyes at Rory, hoping it came off as cute. "What about you? Where would you like to go if you could go anywhere?"

"Bali."

"Oh, me too. For the beaches?"

"Yes, and there's this dessert place."

"Of course." Ellis grinned again at her enthusiasm.

"The chef's American, and he had this great restaurant in the States. One day, he shuts the door, and five years later, he resurfaced in Bali. Opening a dessert place in the middle of nowhere." She slid her knife and fork together on her plate and leaned back in her chair. "He sources locally and everything, I mean everything, like chocolate and sugar and vanilla, is fresh. Nothing comes out of a packet or a bottle. And every plate is a work of art. I saw a Netflix special on it. I was salivating ten minutes into the show."

"I guess you don't have to physically go somewhere to travel." She waved a hand over the table. "You took me somewhere new with this meal, and we never left my dining room."

"The evening is still young."

Ellis tucked a piece of hair that had escaped the ponytail behind her ear. Now that the real reason for the evening sat on the table next to the empty plates, Ellis's stomach churned. There was no dinner or small talk between them and the main event.

Rory must have seen her sudden discomfort because she stood and laid a hand briefly on Ellis's shoulder. "I should clean up." She gathered the plates and headed into the kitchen.

Alone at the table, Ellis pulled in and released a deep breath. She felt a deep attachment to Rory, and she was pretty certain Rory felt something too, but she was scared. Was their connection real or manufactured from her own need? Her heart started to pound.

Only one way to find out. Clasping a hand over her chest, she forced herself from the chair.

Rory, her back to the door, was at the sink swirling a little soap into her skillet. Without looking around, she said. "I'm a die-hard soaper."

"Excuse me?"

"There's an ongoing debate in the culinary world about how you wash your cast-iron pans. I had two friends at the ICE Culinary Institute who fell out over it." She flushed the pan with water, grabbed paper towels, and wiped the surface dry with even strokes. "Personally, I think a little mild soap's not going to hurt anything. Because it's the priming that makes the difference." She set the pan on the stove and dribbled a little olive oil in its center. She turned the burner to high heat, and they both watched silently as the pan began to smoke. Wading up more paper towels, she rubbed the oil into the metal. Her touch seemed firm and light at the same time.

A shiver ran down Ellis's spine.

"It's about seasoning and being protective." Rory fixed her with warm eyes.

Ellis felt the tug of desire. Who wouldn't? "Are we still talking about the pan?"

"Oh my God." Rory burst out laughing. "I seriously have no idea. I was trying for a cute moment, you know, to lighten the mood. You seemed a little tense at the end of dinner, and my mom is good at coming up with metaphors that change everything. I sound like a crazy person, however." She reached over to turn off the stove and wiped her hands on clean towels.

"You kind of did." Ellis chuckled. She anchored a finger in Rory's belt and pulled her close. "But it worked."

"How so?"

"I would very much like for you to prime my pan," Ellis said and took in a ragged breath.

❖

Ellis's bedroom was exactly what Rory had expected. Like the rest of the house, it radiated charm and sophistication. The golden hardwood floors from the rest of the house ran here too, and a plush queen bed with an expensive puffy duvet sat under high windows. The room looked out on the small, flowery backyard through a sliding glass door. The orange tulips in their crystal vase rested on one of the bedside tables.

When had she done that? *Nice touch.*

"This is a great room." She glanced around and reached for Ellis's hand, interlacing their fingers and squeezing tight.

"Thanks." Ellis's voice cracked with many emotions.

Despite her declaration in the kitchen, she seemed nervous. Not that Rory wasn't too. She was hopeful that they would have lots of fun once they tumbled into bed. Ellis might be all buttoned up on the outside. On the inside, still waters often ran deep.

The first time with anyone, though, was almost more about building emotional intimacy than physical intimacy. And that was always scary if you cared about that thing. And with Ellis, Rory absolutely did.

Pulling Ellis with her, she sat on the bed. She slid off her shoes and drew Ellis, still standing, between her knees and rested her head, cheek-side down, on her lower chest. Ellis's heart pounded away, adding a living, breathing soundtrack.

Reaching down, Ellis smoothed a gentle hand over her hair and then hugged her close. Rory let Ellis lead, knowing that she needed to ease into foreplay at her own speed.

Ellis leaned down to kiss the top of her head, her cheek, and then her collarbone. Rory bit back a groan when Ellis dropped to her knees and reached up to brush the skin under Rory's shirt, the exact place she had just kissed. She slid her hand down Rory's blouse to the top button and caught her breath.

"No bra," she said.

"I know." Rory gave her a half-smile. "Easier that way."

Ellis fumbled with the first button but picked up steam on the way down. With each drop of her hand, she exposed a little more skin and sent shivers to Rory's toes. When the blouse was fully loose, she pushed it off Rory's shoulders. It pooled around her waist. Ellis's gaze watched it fall and then rose to Rory's face, her bare shoulders, and finally, her breasts.

Rory sucked in a breath. She knew she wasn't movie-star perfect. Her shoulders were a little too broad, her breasts a little too small, and her waist a little too long. But Ellis was staring at her with such longing and need, it didn't matter one bit.

Rory gently tugged at the hair tie at the back of Ellis's neck. A wave of copper fell around her face and over her shoulders. It caught what little light was in the room and shone brightly. "It's so lovely. You should always wear it down."

"It gets in the way," Ellis said, her voice like rough silk.

Rory imagined Ellis hovering over her, fingers caressing sensitive places, her long hair brushing against her skin, adding to the intensity. "Not all the time, I think." She cupped Ellis's face, stroked it with her thumbs, and brought it upward. Her scent was clean and fresh, and Rory claimed her in a kiss that was long and sweet. Desire tugged hard at its edges, and Rory waited until Ellis tentatively reached out with her tongue before she gave in to her own feelings. Only then did she hungrily slip inside Ellis's mouth, exploring and tasting her warmth. Ellis's breath hitched in response. Rory's nipples, bare to the air, hardened into aching points.

Nibbling the curve of her bottom lip, Rory slid her hand from Ellis's face to her wrist, caressing her shoulder and arm on the way down. Once there, she lifted Ellis's hand to her own chest.

Ellis whimpered in excitement, broke the kiss, and met Rory's gaze. The air was electric and heavy with anticipation, and when Rory nodded, Ellis dropped her hand and slid it over the crest of one breast. She reached beneath to cup it and finally kneaded it. Her caress was light and a little unsure, but Rory felt it to her toes. It had been a long time since someone had touched her like this, and her body arched into the outstretched hand.

Ellis took the hint. Her finger slid over the nipple, rolling at first and then gently pinching and tugging. Just when Rory couldn't take it anymore, Ellis kissed it. She surrounded the nipple with humid heat, her tongue curling around the aching tip.

"Oh God," Rory moaned.

Ellis's only answer was to suck harder, her tongue now stroking the underside of the stiff tip with true artistry.

Rory clutched the duvet as she marveled at this new development. Ellis might have been uncertain about falling into bed, but she was surprisingly skilled now that she was here. Rory had fully expected to take the lead in their lovemaking. Happily, she had been wrong.

The hand at her other breast slid lower, against the flat of her belly and began to play with the waistband of her pants. Rory's head tipped back with anticipation of where those fingers might go next.

As if reading her mind, Ellis gently pushed her back against the bed. "I want to be inside you."

Her words sent heat whooshing through Rory's body and caused her hips to tilt upward, almost of their own accord. "Yes, please."

Ellis pulled off her pants easily. Her underwear came with them, and Ellis licked her lips at a naked Rory lying in front of her.

"Your turn," Rory urged.

Ellis grabbed the bottom of her sweater. She slid it over her head in one fluid motion, revealing a lacy bra and freckled torso. She then wiggled out of her stiff pants and let them drop to the floor. Her panties matched her bra, and like a thousand stars, freckles ran down the length of her legs.

Rory tried to sit up, and Ellis pushed her back as she climbed onto the bed. "Still my turn." The need in her voice made Rory squirm with pleasure.

She gave in as Ellis returned her attention back to her breasts and then ran her hands over her stomach. Her long hair tickled Rory as she moved. It felt exquisite against her skin, as Rory knew it would.

As Ellis finally made her way down her torso, Rory spread her legs. She was ready. Ellis drew circles on her skin, gradually, slowly coming closer to the one place they both wanted her to be. With every rotation, Rory's center throbbed. When Ellis finally found her way between her legs, Rory gasped. Ellis slipped a finger inside.

Ellis moaned. The noise was as guttural as any Rory had heard, and she responded in kind. Ellis stroked deeper, added a second finger, and Rory arched up to meet her. They easily, almost comfortably, found a rhythm. In and out. Sliding and stretching. All of it sent one wave after another of pleasure through Rory's body. Ellis's fingers seemed to be everywhere at once, toying with her and teasing her to new heights. She bucked upward, her eyes squeezed shut, and her muscles continued to tense.

Until Ellis found her clit with her other hand and swirled her fingers around it. Rory pushed against her and gave in to the inevitable. She climaxed with a cry. Convulsing with the release, she throbbed around Ellis's fingers, sucking them deeper with each spasm of her orgasm. Ellis moved gently inside her until Rory, spent, fell back against the bed with a groan.

"Oh, God. That was…" No words came to her. She didn't know how to describe what had happened between them, at least on her end.

"That was what?" Ellis's voice was thick with her own need and cut Rory to the core.

"Let me show you," she said breathlessly and pulled Ellis up. They lay face-to-face on the bed. Her eyes had gone heavy-lidded, and Rory rained tender kisses on them and on her cheeks and lips. She thrust her fingers into Ellis's silky hair and took her mouth in a long, deep kiss. She pulled her into an embrace with her entire body, hugging Ellis with her arms and thighs. She felt Ellis's length against her, supple and yielding to her at every place they touched.

Sliding her hands up her back, Rory fumbled with the bra clasp, and when she couldn't get it, sat back to laugh at her own incompetence. She knew how to define their experience: truly intimate. She had lain naked in front of Ellis and let her touch her in the most private ways. The resulting orgasm had been amazing and wonderful, but it wasn't the best part. She had opened herself up to someone who'd taken this trust like a gift, and now she felt emotionally connected, as if little threads of gold tied them together. That is what had rocked her world.

"Help me," she said with a grin.

Ellis also sat up, reached behind, chuckling slightly, and flicked her bra open herself. "I get it. Next time, no bra."

Rory also sat up and pulled it off her. "I'll hold you to that... Oh. Wow."

Despite the smile playing over her lips, Ellis was clearly turned on. Her breasts were firm and round with arousal, and her nipples were tight and flushed. Apparently, her tendency to blush went everywhere. It was beyond endearing.

"You're so lovely," Rory said and buried her head in Ellis's breasts, kissing and caressing them with her mouth. They were heavier than her own, slightly more than a perfect handful, and Rory ravished them, kissing and nibbling and sucking.

Ellis groaned and melted under her hands. Rory wanted to feel her everywhere. She nudged her back on to the bed and lay with her front to front, touching from head to toe. Rory nuzzled her ear and ran a foot up her shin. The positioning was a little awkward, but it worked, and when Rory finally moved, gliding through the slickness to the entrance of Ellis's body, she could feel the shivers travel everywhere.

Ellis was wet. Rory slid easily to her most sensitive places. And almost by accident, she curled her fingers into a spot that made Ellis cry out and quiver. "Open for me," Rory breathed into her ear.

She arched upward with a gasp. Rory pushed inside deeper and found that spot again and again.

Ellis climaxed with a force that left her shaking, and when it subsided, she rolled into Rory's arms, burying her head against her shoulder. Rory slung a leg over her thigh and drew her in as close as she could. They said nothing; it wasn't disconcerting or embarrassing. Rory knew that whatever questions Ellis had had at the start of the evening were resolved now. And from the way she still clung to her, she had faith in the answers and the connection they'd achieved.

They lay still, wrapped in each other's arms for a long time. Rory was convinced Ellis had fallen asleep. She started to pull a strangely heavy blanket over both of them when Ellis sighed contentedly into her shoulder.

"My pan is going to need a lot of priming."

CHAPTER FOURTEEN

E llis opened her eyes to morning light streaming in through the sliding glass doors. Normally, she ran a sheer curtain over the doors at bedtime. Last night, in all the excitement, she'd forgotten. Now, a warm, almost springlike luminescence flooded the room. Totally appropriate because after last night, she felt, what…reborn?

Yes.

She stretched against the sheets, trying not to disturb Rory curled up beside her. Her muscles were loose and relaxed. A calmness floated in her body, and no part of her was tense. Morning afters had been rare in the last few years. When they had happened, she'd woken up restless, ready to bolt. This, however, felt more like a morning before. Before all the wonderful things that would come next. She grinned at the corniness of her own thought and rolled onto her side to get closer to the woman who'd brought this new phrase into her life.

Rory stirred, stretching here and there, and finally, her eyes fluttered open. "Hi," she said.

"Hi." Ellis caressed her face. "Good morning."

Rory pulled the hand to her lips and kissed it. "How are you?"

"Honestly?"

"Always. Now I'm a little worried."

"Don't be." Ellis snuggled into her shoulder. She couldn't meet Rory's gaze as she said, "Great. You stir me up and calm me down in all the right ways."

Rory wrapped her arms around her. "That may be the nicest thing anyone has said to me."

"Nicer than, I have an espresso machine in the office, and I'll make you coffee whenever you want?"

"Yes. That comes a close second, though."

They both chuckled, and Ellis relaxed completely. So much so that she fell back asleep, something she almost never did.

When they woke up for real, they decided to ditch the office coffee and head up to Sunset Boulevard for brunch. They ate on the patio of an adorable French bistro whose gimmick was eggs Benedict in a dozen different combinations. After one sip of her latte, Ellis confessed that it beat anything the office machine could produce.

After brunch, Rory kissed Ellis on the cheek and said, as if they'd been dating for years and not weeks, "I know you have work to do. I'm going out to shop for the ingredients for the pie. Is it still okay if I make it here?"

Ellis had to admit that yesterday, she had worried about mixing business with pleasure. That if the evening went badly, committing her kitchen for the pie would be awkward and unpleasant. Now that the moment was here, nothing seemed more natural. And even better, it boded well for the future. Together, they could be effective individually. Pretty much her love language. "Yeah, that works for me."

And it did. She was wildly productive at her desk, and hours later, Rory knocked at the inner office door. Ellis glanced at the time on her computer and leaped to her feet. When had it gotten so late? "Dang. The courier, they—"

"Don't worry." Rory smiled. "They came. The pie, the picture, everything is already there, and Gina texted. Diane loves them."

"That's great." Ellis sank back into her seat and glanced at the clock again. "The reveal's in an hour."

"I'm going to head home and catch it there. I came in to say good-bye."

Ellis fought the lesbian *urge to merge* only for a moment before she said, "You want to stay? Catch it together? We can get takeout." Maybe it was all the oxytocin surging between them, but she wasn't quite ready to send her off, yet.

Rory nodded. "Or we can have the leftovers from last night."

"Even better."

Not long after, Ellis threw Diane's live stream to her oversize TV in the family room. "Ten minutes," she called to Rory, who appeared with two full plates. They plopped on the couch, balancing dinner on their knees and ate while they waited for Diane Cortez, and possibly Rory's future, to go live.

Exactly on time, Diane's feed popped on the screen. The web star sat against a background of pink and blue foil curtains and bounced in her chair with obvious excitement.

"Oh my God. I can't believe today is the day I find out the sex of my little bundle of joy. As you can see, I dressed up for the occasion. The top is from Delivered." She ran her hand up and down a lovely, flowered top that gathered at the neckline. "And the jeans are also from Delivered with the right amount of stretch and freedom to make you feel stylish, even in your seventh month." She stood and spun for the camera. Her hair, loose and free, spiraled out as if she was on a fashion shoot.

"She knows what she's doing," Ellis said.

Rory slid her plate on to the coffee table. "I can't believe how nervous I am."

Back on screen, Diane sat, flicked her hair behind her shoulder, and looked straight into the camera. "Before we begin." Her voice turned almost serious. "I know that I'm sitting in front of blue and pink, and I'm all too aware of the extreme gender binary my child is being born into. He, she, they, ze can tell me what their gender identity is when they grow up. For now…I can't wait to find out what their biological sex will be."

"Wow. I wasn't expecting that," Rory said.

"Me neither. Yolie did say she was an ally."

Diane got up, and focusing on her large baby bump in full view, the camera followed her into the kitchen where her husband, a handsome athletic type, waited.

"Hi everyone," he said, waving to the camera. "This is what we did. We got our doctor to put the sex of the baby in an envelope, and we took it to the same person who did London Green's proposal pie."

Diane snuggled into her husband's side. "One degree of separation from a superstar. Can you believe that?"

Rory Hatten and an Upper Crust email flashed at the bottom of the screen.

"Nice," Ellis said.

"All Gina."

The camera switched to an overhead shot of the pie sitting on a blue and pink plate on a white marble counter. The warm golden tones of the crust practically glowed on the screen.

"It looks wonderful." Ellis studied the frame.

"I used every single one of my styling tricks."

Ellis reached over and squeezed her leg as the shot on the TV swung back to the happy couple.

"You ready?" Diane looked at her husband as if he hung the moon.

"You bet, babe."

Ellis said, "For people who already know the sex, they're playing this well."

"They are. I guess all reality TV is a lie."

Back on the screen, Diane grabbed a large knife from off camera, and her husband tapped his phone. A dramatic drumroll played, and together, as if they were cutting a wedding cake, they sliced into the ball-shaped end of the rattle. The framing jumped to a close-up, and dark blueberries and lighter blue cream burst forth. The contrast in colors and textures was stunning.

There was a gasp and a happy shout.

For the life of her, Ellis couldn't say whether the noises were coming from the TV or her own mouth. For a second, both couples reacted the same way to the same moment. For different reasons of course, and Ellis marveled at how the experiences meshed.

"It's a boy!" Diane said and threw her arms around her husband. He threw a fist into the air as if he had won the World Cup. They danced and kissed in celebration for the live stream, and when Diane turned to the camera, tears glistened in her eyes.

Not real. Ellis sat back against the couch.

"Oh, wait. We also got this." Her husband pulled a handmade square envelope into the frame. He held it up to the camera. *Parents to Be*, in big black letters, filled the screen.

He passed it to his wife, and she opened the envelope, pulling out Rory's watercolor. The camera saw only the plain back. What it did catch was her eyes that went soft and round with emotion. "This is wonderful," she finally choked out.

"Oh, this is good for you." Ellis's hand, still on Rory's leg, squeezed harder this time. Her gaze was glued to the screen since this was a real surprise. Neither of them had known that Rory had delivered two treats, not one.

"What is it, babe?" her husband asked.

Unable to speak, she turned the watercolor to the camera, and he had to scoot out of frame to peek. The graphic version of the rattle, coincidentally cut in the exact same place as the real one on the plate, filled the screen. The colors popped more than in real life.

They must have really good lights, Ellis mused as Rory's hand clamped on hers in excitement.

"It's a boy," Diane's husband's voice drifted in over the artwork as he read the words. "It's a boy," he said again, this time with a catch in his voice.

The camera zoomed out to capture Diane and her husband falling into each other's arms with true joy. Laughing and crying at the same time, it seemed that they'd forgotten that they were being filmed and only remembered the miracle of a new baby.

"How wonderful. That's real," Ellis said, her thoughts finally bubbling to life.

She wasn't the only one who thought so. Rory's phone started pinging with several texts, and soon, they were lost in a different reality of congratulations and happy emojis.

Ellis stared at the messages popping up on the phone. "You're going to be very busy."

"If I can find a place to cook." Rory turned to look at her.

Ellis met her gaze. "That place could still be right here with me."

"Seriously?"

"Yeah. Let's try it and see if it can work."

Rory pressed her palm to her heart. "I'm pretty sure I never said thank you. For everything."

Ellis smiled. "And I'm very sure you don't have to."

Over the next few weeks, Rory marveled as Upper Crust got some traction. Diane's livestream started trending. The moments of true happiness at the end of the video were perfect shareable content, and traffic on her site multiplied. The watercolor got almost as much play, and thanks to a case of FOMO, others wanted a Rory Remembrance, as Gina called it, for a life event.

Gina started booking everything from surprise birthdays to getting a new labradoodle puppy. In just a few weeks, Rory's desserts and art keepsakes became an ideal gift experience for a jaded LA audience. Most of the fun was dreaming up original ways to post the reveal on social media. It was a perfect storm, and Rory was riding the wave.

She limited the bookings, though, since she didn't want to take over ETA or monopolize Gina, or more importantly, throw herself on Ellis's hospitality too often. Happily, they settled into an easy rhythm where she would bake on Sundays and one random weekday, staying over the evening before. On the nights they spent apart, they texted or FaceTimed, and while the sex was getting better and better, the real excitement came with these bedtime talks.

One night after they'd said good-bye, Rory snuggled into her comforter and tried to figure out why they gave her such a thrill.

Not that they were saying anything earth-shattering. They told each other about their days, their families, their likes, and dislikes, nothing important. But she felt like Ellis was really listening, and she returned the favor.

When they fell into this deep listening zone, the vibrations of their conversation changed. Ellis valued what she said. There was no judgment, and for the first time in a relationship, Rory trusted her partner to hear who she was beneath the words, which as her mom had pointed out, were too direct at times.

She loved how she felt when she hung up the phone, and she was beginning to suspect that she loved more than the feeling. In the darkness of her bedroom, she blew out a long breath and shook the thought from her head. She wasn't ready to go there yet.

The next Saturday, the shrill ringing of her phone once again woke her from a dream. Why didn't she learn to put it on silent mode? Maya, Meadow, her mom? Why couldn't they let her sleep?

When she opened her phone case, the adorable picture of Ellis she had taken at the French bistro weeks ago greeted her on her screen. "Hey," she said, sleepily. "I think I was dreaming about you."

"Rory?" It was Ellis, but she sounded different, all choked up.

Her chest tightened. "What's wrong?"

"I got another goddamn video with London and Maya, and this time, there was no one there to stop it.

"Are you kidding me? What—"

"I don't want to talk about it over the phone. And I need to see London before anything else. Can you come over? In two hours?"

"Yes, of course."

"I mean, there's nothing you can do, but I could use some moral support."

Of all the people she could call, Ellis had reached out to her. "I'll be there."

Rory showered, dressed, and packed for a sleepover. On the drive to West Hollywood, she worried about what situation would greet her when she knocked on Ellis's door.

At first glance, Rory couldn't tell anything was wrong. As usual, even for the weekend, Ellis was dressed impeccably in a print dress belted at the waist and casual black flats. Her hair swung in a high ponytail, and golden drop earrings dangled from her ears. It occurred to Rory that her style was her armor against the world, and she needed it today more than ever.

Only her lips gave her away. They were pinched until they were almost bloodless, and she quickly waved Rory in as if a dozen movie monsters were hiding in her bushes.

"Okay," Rory said as soon as she was standing in the hallway, the door shut behind her. "What exactly is going on?"

"God, I wish I knew." She headed toward the kitchen. "It started with an email this morning. Let me show you." Her computer and a steaming mug of coffee rested on the marble island. "Here. Sit," she said and slid the coffee over. Fine lines of worry creased her brow, and yet, she had still taken the time to make coffee.

"Thank you," Rory said, appreciation ringing in her words.

"You're welcome. You may want a stiff drink instead after watching this. Jesus Christ, I stood a foot away from her and told her no more videos." Ellis angled the computer so Rory could see. The empty backyard from the beach house was frozen on the screen. She noted it was the exact same frame from the recent social media posts. The blue pool sparkled next to the ratan chair, and the Pacific Ocean rolled far in the background. Anyone who saw London's true love posts would instantly recognize the location.

"You ready?"

"I guess so."

Ellis hit the spacebar, and the video began to play. There was no sound, only a picture.

But what a picture.

Maya, wearing a man's dress shirt, led London into frame. She was dressed in a pink robe, belted at the waist. They stopped by the chair and kissed. London, facing away from the camera, brushed back Maya's hair and leaned into her as if she was something delicious to eat.

The shot was wide enough to capture both of them, the chair, and a bit of the pool. London was angled with her back to the viewer, but she didn't cover up Maya. Clearly, the goal was to document what would come next and keep both in the frame. The shot didn't resemble pornography with its changing angles and close-ups. This felt more like a hidden camera and blackmail.

On the screen, Maya slipped London's robe off her shoulders, and it slid down her backside. She was wearing nothing underneath and returned the favor by unbuttoning Maya's shirt. Within a minute, they were both standing naked in the backyard. London pulled Maya into a deep embrace and kissed her, hard. She licked her way down to Maya's breasts and sucked at them. Maya writhed with pleasure under her touch. Then, she pushed Maya onto the chair and sank to her knees. Grabbing Maya's ass, she pushed her into position.

With one knee on the rattan's armrest and the other on the far end of the chair, Maya was spread wide, giving London and the viewer a full, panoramic view.

London slid a hand up one thigh to her ass. She squeezed hard, and Maya bucked in pleasure. Then she dropped into Maya's center, her blond head bobbing up and down as she pleasured her fiancée. In response, Maya clutched the chair, and in the performance of her life, threw her head back with passion.

London's body blocked the most intimate actions, but she attacked Maya's midsection with wild abandon, as if she couldn't get enough.

Rory hit stop. "Do I have to watch the whole thing?" She was no prude, but she was beginning to feel very uncomfortable watching two people she knew have this kind of sex. There was nothing intimate about it. No joy or love. Rory didn't know her well at all, but London was sensual, and something seemed off. London came off more like a porn star than a fairy-tale princess. That, Rory gathered in a flash of understanding, was probably the point.

"No, we don't have to finish. They go on like this until Maya climaxes." She scrubbed through the video until Maya grabbed London's head between her legs. She stared up at the sky and opened her mouth in a silent cry of release. "And then, they get up and leave." She moved the cursor farther on until Maya was now leading London off screen. She moved sharply, aggressively, as if she was in control, and London was her sex toy. None of it was good for London. Maya, possibly, if she wanted a very different type of career.

In front of her, Ellis's hand trembled. Rory took it off the computer and held it in both of hers. She was trying hard to keep it together. Rory squeezed gently, telling her silently that she didn't have to. At least, not all by herself. "Who sent it?"

"Someone who calls themselves Movie Watchdog. In a nutshell, they don't believe that this is the kind of behavior that Princess Carina would engage in."

A thousand questions marched through Rory's mind. "What do they want?"

"This is where it gets unbelievable. They want London to withdraw from *Dazzled*. They want someone more morally aligned with the innocence of the original cartoon. If she doesn't do it of her own accord, they say that they will send the video to Prodigy."

"And they're not asking for money?" Rory had been certain blackmail was the goal.

"Not yet. They're either crazy and focused only on *Dazzled*, or they're super savvy. To distribute something like this, the participants need to be aware they're being filmed, and they need to sign away the copyright."

"Unauthorized sex tapes are released all the time."

"Not really. Either the celebrity is secretly in on the release and has signed off on it, or they pay to kill it. Sex tapes are usually a way to monetize attention or promote a more legitimate production."

"I don't get it. How did they get their hands on this? And why on earth would London shoot something like this?"

"That's the weird thing. She says she didn't. And when I asked if Maya did, because that makes more sense, she said it would have been impossible." Ellis held Rory's hand like a lifeline.

"Because?"

"Because she swears right and left that they never had sex by the pool. I got a whole rundown of all the places that they did have sex, and don't ever sit in that living room again. But never, not once, by the pool."

"Let me get this straight. She's saying there couldn't be a video."

"That's her crazy logic."

"Clearly, someone set up a camera and shot it from their backyard. The proof's right there."

"I know." Ellis glanced around as if looking for answers. "I mentioned that. London wouldn't even look at it. She wouldn't wake Maya up to ask her or let me talk to her. She said she was way too busy to figure this out. She said I needed to deal with it."

"Wow. That's selfish." Rory slammed her mouth shut. It was too late. The words were out there. The unspoken rule between them had been they both could diss Maya whenever she deserved it, but London was completely off-limits. "Oh, shit, I'm sorry."

"Don't be. You're right." However, Ellis untangled her hand from Rory's and rubbed the back of her neck. "London's never had to deal with any of the unpleasantness of her life. I mean, it's my job, I suppose. The lawyers and the PR firm are already on it. You'd think, though, she would want to strategize about what happens if Movie Watchdog does send the tape to Prodigy or how to get them not to."

"Yes, you would," Rory said evenly.

"Movie Watchdog wants London to issue a press release Monday morning saying that, after careful consideration, she's exiting from *Dazzled*. I mean, that's not even close to the way it works. And if she doesn't, the tape goes to Prodigy. If Prodigy feels their reputation is worth more than money, and they might, they could delay the shoot and recast. Or they could use it to renegotiate the contract and not in London's favor. It's a fucking mess."

"So we hurry up and wait and see what happens after Monday?"

Ellis bit her lip and nodded. "The lawyers have already hired a fixer, but there's not much to go on. Yes, we wait. Something I'm not very good at." She sat beside Rory at the island and put her head on her shoulder. "Thanks for coming. It's easier not to go off the deep end when you're here."

She put an arm around Ellis and hugged her close. "I'm glad you called me."

They sat for a minute in silence. Rory could almost hear the thoughts whirring in Ellis's head. "The thing that kills me," Ellis said, her voice soft. "Is not the sex tape. It's the fact that London looked me in the face and lied to me about making it. I thought we were in this together. I thought we were friends." She waved at the screen where London still stood buck naked. Her head and face were down, as if she was carefully watching her steps, but her front was exposed to the camera from her neck to her toes. "For Christ's sake, she's right there in living proof."

Ellis sucked in a quick breath. "Wait a sec." She pulled the computer closer and leaned in to peer at the screen.

"What?" Rory asked after a long beat.

"Can you make the picture bigger? Zoom in?" Her finger hovered over London's groin. "Right about here."

"Sure. How?"

"I don't know. Push a button. They do it all the time on those FBI shows."

"That's TV," Rory said, not unkindly. "They can do all sorts of things, and happily, I've never worked for the FBI. Wait a sec. Give me your phone."

Ellis grabbed her phone, opened it, and handed it over.

Rory focused and took a picture of the computer screen. "Now try to zoom in. Will that work?"

Ellis pinched the picture with two fingers, and London's bare midsection magnified. Her eyes widened. "Holy shit," her voice shook with emotion. "She was telling the truth. It's not her."

"How do you know?"

"Look." She pointed to right above London's vulva.

"I don't see anything?"

"Exactly. When London was in preschool, she had a bad teeter-totter accident, and a bolt cut her. It left a nasty scar right there. We should totally see it."

"Maybe she covered it somehow. Like, with makeup. I mean, if she knew she was being filmed—"

"No, we've tried. One year, she wanted to wear a see-through dress to some award event. Even after makeup, you could still see it." She jabbed her finger at the screen. "This is not her. I mean, the face is, but the body's not."

"Who is it?"

"I've no idea."

"You don't think this is faked like…a deep fake?" Rory asked.

Ellis lifted one shoulder and a palm as if even she couldn't believe it. "It would explain a lot. And I hear they're getting easier and easier to make."

"You think some crazy person made a tape to influence the casting of the biggest movie of the year?"

"The world is a strange place these days. Anything's possible."

"You think Maya's a fake too?" Rory asked.

"She has to be, right? I mean, it looks like her, but there's no way Maya would do something that stupid. She has way too much to lose." Ellis bit her lip, and Rory could almost see the thought, no, the betrayal, rolling around in her mind. She clearly didn't want to go there.

"Okay. But how would strangers get access to the backyard?"

"Cut and paste? I mean, the backyard is all over the internet." She rubbed the back of her neck. "I'll call everybody and let them know. But I can't sit around and do nothing. Is there any way we can prove this is a fake?"

Rory licked her lips before she answered. "You're not going to believe this. I think we can."

Chapter Fifteen

Two hours later, Ellis drove into a quiet cul-de-sac in Rory's North Hollywood neighborhood. Rory directed her to a small bungalow on the left. It was cute, painted a cream color with matching decorative stone accents and bright green bushes.

Despite the obvious curb appeal, Ellis frowned as they got out of the car. "I'm not sure about this."

"We don't have to stay. We can even go right now if you want. She's good, though. Video editing and special effects are how she pays her bills."

Rory's tone was comforting. In fact, she had been a rock all morning—rushing over at the crack of dawn, treading lightly with Ellis's emotions—and here she was, again solving a big, big problem. It was nice, Ellis reflected, to be able to lean on someone.

"No, I need answers. Let's give it a shot." She came around to Rory's side of the car.

As if on cue, a Jeep that could survive the apocalypse zoomed around them and took possession of the driveway. An attractive brunette with an expressive face jumped out of the driver's side and strode over in a huff.

"*Hola*. I see how it is. We're back to being friends when you want a favor?"

Rory raised up her palms in defeat. "Yeah, I know it looks bad, Alejandra. Thanks for meeting us."

"Whatever." She grinned, and Ellis gathered that her bluster was mostly show. "It takes more than a little ghosting to get rid of me," she added and leaned in to kiss Rory loudly on the lips. To her credit, Rory stepped back as soon as Alejandra made contact, but Ellis was surprised by the jolt of jealousy that hit her.

Alejandra tilted her head toward Ellis. "This the agent?"

"Yes, and my girlfriend, by the way."

"Oops. Sorry. I take back the kiss." She stuck out a hand to Ellis. "I'm going to be clear. I'm helping today because Rory's good people, and I'm kind of curious about what's going on, and I wouldn't mind an interview with your client when this is over. She'd be a huge draw for my *Fresh Beginnings* podcast. I'm just starting out."

"Rory mentioned something about that." She was a little nervous about looping in a desperate entertainment reporter. Rory said they could trust her, and she trusted Rory. "And let me also be clear, this is off the record," she added anyway.

"Yeah, yeah. Rory made me promise. And I don't break my promises. Should we go inside?" Without waiting for an answer, Alejandra moved down the path and opened the door with a key. "Beso, I'm home," she called out into the empty house.

The sound of skittering echoed noisily until a large black and white dog rounded the corner. Barely glancing at Alejandra, he launched himself at Rory, whining with joy. She dropped to his level, and Beso, happy beyond measure, tried unsuccessfully to climb into her lap and finally settled for licking her face.

"Traitor." Alejandra surveyed the scene. "He's called Beso because he loves to kiss. It's endearing at first and then, super annoying," she explained to Ellis. "Come on. The office is back here. Beso, down."

The dog obeyed but glued himself to Rory's side as they followed Alejandra. Ellis also stepped close and whispered, "How long did you guys go out?"

"Not that long. Dogs really like me."

"Mmm-hmm."

Alejandra invited them into a plush home office. A long desk with three monitors, speakers, and a huge computer tower were against one wall. A green screen, standing LED lights, and a nice DSLR camera on a tripod were set up on the other. If nothing else, Alejandra was committed to both her jobs.

She plopped down in a black and yellow gamer's chair by the desk and stretched out her hand. "You have the video?"

Standing behind her, Ellis handed over a flash drive, and she slid it into the tower. Moments later, London and Maya popped up in triplicate across the screens. Ellis groaned. Three naked Londons added insult to injury.

"We think London may be fake." Rory pointed at the middle screen. "Can you tell?"

Suddenly all business, Alejandra played the video from the beginning, slowing it down here and there and stopping it completely when London went down on Maya. "Does she have her back to us the whole time?"

"Mostly," Ellis said impressed by how professional Alejandra was. Her face had stayed completely blank as one of Hollywood's biggest stars had been disrobed right in front of her. "We only see her face at the beginning and the end."

"Smart." Alejandra rewound the video to the top. "And the framing is too. It's far enough away that no one's looking at their faces." Alejandra played the video frame by frame. "Because... if you did..." In slow motion, London and Maya paraded to the chair. "You'd see that."

London froze, her face in profile. "Look at her ear." Alejandra pointed to the screen.

Ellis peered closer. "I don't see anything."

"How about now?" Alejandra tapped her keyboard, and a close-up of London's face popped on the screen.

"You have special software to do that?" Rory asked.

Alejandra nodded.

"See?" She nudged Ellis.

"What are we looking for?" Ellis asked.

With her cursor, Alejandra circled London's lower ear lobe. Now Ellis could see it. The bottom portion of her ear was slightly blurry, and it didn't quite match up with the hairline.

Alejandra bounced in her seat with excitement. "They must have hired an actor who looked like her body-wise—most importantly, had hair like her—and did a face swap. There are tons of programs on the internet these days if you know what you are doing. And the technology is getting better all the time."

Ellis took a step back. London had told the truth. And she hadn't believed her.

Alejandra continued to advance the frames. "Oh, and here, look. When she puts her hand up to brush back her hair, her finger disappears. Just for a second. See."

She toggled back and forth between two frames. One of her fingers in the air and the next, the finger was, like magic, gone.

"We didn't know how to look at it," Rory announced the obvious.

"What about Maya? The fiancée. Is she fake?" Ellis asked.

Alejandra scrubbed through the video, slowing down and zooming in at different times. Ellis waited with bated breath. So much hinged on her answer.

"I'm no expert. She's facing the camera most of the time, and I don't see any telltale signs like digital glitches and discoloration or weird mouth movement. And watch her face."

In real time, Maya grabbed fake London's head as she climaxed.

"Look, she's blinking like crazy," Alejandra said as if she had explained the secrets of the universe.

"And that's important because?" Ellis asked.

"From what I know, most of the neural networks that produce synthetic media never learned about blinking. You got to pull the data points from photos you already have, and in those pictures, almost everyone has open eyes. The upshot is, deep fake faces blink far less than normal people. They're on the verge of correcting that. Well, big-time AI is."

"Oh my God. She's real?" Ellis's shoulders tensed.

"I would say so." Alejandra spun in her chair again. "And I would also say whatever's going on here, she's possibly in on it."

"Damn. I had really hoped she was fake too." Sighing deeply, Ellis met Rory's gaze over the chair and Alejandra's head. Rory mouthed the word, sorry.

Ellis clenched her jaw and nodded. This changed everything. What was Maya up to? If she had been in on the video, then she knew who Movie Watchdog was. Unless...Fuck, Fuck, Fuck. She *was* Movie Watchdog?

A searing heat flushed through her. What on earth was Maya's endgame?

There was only one way to find out.

❖

Rory watched, helpless, as Ellis flushed red. Freckles popped up all over her face. Normally, she was good at keeping her feelings at bay. Now that they were out, they ran like wildfire. And for the first time that morning, Rory wasn't clear how to help her.

"Thank you, Alejandra," Ellis said surprisingly evenly. "I appreciate your help. I'll have our lawyers send over an NDA, and if you sign it, I will get you enough celebrities who have big break stories to launch your podcast. Not London but others who'll be glad for the attention." She held out her palm for the flash drive.

"I will totally take that deal." Alejandra jumped up and grabbed it from the tower.

Ellis closed her hand tightly around the flash drive. Her fist turned red with the effort. "We'll show ourselves out," she said and walked into the hallway.

"Some shit hit the fan, I assume?" Of course, Alejandra was fishing for information the second they were alone.

"You have no idea." Rory hurried out before she pressed her further.

While Ellis uncharacteristically tapped her foot at the opened front door, Rory gave Beso and then Alejandra good-bye hugs.

"Answer my texts this time," Alejandra said, hugging her back, hard.

"I will, but you don't need me anymore."

"It was never just that. Like I said, you're good people."

Ellis apparently had enough of waiting. She grabbed Rory's arm and guided her out the door.

Alejandra called after them as Ellis hurried down the path. "We should all go out sometime. We can meet at the Honey Pot for a drink."

Ellis didn't respond. The silence continued in the car as she gunned the engine and made a quick U-turn. She was as stiff in her seat as when they'd first met in London's kitchen.

"That was nice of you offering up your actors." Rory hadn't seen this Ellis for a while now. She had forgotten how cold and bottled-up she had been.

"She did us a favor," Ellis said tersely.

"Yeah, but you didn't have to help her."

"Women should help women whenever they can, especially in this business." Her tone was still clipped. "It will be good publicity for my clients too."

"True." Rory slipped her hand onto Ellis's thigh and rubbed her quad, which was tight as a twisted rope. After sliding her thumb up and down the muscle repeatedly, Ellis's chest expanded with a full breath, and the tension finally broke.

"Actually, I kind of liked her," she said and relaxed a little into her seat.

"She's great…in small doses." Rory laughed and glanced over to see the ghost of a smile on Ellis's lips. "Are you ready to talk about this? What exactly are we doing now?"

"Hiring a hit man. Can you make that happen too?" The smile spun into a grimace.

At least she was talking. "No, seriously."

"Oh, I'm serious. Maya's going to die. You're right, though, maybe it would be easier if I did it myself."

"Ellis!"

"Okay, okay. I'm going to drop you off at home, and then I'm going to Malibu to get some answers. And short of murdering anyone, I'll do whatever it takes."

Rory licked her lips and tried to channel her mom. "I'm all for answers. Are you sure this is the right time?"

"Meaning?"

"Meaning, you're riled up, and take it from me because I've had way too many bad outcomes, you shouldn't ever go in angry and say whatever you want."

"When you have a viper in your midst, you can't wait. She could be striking right now for all we know." She pushed on the gas pedal, and the car whipped around a corner.

Marveling how the tables had turned, Rory grabbed the armrest as the seat belt tightened around her. "You also shouldn't go into a viper's nest without a plan. Maya's clearly desperate and not as smart as she thinks. That's a deadly combination."

Ellis took in a deep breath and rubbed the back of her neck until she finally said, "New plan. I'm going to make London want to kill her."

Little by little, Rory talked her down. Mostly, she encouraged Ellis to get her frustrations out. With Maya. With London, who refused to take the video and her future seriously. With a job that gave her no free time. And when they finally eased into Ellis's garage, she was back to driving with both hands on the wheel and a gentle touch on the gas pedal.

"You sure you don't want me to come?" Rory asked later as they both stood in the kitchen. Ellis had texted London, and under the deception of bringing a travel document over for Maya to sign, had set up a meeting for the three of them.

"I would love that, but I don't want London to think that we're ganging up on her. And I'm already coming in under false pretenses."

"I hope you can find a way through this. Maya has only one place to go, and she's paid the rent until next month."

Ellis's forehead wrinkled and then smoothed. "Oh, you mean your apartment."

Rory nodded.

Ellis hooked a hand in her jeans pocket and pulled her closer. "That's the easiest solution today. Why don't you move in here for a while? Just until all this is settled."

"Ah…" It wasn't that she didn't want to, but she didn't want Ellis to think she was forcing her into anything. "I wasn't angling for that."

"I know. It was my idea. You don't have to if you don't want to, but everything's easier with you around. I might have gone off the deep end earlier, and look at me now. I'm back to being me again. You made that happen."

Rory sucked her bottom lip into her mouth while a thousand reasons she should say no ran rampant in her mind.

"And," Ellis continued, "you could take more bookings for Upper Crust. Get that up and running and…" Ellis took a deep breath. "Here's the real reason. I don't know what I'd do without you."

"Silly." Rory grinned. "I'm not going anywhere."

"Does that mean you'll stay?"

A warmth brimming over with love flooded through her. She had never felt so full. And with it came clarity. She knew she answered some sort of need in Ellis. That she grounded her in a good way that had allowed the morning to play out as well as it had. And it went both ways. Ellis had allowed her to stop and take ownership of her life. Ellis had created the space for her to pause and breathe before reacting. They weren't just falling head over heels like in the movies; they were creating a relationship which was a thousand times harder and much more real.

"Yes, I'll stay until this is sorted out," she heard herself say. As soon as the words were out of her mouth, the arrangement already felt much more permanent.

Rory dropped her hands to Ellis's hips, looked into her eyes, and drew her even closer. Her heart thumped in her chest as if this was their first kiss. Maybe it was. The first of their new reality. Their lips brushed, and Ellis moaned in her sea animal way.

This time, they both giggled, their lips pulling back into grins and their teeth knocking against each other. The kiss quickly became awkward and fumbling, but Rory held on tighter, and Ellis completely relaxed in her arms. Then, it was a full-body kiss, where they wound arms and legs around each other. Rory almost lost her balance as Ellis wrapped her foot around her ankle. There were dozens of places where they connected. When they finally separated, Rory thought it was a kiss for the ages.

She locked eyes with Ellis, unwilling to let the connection between them fade now that they were no longer touching.

"Now, you go, and you get her."

"Damn right."

CHAPTER SIXTEEN

At the beach house, the afternoon sun flooded through the floor to ceiling sliders, bathing the living room in light. Ellis stood in its warmth as she waited for London to get Maya from the pool deck. Now that she had heard the sordid history of the furniture in that room, standing seemed the wiser choice.

A side door opened, and London glided in as graceful as a billowy cloud. She wore a one-piece bathing suit that hid her scar and also emphasized every curve. She had answered the door this way, and now with a start, Ellis realized she had covered up with the same silk robe from the video. Maya bounced in behind her. She was dressed in a skimpy two-piece, leaving nothing to the imagination. Ellis didn't know if it was the sex tape talking, but today, she seemed coarse and unrefined against London's natural elegance. Even throwing on a cover-up and slipping on flats didn't help.

"Sorry to interrupt your afternoon." Thankfully, to her own ears, she sounded professional and calm and not the raving lunatic of a few hours ago. *Thank you, Rory.*

"It's all good," London said. "It's too cold out there anyway."

"You have more papers?" Maya plopped on a love seat that apparently had seen a lot of action. "I thought I signed everything."

"You have. I've come because I got a very disturbing email this morning."

London rolled her eyes like a young child. "Oh, come on, not this again."

Maya turned directly to Ellis. "What email?"

Ellis studied her. Her face was open and genuinely curious, as if this was the first she was hearing about it.

A breath caught in Ellis's throat. Could she be wrong? Her gut responded with a hard kick. *No, she's a better actor than anyone ever thought.*

"It's nothing. Ellis got a sex tape," London jumped in. "I told her it was fake and to let it go. These things happen all the time. Better get used to it if you stay with me." She ruffled Maya's hair and then focused on Ellis. "Clearly, you showing up here—again—means that you didn't believe me in the first place."

"Oh no. I believe you. It's fake. I verified that with an expert." Again, she fixed her gaze on Maya, who stared up at her nonplussed, taking easy breaths, her hands resting loosely in her lap.

Instead, it was London who broke. "For fuck's sake, then, Ellis, I already told you, let the lawyers or Mark—"

"Wait." She held up her hand. "Let me be clearer." Her glare bore into Maya like hot lasers. "At least, half of it is."

London let out an exasperated breath. "For the last time"—she infused every word with clear annoyance—"I didn't have sex out by the pool."

"I know." Ellis laced her arm through London's and spun her around. They both looked at Maya. They were the audience to her performance. "She did."

Under the dual attention, Maya cracked a little. She tugged on the bathing suit tie around her neck.

There it was. A surge of adrenaline raced through Ellis's body, and she resisted the urge to pump her fist in the air. Because she hadn't forgotten that whatever was good for her was very, very bad for London.

"What do you mean she did?" London threw off Ellis's arm. "What are you talking about?"

Losing no momentum, Ellis quickly pulled her computer out of her workbag on the floor. "Let me show you."

Maya watched as Ellis set up the computer on the coffee table, and some color drained from her face. Still, she said nothing. Ellis gave her grudging respect. She wondered what she would do if the tables were turned. She would never lie to Rory, for one.

Finally, she angled the screen so they could all see it and pushed the space bar. Already knowing the video by heart, she observed London and Maya as they regarded it. London's whole body sagged as the scene played out. By the end, she was tapping her chest right above her heart.

Maya, on the other hand, sat defiant, shoulders back and chin thrust out. There was a visible tightness around her jaw.

London finally snapped the screen down. "Is she right?" Her voice was thick with pain. "Is that you?"

The enormity of what she was doing hit Ellis with a hard blow. She longed to put her arms around London and hug the hurt out of her. Whatever Maya's true feelings were, London had loved her or thought she loved her, which was the same thing in London's world.

"Well?" London demanded.

Maya's gaze darted around the room until she clearly settled on a strategy. "Let me explain."

Ellis almost laughed. Had that line ever worked? Either in the movies or real life?

"Go ahead," London said, more like a threat than permission.

"I don't want to go to Hungary."

"What?"

"I mean, I would love to go anywhere with you, but not right now. I need to stay here for my career. I got that offer for that web series, and you made me turn it down."

"I told you. It wasn't a real production. The funding wasn't there, and the producer was pulling promises out of his ass."

"We never actually had that conversation."

London cocked her head. "Wasn't it obvious? That show had disaster written all over it."

Ellis bent her head to study the floor. She didn't want this peek into their relationship. London was probably right about the show, and she could also see her not communicating it. London expected people to read her mind. For the first time, she almost felt sorry for Maya.

She glanced her way. Either she was changing tactics or was now fighting back real tears.

London didn't seem to notice. "Besides, I told you that as soon as we got back, I would take care of it. I would make you a star."

"I wanted to do it myself," she said in a quiet voice.

A flutter of guilt twitched in Ellis's stomach. That was a reason she, herself, could totally appreciate.

London pointed to the computer. "So you made that? How the fuck did you even do it?"

"I had a friend come over when you were down at Prodigy, and then I hired a computer guy, and he changed the face."

"How did you find the money for that?"

Ellis bit her lip. She wanted to know that answer too.

"My half of the lap dance money."

"You were in on that too?" London's eyes widened as the truth clicked in her mind. "You were going to send the lap dance to Prodigy, and when that didn't work, you did this."

London's chilly tone sent a shiver down Ellis's spine. Stupidly, she hadn't realized it would be this emotional. She crossed to the other side of the room to give them some semblance of privacy.

"I wanted both of us to stay in town," Maya said, desperation in her tone.

"Oh my God. You were going to ruin possibly the biggest role of my career so you could stay here and do some stupid web drama?"

"You were the one who told me not to give up on my dreams. And you didn't have a problem with the lap dance."

"That's because there, you weren't cheating on me." London had finally arrived at the heart of the matter.

"Cheating? I…didn't cheat. It wasn't real sex."

"It looked real to me."

"It didn't mean anything." She made one last attempt.

London took one quick step and towered over her. "It does to me."

Across the room, London's comment hit Ellis like another blow. Everything was clear now. Of course London was upset that her girlfriend, no fiancée, had let someone else go down on her, fake or not. Regardless of what she had said on her balcony weeks ago, she was more upset that the video had cast Maya in the starring role, not her. Their relationship could never recover from that betrayal. London always had to be the one in a close-up.

On the love seat, Maya knew it too. Her body shrank in on itself as if her fight and bravado had dried up with those four words.

"You can go now." London's dismissal was loud and clear.

"What? Where?" Maya asked choking back a sob.

"Figure it out. You don't seem to be short on ideas."

"I… I…" She had no words, and she closed her eyes on this horrible new reality for a long beat.

Eventually, Maya stood in a daze and circled the room to collect her phone and a new Prada backpack by the door. Her sex appeal, hugging her earlier like haute couture, now hung in ragged tatters. She glanced at London, the hope for a reprieve written all over her face.

London dealt the last blow. "Someone will get the rest of your things."

Maya hitched the backpack over her shoulder and opened the front door. Bright light flooded in, and she was quickly eclipsed by it as she exited.

Ellis wheeled around to face London, ready to rush to her, ready to hold her and let her cry it out. She, however, stood in the center of the room, still in character, as if she was waiting for a director to call cut.

"London? You okay?" Ellis asked, knowing what a stupid question it was.

Turning her head almost in slow motion, London met her gaze. "You know what this means, right?"

Ellis shook her head and took a step toward her in case she needed to pick up the pieces of London's broken heart.

"You're going with me to Hungary."

❖

Rory looked at her phone for the millionth time that afternoon. It had been hours since she had kissed Ellis good-bye and sent her into battle, and still, no text. Not that she had expected one. Ellis was in one of the most difficult conversations of her career, and her dealings with London had always sat outside the rest of the world. Rory didn't want to add personal stress to that. She did want to know, though, if Ellis and London and Maya were okay.

Instead, she dove headfirst into her own work. She spread out on the marble island in the kitchen, made a grocery list for the pies, and pulled her brushes from a new canvas case. Her mom had squealed with joy, completely living up to her name when Rory told her how well the watercolors were being received.

"I knew it," her mom had said. "You're very talented."

"Talent almost always needs a good idea first."

"Then, you're lucky I'm talented with good ideas."

Now, looking at the art pieces in front of her, she knew her mom had been right. The bright, saturated colors of her drawings popped against the white marble. The happy messages sang out with her mom's joy. Even better, she loved making them. Maybe this could work. She could say good-bye to the back kitchen of dumb cooking shows and hello to a new career simmered in this perfect kitchen.

Ellis's key clicked in the front door, and Rory's smile widened. She hustled to the front hall to greet the woman who she was now kind of, sort of, living with. Her smile died as soon as she rounded the corner. Ellis's shoulders sagged, and her arms hung limply at her sides.

"Oh my God. What happened?" Rory rushed over to take her workbag before it fell to the ground.

Ellis pursed her lips and shrugged.

Rory guided her into the living room, sank her into the cushiony couch, and removed her flats. She sat on the coffee table and took one of Ellis's feet in her hands. Rubbing into its arch, she asked, "Are you too tired to tell me everything?" Curiosity burned through her, but she understood that Ellis might need time.

Ellis slung her head back against the sofa and closed her eyes. "It was awful. I went in there with righteous anger. I was certain I knew who the villain was and who the good guys were."

Rory's breath caught in her throat. "Maya didn't make the video?"

"Oh no, she made it. She totally caved and told us everything. It was like one of those legal shows where the prosecutor asks one simple question, and bam! Everything comes tumbling out. Thank you. That feels so good."

While Rory rubbed one foot and then the other, Ellis replayed the conversation, finishing with, "London was angry enough to kick her out. But, shit, she might have done it because she was jealous."

"Jealous? Of who?"

"Maya." She opened her eyes and raised her head. "I think in the end, London, despite her lip service, wanted to control the narrative of their relationship, and she wasn't going to give any part of that away. Even when it became clear that Maya had real reasons for doing what she did, not good ones," she added hurriedly, "but ones that made sense with London's personality. I felt a little sorry for Maya. I texted her to see how she is. Not surprisingly, she hasn't answered."

"That's rough." Rory blew out a long breath. "What did London say?"

"She said…" Ellis dropped her gaze and slid her foot out of Rory's hands.

For reasons she couldn't quite identify, Rory's chest tightened as Ellis put both her shoes back on.

"Not much. It was almost like it had never happened to her. She talked about Hungary… and the…shoot."

Rory resisted the urge to grab her hand. The pauses, the dropped head. Something else was going on, and while she wanted to know, needed to know—they should tell each other everything— she could wait. Ellis was clearly spent. London would be gone in three days. All Rory had to do was help Ellis to that finish line, and time would be theirs. To grow this thing into something deeper than her relationship with London.

"Come on," she said. "Let's get you a glass of wine, maybe a hot bath, and no work tonight. You hear me?"

The evening played out almost as planned. There were two glasses of wine and a quick check of emails before bed, but the bath was long and luxurious. Rory poured a generous dollop of lavender bath foam into the tub, arranged glowing candles around the room, and set up Ellis's phone in the corner to play her favorite meditation podcast.

"Stay here for as long as you need," she said as she closed the door behind her.

"Thank you." The reply was muffled but heartfelt.

In the kitchen, Rory opened the refrigerator door. She would bet her bottom dollar that Ellis hadn't eaten all day. The fridge, not surprisingly, was almost empty. She pushed a sixpack of diet sodas out of the way to discover two imported cheeses in the back. Crackers she found unopened in the pantry. She cut up a slightly withered apple and made the world's simplest charcuterie board.

While she waited, she added items to the grocery list. They hadn't talked about the finer points of her temporarily moving in. She didn't want to act or feel like a guest. She planned a few simple meals for later that week and riffled through the pantry, taking stock of what she would need.

"Oh, here you are." Ellis finally wandered into the kitchen, looking much better. Color had returned to her face, and her hair hung loose over her shoulders. She wore classic silk pajamas, black with white trim. Rory marveled how put together she always looked, even now. Opposites attract, she mused.

"Is this for me? I'm starving."

"I thought you might be."

She placed her hand over her heart in thanks and sat at the island to eat. They chatted about replanting the flower bed in the front and a possible trip up the coast to visit the redwoods. The conversation was set almost exclusively in an unformed future. Ellis stayed far away from the day's events, and Rory followed.

The next morning, Rory woke up in Ellis's bedroom, and felt as if she really belonged. No longer just an overnight guest, she had claimed her side of the bed and rearranged the bedside table to accommodate her phone. Ellis had even put her toothbrush into her holder last night. Not that they were getting married or anything, but it felt right.

When Ellis opened her eyes, she checked her emails. Nothing from Maya or London, so they walked up to their French bistro for breakfast and the wonderful lattes.

"We have to stop eating like this," Rory said as she dug into a yogurt, fruit, and granola parfait.

Ellis reached over with her spoon for a sample. "Why? It's delicious."

"It should be. There's as much sugar in this as there is in chocolate cake. You're right, though. It's delicious." She ate another bite. "The blueberries are healthy, I guess." She dug one out and handed it to Ellis on her spoon. She plucked it off and popped it into her mouth.

"Speaking of healthy," Rory continued, "I was thinking that I might make dinner to earn my keep. Salads and some meatless meals. If we're going to splurge on the weekend, maybe we should try to balance it out during the week?"

Across the table, Ellis's posture stiffened, and her mouth pinched inward.

"Or we can add chicken?" Rory's muscles tensed too. "Shit, too much domesticity too fast? I can—"

"Look." Ellis placed her fork on her plate, and her hand seemed to unconsciously go to her neck and started to rub. "I need to tell you something."

Rory tamped down sudden nausea rolling in the pit of her stomach. "*Okay.*" She drew the word out into two long syllables.

"I didn't exactly come clean about everything yesterday." She stopped and cleared her throat.

Rory said nothing. Bad news was knocking on the door, and she wasn't going to help Ellis open it.

"After Maya left," Ellis finally started again, "London told me that I had to go with her to Hungary."

"Of course she did." She didn't know why she was surprised. Ellis had directly told her last night that London needed to control the narrative. She just hadn't realized that London was telling her story too. "What'd you say?"

"I said I would."

Rory felt as if Ellis had punched her in the gut. She was a fool. She had thought to get London on a plane and have Ellis all to herself. Then, they could shape this beginning into something that might last. But the reality had always been staring her in the face. Ellis was wrapped up in London hook, line, and sinker.

"Just to get her settled," Ellis rushed to add.

Rory blew out a breath that she absolutely knew she was holding and raised her palms in the air. "Which is for how long? A few days, a few weeks, the whole time?"

"I don't know," she admitted, her voice small and thin.

"I know we basically just started, but where does that leave us?"

"Nothing between us has to change." Ellis grimaced as soon as she said it, as if she knew she was losing control.

"Are you kidding me? You're naive if you think that. Everything will be different. At the very least, you'll be sleeping in Hungary. I'll be sleeping in America. One of us will be in the wrong bed."

"We can Zoom and text. Maybe you can even come over to the right bed. Rory,"—panic crept into her voice—"this is a short-term problem."

"And what about the next time London gets a career-changing role? This is not just about a couple of months in Hungary. It's a deeper problem."

Ellis shook her head, seemingly to reject that idea, but Rory could tell that she had hit a nerve. And even worse, both of them knew she was right.

"I feel like I have to go." Ellis swallowed hard, and her voice quavered. "I feel responsible, in some way, for the disaster that was London and Maya, and maybe this is how I make it up to her."

Rory sighed heavily again, ran a hand through her hair and tried to see the situation objectively. Ellis's job, quite literally, was to protect London from the Mayas of the world. She was contractually responsible for her career, her happiness, her whole life. And if Rory was being honest, she should shoulder some of that blame. After all, she had run interference for Maya in London's kitchen.

Still…she bit her bottom lip. Emotionally, it was a different story. None of them had known how Maya and London would play out. Right from the start, everyone's expectations had been wildly different. It was no one's fault. No, that wasn't correct. This was on London, who did only what she wanted, consequences be damned. Like a black hole, she created chaos that destroyed whatever was in her orbit. Why couldn't Ellis see that?

And even worse, Rory realized that she was now circling London too. How long before she fell beyond the event horizon? Shit. Was it already too late for her to escape? Nope. She still had time. She grabbed her phone, then her wallet, and stood. She could hear her mom's voice as if she was there:

Don't do it, sweetie. Don't say it.

I have to. Maybe if I do, I can get Ellis out too.

"I totally get it. You need to protect London. And I also get that she doesn't have anyone else, and as hard as you seem on the outside, you are vulnerable and warm on the inside. But this is not the time to be the beanstalk."

Ellis scooted her chair back as if moving away from what would come next.

"This is your time to be Jack. To chop down what is holding you back and to go after what you want. Maybe that's me, or maybe it's not. Fact is, you need to choose yourself over everyone else, including London. Don't always put her first. She doesn't deserve it. And more importantly, neither do you." She opened her wallet and dropped her share of the bill on the table. If this had been scripted, she would spin on her heel and stride out of the restaurant, head held high. She had said her piece.

In reality, she turned to the gate on the patio and froze. Her things were at Ellis's, and she didn't have a key. Hand clenched against her thigh, she waited until Ellis also rose and tucked more money under Rory's.

They walked back to the house in silence, at least three feet away from each other. Rory scooted in the door and gathered her things in a flash. She could always come back and get whatever she'd missed when Ellis had left for Europe.

On her way out, Ellis grabbed her arm and drew her back. "Where are you going?"

"Home, I need some time to get my head around this."

"Why don't you stay here? We can do it together"

She froze. She wanted to with all her heart. She had hoped she had given Ellis a lifeline at breakfast. Was this her grabbing hold of it?

"We only have two days."

The words bored a hole through her heart. Whatever they said to each other, she was still leaving. This was Ellis informing her the decision was already made. She had cycled completely back into professional mode.

"I don't think we can. I'll text you later."

Out by the curb, Rory slammed the car door in disappointment and gripped the steering wheel tightly. "Shit." She feared that this had been their firing, as her mom had said, and they had cracked in the flames. After a lifetime of sitting by her mom's pottery kiln, she knew there was no real way to fix a broken pot.

Thankfully, the tears waited until she was pulling out of the driveway. She drove around the corner, out of sight of the house, and dialed her mom.

"Mom?" she said, her voice heavy with hurt.

"Sweetie. What's wrong?"

"Can I come home?"

CHAPTER SEVENTEEN

"Please tell me you're not serious." Yolie tapped on her desk in their office early Monday morning until Ellis looked at her.

Instead, Ellis continued riffling through her desk drawer. "Serious as a heart attack."

"That's a terrible simile."

"But a fitting one. Oh, great. Here it is." She plucked up her favorite pen and carefully placed it in the computer backpack she was organizing for her trip.

"If that's true, you should reconsider blowing up your relationship and running off to Europe for London."

"That's not quite the way it is." She continued to dig in the drawer.

"Ellis, for goodness' sake, can you stop for a minute?"

Ellis shut the drawer and focused on her. "What?"

Yolie set her jaw before she spoke. "As your employee, I say, go to Hungary. Make sure London rocks Princess Carina, and there's *Dazzled Two* and a video game. Gina and I can absolutely manage everything on this end. I would enjoy having the office to myself, no offense."

"None taken."

"As your friend, though, a good friend, I hope, I say, look at what London is costing you personally. What she's asking now takes your professional commitment to her to a whole new level."

Silently, Ellis rested her elbows on her desk and dropped her head into her hands. Yolie wasn't wrong, but she wasn't quite right, either. There had to be a way out of this where everyone came out relatively unscathed.

Her whole body ached from head to toe. She had barely slept last night, kept awake by the thousand and one scenarios churning through her mind. Even though she hadn't found the right solution, that didn't mean it wasn't out there.

She raised her head. "Thank you, Yolie. It means a lot to me that you care enough to say that."

"Not that again." She shook her finger at Ellis. "That's the exact way you sidestepped the last conversation about London. I do care. A lot. That's not what we are talking about, though. What're you going to do about London?"

"I plan to find a way through this where no one is disappointed."

"Except for you, maybe. And Rory." Yolie shook her head. "She's a keeper, you know."

"I can do it," Ellis said with more certainty than she felt.

"I don't think that's possible."

The phone rang. Saved by the bell. Silently thanking whoever was on the other end, Ellis picked it up before Gina could get to it. "Ellis Turner Agency," she said cheerily and put an end to the conversation.

Light filtered through the canyon, and there was enough bite in the morning air to remind Rory that spring hadn't entirely arrived. She, her mom, and Meadow sat out on the small balcony of her mother's tiny home, enjoying fresh coffee and blueberry cornmeal cake.

She looked at her plate; the cake was chockful of fruit. Last time she was eating blueberries, she'd been happy. "I don't know, Mom. Maybe I can find someone else to book events for Upper Crust. I don't see how I can ask Gina to do it anymore. And where am I going to cook?"

"You made your pies here last night," her mom offered.

"That was an emergency, and it was far from ideal. Thank you, though. I really appreciated it."

Meadow puffed out her cheeks and blew out her breath with a pop. "I don't get it. Are you guys breaking up or not? How am I supposed to think about this?"

"Truthfully, I don't know. We texted a little this morning."

"And?"

Rory sighed. As usual, Meadow's questions and demands exasperated her. If she was honest, though, she needed to unpack this. Who better to listen than her family? A family who wasn't getting on a plane in thirty-six hours to jet six thousand miles away.

"She said she was sorry. I said I was sorry too." There was nothing really to report. The conversation had gone exactly like she thought it would. No forward movement. "Then, I had to explain that I was sorry about how everything went down, not that we were making up." Rory took a long sip from the homemade mug. "Your coffee's always the best anywhere, Mom."

"That's it?" Meadow kicked her bare foot with a sneaker.

"Practically. She asked if I was okay, and I said yes and that I was sad. She said she was sad too."

"That's a start," her mom said.

"Or an end." Rory shrugged. "Who's to say. There are no clean cuts here. It's all so messy."

"That's how life is. Sometimes, the mess makes it better."

She remembered that she had told Ellis the same thing when they were eating burritos. That seemed like a lifetime ago, and now, she wasn't even sure that was true anymore. She was devastated—she had fallen so hard for Ellis—but she couldn't let herself get caught up in the wreckage and turmoil of London's wake. That was the real dealbreaker.

She turned to Meadow. "We didn't break up...yet."

"Well, what did you do?"

"We texted. She told me how important I was to her. I told her the same. It doesn't matter what we say, we're moving backward.

Who can have a real relationship with texts and Zoom calls? Who knows how long she'll be over there, and we'll be apart? At some point, time between texts will get longer and longer until neither of us bothers anymore."

"That's a pretty dismal way to look at it." Her mom frowned at her coffee and her.

"I'm not saying that's what will happen. But… but…" Rory found she couldn't finish her thought. Twenty-four hours ago, she had been so excited about her future. A new relationship, a new home, and a new business. One trip around the clock, and bam, it was gone. But she respected herself too much to allow someone to actively hurt her.

"I don't mean to make this all about me," Meadow said, filling the pause. "How does this affect *Small Bites with Scarlett*? How much longer do I need to be patient?"

Rory's mouth fell open as she stared at her sister. She had no idea how to answer either of those questions.

Surprisingly, her mom did it for her. "Honey, I think you're going to have to let that go for now. Rory has a lot to figure out, and you can help her by not putting more on her plate."

Holy cow. That was sharp criticism from their mom. Meadow went mute, and Rory swung around to stare at her mom, who reached out to pat her hand.

However this Ellis thing worked out, her mom would always be there for her. That wasn't completely enough, but it was a lot. "Thanks, Mom."

"Excuse me, Ms. Green." A lounge attendant in a crisp gray suit bent down to London in the First-Class Hideaway at LAX. "Your plane's done boarding. I can bring you in last now if you're ready."

"Right." She knocked back the glass of champagne on a side table and rose.

"Thank you," Ellis said to the waiting attendant who was so starstruck, she hadn't given her a first glance. Before she got up, Ellis opened her phone case. No more texts from Rory. Just the time and date in big white text. Dinnertime on a Tuesday. She sighed and wondered where Rory was at that moment. She didn't like not knowing.

They had said their awkward good-byes in a brief text earlier that morning. Ellis had told her that Gina would gather Maya's things and bring them to the apartment the next day.

Have u seen her? she had texted to prolong the conversation
Haven't been home yet.

Rory hadn't elaborated. Ellis hadn't pushed, but she did think about it. She wondered if Alejandra was comforting her with more of her kisses. Maybe Rory was with her? That woman was an opportunist if there ever was one.

"Ellis? You coming?" London tapped her foot against the tile.

"Sorry." She snapped her phone case closed and gathered both her carry-on and backpack.

The attendant led them down a long hallway covered with murals of early aviation that connected the private lounge to the public concourse.

"Anything from Maya?" Ellis asked. She hated to leave the country with that loose end flapping around in the wind.

"Nothing. That part of my life is over once and for all. On to something bigger and better."

And she absolutely was. Out of everyone, London had come out of the last few days completely scot-free. As usual, falling out of love for London had been as easy as falling in love. There was the slim danger that Maya could still resurface. If she did, exposing the fake sex tape she had made was more than enough leverage. It was, as London had called it, over once and for all.

"Yep," London said to no one in particular. "Not one thing tying us to this town."

"There's ETA," Ellis said quietly.

"That can run itself now. We'll be away on set. Yolie and Gina can handle whatever is left over. Oh, I meant to tell you, the production office said they would get me an assistant while we're on location, but I'm going to need Gina back when I get home."

Ellis shoved that outrage away for later since they'd reached the end of the hallway. The attendant opened the double door to reveal the noise and confusion of everyday passengers hurrying to make their flights without escorts or separate check-ins or private TSAs.

London broke into a thousand-watt smile and crossed the threshold of the door as if she was on a red carpet of an award show. Half a dozen paparazzi who must have bought cheap tickets rushed to her. Surrounded by the sound of clicking cameras, London adjusted her stance to give them a better shot.

Travelers stopped and stared. Who was this? And then, when she was recognized, they started to gather. "Hey, Princess Carina," someone shouted, "where's your crown?"

"I'm on my way to get it," London called back, completely in her element.

"Ladies," the attendant said over the commotion, "the plane? We don't want to keep them waiting."

Ellis knew they would delay, however. The plane and everyone on it would stand by until London got there. That was how she moved through life, forcing everyone around her to wait until she was ready.

Ellis's pulse sped as familiar heat coursed through her body. Without stopping to think it over, she stepped through the door, standing close enough to London to ruin the pictures. "And there's Rory." Her voice gathered steam.

"Huh?" London struck another pose.

"Rory's tying me to LA."

London waved back to a young girl who'd shyly raised her hand. "You still with her?

"Why wouldn't I be?"

"I thought…" London finally turned and had the grace to look a little sheepish.

Ellis cupped her elbow and pulled her back through the doors to give their conversation a little privacy. The attendant's eyes went wide with despair.

"Sorry. One second," Ellis said to her, and when she had London alone, "You thought what?"

London dropped the smile and the stance. "Oh, you know. I thought since Maya betrayed me, and they were friends, you would..."

"What? Betray Rory?" She slapped her hand over her mouth as soon as she said it. Not to take it back but because she had finally voiced the truth that she hadn't wanted to see, even if many people had tried to tell her. It settled on her heavily and lightly at the same time. "We had a relationship outside of yours and Maya's. Not everything revolves around you."

"Ellis, don't be dramatic."

She almost took a step back. That was the pot calling the kettle black. "I'm not going." *Fuck.* Had she seriously blurted the words out the second they'd formed in her mind? Without thinking about them? Had she just pulled a Rory?

"Not going where?"

Ellis pulled in a deep breath, and this time, gave her words real thought. "With you. To Hungary." That felt a tiny bit better. Actually, a lot better. She had been wrong. There was something very freeing about saying what needed to be said.

"Ellis," London grabbed her wrist and tugged. "Come on. We can talk about this on the plane."

"No." Ellis stood her ground. The heat receded and left only calm in its wake. "The production will take good care of you. You're their star. You don't need me. And I'm beginning to realize that I don't need you as much as I thought."

"That's ridiculous," London said, not angry, just seemingly full of disbelief. "Come on. Get on the plane."

Ellis pursed her lips and shook her head slowly.

"If you don't"—wearied annoyance crept under her words—"we're done."

"Sorry. I'm staying here."

The double door opened, and the attendant stuck her head inside. "Ms. Green, if you're planning to make the flight…"

London cast a pointed look at Ellis. then tilted her head toward the door. Her irises, that swirling mixture of lovely blue and green, asked the question she wouldn't voice again.

Ellis raised one palm in a silent good-bye, and London turned her back on her, probably forever, and met the attendant. "Do I have time to sign an autograph or two?"

The door closed behind her with a heavy, metal finality. Ellis dropped her hand. She had been fired by her biggest client, she was most likely single, and she had no idea how to get out of the airport from here.

Standing under the glaring lights of the industrial hallway, however, everything felt very right.

❖

Rory turned the key in the lock and started to open the front door of her apartment.

"Everything okay?" Meadow, standing by her side, craned her head around her to see.

"Honey, let her get the door open," their mom said from the other side.

"She could be in there waiting for us. Ready to pounce." Meadow pulled her keys from her purse as a weapon.

"For four days?" Rory swung the door open to reveal the empty living space.

The apartment was exactly as she had left it when she had hurried out to help Ellis. A jacket slung over the sofa, art supplies scattered on the coffee table, reusable grocery bags resting by the front door.

Meadow frowned as she strode inside, looking around for whatever Rory had missed. "Did she have somewhere else to go?"

Rory patted her on the shoulder. She had met Maya only twice, so her interest wasn't concern. She had come because she loved drama. She had been hoping for a showdown. Her mom, on the other hand, was there for support. Truth be told, Rory was happy to have them both by her side. If Maya had been there to confront her, Meadow would've totally had her back.

"Maybe she's in her room." Meadow headed for the second door down the hall. She flung it open without knocking and peered inside. "Are you sure you still have a roommate?"

Rory came up behind. All Maya's stuff was gone as if she had never lived there, except for a folded piece of paper sitting like a tiny tent in the middle of the room.

Rory flipped it open. *I moved out. I'll call Gina and tell her where to send my stuff. I'm going to need next month's rent back.*

"What does it say?"

Rory handed the note to her sister. Maya was gone. If nothing else, actors sure knew how to make exits.

"You going to give it to her?" Meadow handed the note to their mom.

"You mean the money? Yeah, probably. It's not worth the stress."

"That's my girl. Move straight on." Her mom smiled. "Why don't I take you both out for a beer. How about that bar you used to work at? It's right around the corner, right?"

"That's a great idea, Mom." Rory wasn't ready to be alone quite yet.

As they were leaving and locking the door, Meadow lectured her loudly on how she should keep the money. That Maya owed it to her. That she actually could put a price on convenience.

The door across the hall opened. A tiny woman with white hair peeked out. "Oh, it's you, dear," she said, "I was afraid those rude women were back."

"Finally, we're getting somewhere," Meadow said under her breath.

"They came almost in the middle of the night and started carting away furniture. I was afraid they were robbing you."

"That was my roommate. My ex-roommate. She's moved out."

"I did recognize her eventually. They were making so much noise, I almost called the police."

"I'm sorry, Mrs. Bradley."

"I never liked her anyway. She never said hello when we were in the elevator together."

"Good instincts. We're going to the Honey Pot. Would you like to come along? I'll buy you a drink as an apology?"

"I'll pass, thank you. *You* have nothing to apologize for, my dear."

"Ask her who the rude women were." Meadow nudged her in the ribs. "Don't you want to know?"

"Not really."

"Elevator's here," their mom called.

As annoying as Meadow was, she was taking her mind off Ellis who, currently, was somewhere over Nevada flying farther and farther away from her.

Rory brought half the crowd with her when she and her family entered the Honey Pot. There was an older couple canoodling at the bar, and Alejandra sat in the back chatting animatedly to Terri, who tapped an order pad on her thigh.

"Rory!" Facing the door, Alejandra jumped up and waved them over. "And family," she added when they made their way to the table. She kissed Meadow and her mom on their cheeks and Rory on her mouth.

Rory didn't back away this time. There was no point now.

"Please, join me." She pulled out a chair for Rory's mom.

"Thank you. She won't stop talking." Terri whispered to Rory. Her hair was frizzed in its old style, and the order pad had no drinks written on it.

"Quiet tonight," Rory said.

"Back to our usual terrible Tuesdays."

"I'm buying the first round. Whatever you all want." Alejandra waved a hand over the table. "We're celebrating. I got the NDA from Ellis today and a list of potential guests for the *Fresh Beginnings* podcast. Thank you very much. She's a keeper."

Meadow opened her mouth, and Rory dropped a hand on her shoulder to quiet her. "That's wonderful. What do you want to drink, Meadow?" If Alejandra noticed, she didn't say anything.

"What exactly are we celebrating?" her mom asked.

Alejandra didn't need an engraved invitation. She was off and running about her podcast.

Rory took the only remaining seat, her back to the door.

By the second round, Meadow and Alejandra were thick as thieves, planning a *Goat Cheese of the Stars* podcast that would probably never happen. Rory sipped her beer and let their excitement swirl around her. It was both comforting and distracting. Too bad Meadow was straight. They would have been a fun couple.

On the table, her phone pinged. She flipped it over and frowned at the message that had popped up on the screen.

"Who is it, sweetie?" her mom leaned over to ask.

A few swipes later, she answered. "It's *Guess Who's Coming to Dinner*. They want me back for the new season. They're sending me a contract."

Joy glanced at a wind-up watch on her wrist. "Now? It's the middle of the night?"

"They send the contracts out at night so no one's in the office if you want to complain or negotiate."

"It's kind of smart." Meadow nodded as if she had been through the process a million times.

Rory pulled up the contract and poised her finger over the document.

"I can't believe you're going to sign it." Alejandra reached out to grab her hand. "You whined about the first season nonstop when we were together."

"I need a job. A bird in the hand," she said and tried to wiggle out of Alejandra's grasp.

An emptiness filled her. So much had happened in the last few months. And with one drop of her finger, she was right back where she'd started with virtually no forward progress. Until she figured out Upper Crust, and that was a big if, what choice did she have?

Alejandra held on tighter. "If you're going to do it, then let your agent get you the best rate."

"I don't have an agent."

"Sure, you do." Alejandra released her hand and pointed over her shoulder to the door. "She's standing right there."

Her heart jumped to her throat.

What if…

No. She tensed. There was no way that Ellis Turner—the woman who had complete possession of her heart—was standing in a lesbian dive bar in NoHo Art's District.

"Rory," Meadow said softly. "Look."

She slowly swiveled, longing and despair surging through her in equal measures.

There was a figure in the open doorway, backlit by the lights from the street outside. They surrounded her like a full-body halo. She stepped inside and came into focus. Her shirt was untucked, tendrils escaped her bun, and freckles cascaded down her cheeks, but she had never looked more beautiful.

"Ellis." The word was both a question and a declaration. Rory's breath quickened, and a shiver etched down her spine. She fumbled to get up and tripped over her own feet as she hurried to the door. "What are you doing here? Shouldn't you be on a plane?"

"That's the thing. I finally realized that this is the place I need to be." She looked at Rory with a gaze that was afraid to hope but hoped anyway.

"In a shabby bar with cheap booze?" It was a stupid comeback, but she was undone by Ellis's arrival.

"No, silly. With you." Ellis flushed a little. She took her hand and laced their fingers. "It took me way too long to realize that working with…no, for London, was like jumping in a big river. It's not easy to get out, and you go wherever her current takes you."

Rory nodded encouragement. She knew how hard this was for Ellis, and she also finally knew not to say I told you so.

"And that would have been okay," Ellis continued, "because sometimes, the greater good is what work's all about. I think, though, I finally get it. I was so worried about disappointing her that I didn't realize I was disappointing everyone else. And most importantly, myself."

Rory swallowed hard. She cast around for the right thing to say, something that contained no judgment. "And you realized all this in the airport?" She winced, again not quite right. She too, was a work in progress.

A smile tugged at Ellis's lips, and Rory squeezed her hand. Thankfully, she had taken it the correct way. "Yeah, crazy, right?"

"Not at all. Awareness comes when it wants." She channeled her mom. That was much better. "And London? Is she…"

"On her way to Hungary, without me."

Rory went weak at the knees. Ellis had done it. She had chosen herself. And now, maybe, she was choosing Rory.

Ellis cupped her cheek and forced their gazes to meet. "Forgive me?"

"For what? Coming to your senses?"

"For taking so long to do it."

Rory became aware of her own heart pounding in her chest. This was the moment where everything would change. Their relationship wouldn't be easy, no real relationship was, and they were very different people.

Ellis's chin quivered as she waited. Her irises shimmered in the low light of the bar like faraway stars. Looking deeply, Rory made the same wish she had months ago at the party. *Please let tonight be the start of something big.* Tonight, however, she meant Ellis.

Rory tapped a loose fist against her chest. "I forgive you with all my heart. And next time, when I've done or said something stupid, you're going to have to return the favor."

Ellis's eyes went soft and glowed from within. "Deal."

Rory let out a happy breath, bent her head, and froze before their mouths touched. "How on earth did you know I was here?"

"Mrs. Bradley. She's a very nosy neighbor." They were so close Rory could feel the words brush her lips.

"Thank God," she said and finally went in for the kiss.

When they surfaced, everyone at the back was clapping. Ellis flushed bright red and grabbed Rory's arm. "Who are all these people?"

"This"—she waved a hand to her mom , who was rapidly approaching—"is my mom."

"Pleased to meet you, Mrs. Hatten."

"Please, just Joy." She sidestepped the handshake and ran both hands down Ellis's arms. "Your glaze is excellent, my dear. Simply excellent."

Ellis turned to Rory.

"Don't ask. And this is my sister, Meadow."

Grinning widely, Meadow pumped Ellis's hand several times. "So glad to meet you. Rory was miserable. And I can't wait to work with you and Scarlett."

"Meadow," Rory said sharply and quickly stepped in front of her. "And you know Alejandra, of course."

"You're part of the pack now." Alejandra stepped up and kissed Ellis on the lips. "I didn't think you'd accept my invitation so soon. Now that you're here, can I buy you that drink?"

Rory pulled up another chair and slid her hand onto Ellis's lap as they sat. She never wanted to be separated from her again. "You okay? You're a long way from Hungary."

"Yes." She closed her own hand over Rory's and squeezed. "Because we'll both be sleeping in the right bed tonight. Together."

EPILOGUE

They had picked a terrible day to shoot. It was unseasonably hot for fall. Without an ocean breeze, ninety degrees in Topanga Canyon seemed like nine hundred, and Meadow's tiny home, despite its air-conditioner upgrade, was stifling hot. Ellis stood outside at the craft service table that, for a food show, was woefully lacking. Even the drinks were warm.

None of it mattered. This episode of *Small Bites with Scarlett* had otherwise been blessed by a lucky star. The goats had been impossibly cute and incredibly camera ready. They frolicked and gamboled on cue. The cheese was delicious; Rory had baked every crew member a tartlet to take home with them. And Meadow was a star. She was funny and approachable and just the right amount of quirky when the cameras rolled. When it aired, this show would send her business soaring.

Ellis glanced at Rory chatting under the shade tarp to someone she had known on Norah's show. Sensing the attention, she turned to Ellis and grinned. There was lasting love in her look, and Ellis grinned back. So much smiling and laughing these days. Sometimes, her cheeks hurt when they climbed into bed.

Rory had officially moved in and then partially out when she rented a small, commercial kitchen nearby. Upper Crust was doing as well as their relationship, especially now that she was promoting Golden Meadow goat cheese. Every tart came with a golden meadow plate from Joy's kiln. Synergy was a wonderful thing.

"Thank you for making this happen." Joy materialized at her side.

"You're welcome, but I think your daughters are the force to be reckoned with."

"Maybe. I know what it's like to be the wind behind that force. You do it perfectly."

"Thank you," Ellis said with real emotion.

Meadow stuck her head out of her house and called to her mom, "Can you get one of your plates? Wait, we need three."

Ellis watched Joy hurry off. Over the last six months, Rory's family had grown more and more important to her. Joy had a natural ability to build people up, and she was trying to emulate that style as ETA grew and changed. Yolie, and Gina too, had signed their own clients. ETA was quickly becoming a go-to agency for both actors and casting agents, not just the London Green show. And Ellis didn't miss being a manager one little bit.

Sometimes, however, when she heard about London's exploits, a tinge of something lurched in her stomach, not guilt or regret exactly, but something. London's star was in the stratosphere. *Dazzled* was in post-production, and by all accounts, the shoot had exceeded all expectations. She was tempted to call to congratulate her. But London hadn't reached out, and a friendship where there was true equity would never be on the table. Eventually, with Rory's help, she had let London go.

Maya remained a mystery. Gina had gathered up her possessions months ago, namely London's gifts, sent them to an address in Silver Lake, and no one heard of her again. Ellis still felt a little responsible when she thought of the way things had ended. Again, thanks to Rory's wisdom, she realized that everyone's happiness was no longer her responsibility.

"I was just thinking about you," Ellis said when Rory brought her a cup of ice.

"Good things, I hope."

"Always."

Rory poured Ellis's flavored water into the new cup and handed it back to her.

Ellis sipped the cool drink. "That's much better, thanks."

A production assistant's voice came through a nearby walkie-talkie. "Does anyone have eyes on Joy? We still need those plates."

"Joy is the perfect name for your mom. Hey—" Ellis swung toward Rory with a sudden thought. "If your mom's name is Joy, and your sister's is Meadow. How did you end up with such a normal name?"

"I didn't."

"Rory is—"

"Not my full name." Rory stuck out her hand. "Pleased to meet you. I am Aurora Borealis Hatten."

"That's a mouthful." Ellis laughed and clasped Rory's hand in hers flashing back to the morning they met. On that occasion, she had shaken her hand too. Then, she had wanted to wring her neck instead. Now, all she wanted to do is pull Rory into a deep hug.

Why not?

She tugged on her hand, and hot as it was, Rory fell willingly into her arms.

God, everything had changed since that first day. She had lost London. She had found this amazing woman in her arms. And she had found herself.

"Makes sense," Ellis whispered up into her ear.

"Why?" Rory asked.

The words were right there. She didn't need to reach for them. "Because you're my shining light."

About the Author

Catherine Lane started to write fiction on a dare from her wife. She's thrilled to have published three contemporary romances: *The Set Piece, Heartwood*, and *Romancing the Kicker* and one fantasy novella, *Tread Lightly*. Thank goodness, her wife, as usual, was right.

They live in Southern California with their son and a very mischievous rescue dog. Catherine spends most of her time teaching and writing. But when she finds herself at loose ends, she enjoys experimenting with soup recipes in the kitchen, paddling her kayak on flat water, and trying, unsuccessfully, to outwit her dog.

Books Available from Bold Strokes Books

All This Time by Sage Donnell. Erin and Jodi share a complicated past, but a very different present. Will they ever be able to make a future together work? (978-1-63679-622-2)

Crossing Bridges by Chelsey Lynford. When a one-night stand between a snowboard instructor and a business executive becomes more, one has to overcome her past, while the other must let go of her planned future. (978-1-63679-646-8)

Dancing Toward Stardust by Julia Underwood. Age has nothing to do with becoming the person you were meant to be, taking a chance, and finding love. (978-1-63679-588-1)

Evacuation to Love by CA Popovich. As a hurricane rips through Florida, so too are Joanne and Shanna's lives upended. It'll take a force of nature to show them the love it takes to rebuild. (978-1-63679-493-8)

Lean in to Love by Catherine Lane. Will badly behaving celebrities, erotic sex tapes, and steamy scandals prevent Rory and Ellis from leaning in to love? (978-1-63679-582-9)

Searching for Someday by Renee Roman. For loner Rayne Thomas, her only goal for working out is to build her confidence, but Maggie Flanders has another idea, and neither are prepared for the outcome. (978-1-63679-568-3)

The Romance Lovers Book Club by MA Binfield and Toni Logan. After their book club reads a romance about an American tourist falling in love with an English princess, Harper and her best friend, Alice, book an impulsive trip to London hoping they'll each fall for the women of their dreams. (978-1-63679-501-0)

Truly Home by J.J. Hale. Ruth and Olivia discover home is more than a four-letter word. (978-1-63679-579-9)

View from the Top by Morgan Adams. When it comes to love, sometimes the higher you climb, the harder you fall. (978-1-63679-604-8)

Blood Rage by Ileandra Young. A stolen artifact, a family in the dark, an entire city on edge. Can SPEAR agent Danika Karson juggle all three over a weekend with the "in-laws," while an unknown, malevolent entity lies in wait upon her very skin? (978-1-63679-539-3)

Ghost Town by R.E. Ward. Blair Wyndon and Leif Henderson are set to prove ghosts exist when the mystery suddenly turns deadly. Someone or something else is in Masonville, and if they don't find a way to escape, they might never leave. (978-1-63679-523-2)

Good Christian Girls by Elizabeth Bradshaw. In this heartfelt coming of age lesbian romance, Lacey and Jo help each other untangle who they are from who everyone says they're supposed to be. (978-1-63679-555-3)

Guide Us Home by CF Frizzell and Jesse J. Thoma. When acquisition of an abandoned lighthouse pits ambitious competitors Nancy and Sam against each other, it takes a WWII tale of two brave women to make them see the light. (978-1-63679-533-1)

Lost Harbor by Kimberly Cooper Griffin. For Alice and Bridget's love to survive, they must find a way to reconcile the most important passions in their lives—devotion to the church and each other. (978-1-63679-463-1)

Never a Bridesmaid by Spencer Greene. As her sister's wedding gets closer, Jessica finds that her hatred for the maid of honor is a bit more complicated than she thought. Could it be something more than hatred? (978-1-63679-559-1)

The Rewind by Nicole Stiling. For police detective Cami Lyons and crime reporter Alicia Flynn, some choices break hearts. Others leave a body count. (978-1-63679-572-0)

Turning Point by Cathy Dunnell. When Asha and her former high school bully Jody struggle to deny their growing attraction, can they move forward without going back? (978-1-63679-549-2)

When Tomorrow Comes by D. Jackson Leigh. Teague Maxwell, convinced she will die before she turns 41, hires animal rescue owner Baye Cobb to rehome her extensive menagerie. (978-1-63679-557-7)

You Had Me at Merlot by Melissa Brayden. Leighton and Jamie have all the ingredients to turn their attraction into love, but it's a recipe for disaster. (978-1-63679-543-0)

All Things Beautiful by Alaina Erdell. Casey Norford only planned to learn to paint like her mentor, Leighton Vaughn, not sleep with her. (978-1-63679-479-2)

Appalachian Awakening by Nance Sparks. The more Amber's and Leslie's paths cross, the more this hike of a lifetime begins to look like a love of a lifetime. (978-1-63679-527-0)